Loved me at my DARKEST

EVIE HARPER

you loved me series 1

YOU LOVED ME AT MY DARKEST

Published by Evie Harper, First Edition August 2014

Cover Design: Louisa Maggio at LM Creations
Editing: Becky Johnson, Hot Tree Editing
Proofreading: Jenny from Editing4Indies
Proofreading: Bel Burgess
Formatting: Max Henry at Max Effect
Images: Shutterstock

I dedicate this story to

my sister, Sarah

If God asked me to choose a sister for every lifetime I was given, I would choose you every time.

I love you.

WARNING

This content contains material that maybe offensive to some readers, including graphic language, dangerous and adult situations.

Some situations may be hotspots for some readers.

prologue

HOPELESSNESS WRAPS AROUND MY BODY LIKE A TIGHT cord. Alone and beaten, each breath comes quicker. My eyes are almost swollen shut, with only tiny slivers of light shining through to let me know it's daytime. Thick, rough rope scrapes harshly against my wrists. A dirty white dress, held up on my shoulders by thin straps, covers my shaking body.

What have I done? I failed in my escape, caught in the grasp of evil again. Have I failed Lily too? Will I die down here—never being able to let my sister know how thankful I am that she did everything she possibly could do to save me? I would give up anything in this world to tell her how much I love her, and to tell her to keep fighting.

So many hits to the head has left it pounding like it

never has before. I've vomited twice already. I dread more may be coming up. My lip quivers and my chest expands heavily. Tears squeeze through my swollen eyes and spill down my face.

I hear the door opening, and I sense movement near my body. Hot breath heats my cheek letting me know someone's there. "Sasha, you need to reveal to us who helped you, or things are only going to get a lot worse for you." A gruff voice I know all too well causes bile to rise and threatens to empty again.

I turn my head away and say, "I will never give up who helped me." Only my words come out all wrong and slurred. *What's wrong with my speech?*

He sighs. "Fine then, the hard way it is."

I laugh in my mind. Given what I have already been through, I thought that already was the hard way.

I'm pulled upwards by the ropes around my wrists, and he begins walking. I fall to my knees as soon as I try to take my first step.

"Get up," he growls.

My hands are yanked up, and my shoulders scream from the pain. A whimper tries to escape but can't get past the lump in my throat. He grips my elbow and pulls me along with him.

Light explodes between the tiny cracks in my swollen eyes and heat from the sunshine hits my skin. I realise I'm outside. I smell the salty ocean air and feel the chilly breeze. He continues to walk me for a moment, and then stops. I'm pushed to my knees, and then my hands are lifted above my head and tied to something round. I feel it with my fingertips; it's hard and rough, and feels like a wooden pole.

"Now, boys, watch and learn. This is what we do to slave girls who try to escape and protect traitors." I can hear the sick excitement in his voice. He has been gunning for me ever since I arrived.

My head is still thumping painfully, and my chest is rising and falling fast, waiting for the first punch to come. Trying to predict from which angle, so I can brace for the pain, I feel it.

A scream is ripped from my throat as a searing sensation runs down my back. I arch in response to the blistering pain. I sob when I realise he's whipping me.

I try to move forward to get away. When I feel it again, I scream. My back forces itself forward, trying uselessly to get away from the attacking whip.

Trying to force my hands out of the ropes to defend myself has caused my wrists to throb with pain. I want to crawl into a ball and try to protect what piece of untouched flesh I have left.

I scream again as the whip slashes through my thin dress and skin. The pungent smell of metallic fills my nose. The sliminess of my blood as the whip flicks down my back, seeps downward. The pounding in my head is growing. My eyes are begging me to open them to see, to escape. My body arches again along with a piercing scream from another strike.

Tears overflowing through my swollen eyes, I can taste the saltiness on my lips. My head sags to my chest, my breathing heavy. I sense my body going faint. I'm so tired.

The promise of unconsciousness whispers on the edges of my mind. Darkness begins to envelope me.

All of a sudden, I hear screaming in the distance. I recognise that voice. It's Lily. She's getting closer. Oh, thank God, I can tell her how much I love her. How much she has been the best big sister anyone could ever ask for, and demand that she keeps fighting.

Suddenly, I'm turned over. I hear her sweet voice talking to me; she's crying. Lil's arms feel so warm around my body. Home. I'm finally home. *I love you, Lil.* I try to say except my mouth won't move. I scream it in my mind to her. *I love you, Lily!* These are my last thoughts as darkness surrounds me and the light drifts away.

Carefree and Flying High

TAKING A SEAT AND LOOKING THROUGH THE ENORMOUS glass window, I watch a plane move down the runway, building up speed, until it's up, and flying into the sky off to some exciting place in the world.

I look down at my bags, butterflies fluttering around in my stomach. Finally, a packed suitcase and passport in my hands. I'm finally here, Sydney airport, and I'll be getting on a plane and leaving Australia, my home. I love my home, but seeing the world has always been a dream of mine, and today that dream is finally coming true. I, Lily Morgan, will be getting on a plane to travel the world. Excitement vibrates through me like fireworks ready to show the world just how happy I am.

I look around the airport terminal at the people

bustling around me; some on their phones, a couple trying to get their children to behave, and others just sitting, looking out at the runway. I wonder if they are like me, in awe of doing something they have only ever dreamed of.

I feel movement on my denim shorts and look down past my white shirt to see Sasha poking me. I look over at my sister. She looks like she's ready to burst with joy as well.

"Lil listen." Sash is jumping on her bum like a little kid, her yellow dress bouncing with her. She points to the ceiling, and I hear the man on the voiceover announcing our gate is ready for boarding. People start walking over and lining up with their tickets.

We've been talking about going overseas since high school, but we kept putting it off. Then three years ago, our parents were killed in a car accident. A drunk driver ran a red light and hit my parents, striking the passenger's side of the car. They both died instantly from the impact. Sasha and I crumbled when we lost our parents, but we managed to pull ourselves through some pretty tough times and have slowly moved on with our lives.

My eyes start to water and I feel a familiar palm squeeze my hand. I look over, and Sash gives me a sad smile. She knows what I'm thinking about, and like always, she is there for me. I bury my pain and put a smile on my face for her; she has suffered enough. I don't want to remind her of how much we have lost.

When our parents passed, the first place we went was the family farm. We climbed up into our childhood tree for the first time in many years. We cried together and said our goodbyes to our parents.

Sash may be my little sister, but she is also my best friend. Living on a farm far away from any neighbours, we only ever had each other, and that's all we needed. Being only two years apart, we were always into the same things. We shared secrets and practiced kissing on the back of our hands, giving each other tips. All of this in our favourite tree, we would climb, sit and talk in our willow tree for hours after school until mum would call us in for dinner.

Many people ask if we are sisters, but we can never understand how people pick us out. We don't think we look alike. Sash has Mum's beautiful straight, light brown hair, blue eyes, and her outgoing personality. At twenty-eight, I have more of my dad's dark blond, thick straight hair and his green eyes. Sasha's and my body types are similar though, generous in the bust area but not over-the-top. We're both tanned and athletic from growing up working on the farm.

With our parents gone and no one to keep the wheat farm going, Sasha and I decided to move back home. It's been in our family for four generations. One day we knew one of us would take it over. It meant too much to our dad to just see it go to a stranger.

It was hard at first to live where our parents had. Sometimes I think I can still hear my mum call us in for dinner or hear my dad's laughter. My parents were in love; not just any love, they were soul mates. They never fought. They argued, but not for long, and usually only if they believed the other was going to get hurt or letdown.

They would have done anything for each other. I suppose it was right they died together. I think if one had lived, they would have died of a broken heart anyway.

After working the farm for three years and acquiring some trustworthy employees, Sasha and I decided it was time to do some travelling. We didn't want to keep putting it off and one day regret never doing it. It's what our parents would have wanted. Mum and Dad were both adventurous. They wanted Sash and I to see the world before we settled down.

We have no set plans, but our first stop is New York City. It's the one place we both want to visit first.

"Lil, let's go line up," Sash's excited voice sends butterflies to my stomach.

We stand from our seats, pick up our suitcases and start toward the ticket desk. My heart beats wildly, and I have a huge smile. I glance at Sasha and see she has the same sized grin on her face. Yep, this is going to be a trip of a lifetime.

I clock her as soon as she gets off the plane, fucking perfect. One of the most stunning smiles and perfect bodies I've ever seen. Every man turns his head as she walks by. It helps she has a mini version right next to her.

Country girls, easy to pick with their clothes. And first-time travellers. The dumbstruck look on their faces says it all.

She would be fucking perfect for what Marco's looking for. He'd probably fall all over his feet to have her. A pang

What a day! Every day in New York is full on and different. Today we visited Times Square, and it was amazing. Another place and another memory I will always cherish.

We get back to our room and drop to our beds exhausted. Our legs are killing us from all the walking. On our way back to the hotel, Sash and I decided it's time to move on. The last two weeks have been wonderful, but it's time to see more wonderful places. New Orleans will be our next stop. We booked a flight for tomorrow night. Excited about heading to a new place, the air hums with our renewed energy, ready to leave New York with a bang. We settle on a rave party we saw signs for today. *Bring on our final night in New York City!*

Standing on the balcony looking out over the sea of dancing, sweaty bodies, all I can think about is her. I need to get her out of my head and feel another woman's warm pussy around my cock. Yeah, that will make me forget about her. I need to burn this energy off, so I don't go back to the hotel and wait around like a pathetic loser to catch a glimpse of her.

I'm scouring the dance floor, looking for any woman who looks like she will be an easy fuck, someone who won't want the bullshit talking beforehand. That's when I spot Mick walking up the stairs to the balcony.

"Well, fuck, you eventually decide to turn up when I ask. Where the fuck have you been for the past two weeks? You haven't answered any of my calls. Marco's been asking for

progress reports, you find anyone?"

I have. She's perfect. But I can't do it. She's too innocent, too fucking special. "No, I didn't find anyone who matches what Marco wants," I reply, still scanning the dance floor.

"Well, I found someone an hour ago, and she is exactly what Marco asked for. She comes with a bonus as well, plucked them right off the street, easy as pie."

Mick pats my shoulder and says, "So it's time to go home now."

Thank fuck, they finally found someone. I can leave this fucking city and stop my growing obsession for this woman from getting any worse.

I push back from the railing and follow Mick down the small hall and out the exit doors, where we walk down the stairs on the outside of the building. There're two black vans parked at the underside of the stairs.

"Take the second van, Jake. It has the package. I'll lead in the first van, with the bonus package."

I nod and walk to the van. Opening the door, I take a step in and freeze. All the blood drains from my face, and my heart completely stops. I'm looking straight at her, Lily Morgan. Bound and gagged, she's staring up at me with wide, terrified eyes.

In the end, the innocent lamb was caught by the blood thirsty fox, just by another fox.

Nightmares Do Come True

TEARS STREAM DOWN MY FACE, MY HEAVY BREATHING steering my body into a full-blown panic attack. *Breath in, breath out, breath in, breath out*. The haze starts to clear, my calm breaths helping. My ankles and calves are numb, and my shoulders are aching from kneeling on rough flooring, gagged with my hands tied behind my back.

Sasha and I were on our way to the underground rave when two black vans parked next to us. Oblivious to the danger, hands and bodies were suddenly pushing us into the vans, me in one and Sasha in the other. It's eerie to remember how easy it was just to take us; we didn't even get one single scream out before the doors were closed and the van sped off.

Inside the van, I was grabbed by a man from behind,

his hands pulling my arms backwards. I twisted and thumped against him to get out of his grasp. I fought fiercely, but it wasn't enough. With all his strength, the man leaned down on my back, and I fell to my knees, a ripping sound came from somewhere on my short blue dress. The man pushed me facedown to the floor, and my hands were tied behind my back. I screamed and jerked, but no one could hear me, and no one was going to save me. A gag was forced over my mouth and tied around my head tightly.

That man is now sitting to my left. Despite his short black hair, scrawny face and body, he was still strong enough to overpower me. The van comes to a stop, and we sit silently, unmoving. I have no idea how long the van parks for. All I can do is try to calm my breathing and hope they only wanted to scare us and would soon tell me what they wanted. *Please be money. Please just want money.*

The van's door opens and a man steps in. He looks at me, and then freezes. He seems shocked, as if he knows me, but that's not possible. I would remember him. He looks early thirties with messy hair, short on sides, little longer on top with a sharp jaw and dark three-day-old stubble, very masculine and ruggedly handsome. He is wearing jeans and a black leather jacket; he is tall with broad shoulders, and a tattoo peeks out from his black shirt just below his neck. His eyes are dark brown. His body screams power, but his eyes show softness.

If I had seen him out somewhere, I would instantly think he was out of my league. I can only imagine what a smile on his face would look like. It would probably make the most faithful woman think about stripping him naked.

Our eyes are locked together, the stare intense. My first instinct is to ask him to help me, but my hopes dissolve when I hear, "Jake," from the man who tied me up.

Hearing his name shakes him from our locked gaze. Jake nods his head toward the man near me, closes the van door and takes a seat on the floor straight across from me.

"Jake," the man to my left again says his name, sharply this time.

Jake flicks his brown eyes up, and he quickly catches a black bag he is tossed, placing it on the floor beside him without even looking at it.

I feel uneasy as he keeps watching me, yet my cheeks heat from his attention, but it's nothing compared to the fear pumping to my heart, doubling its speed.

My stomach knots as my body rocks sideways from the van driving again. *Where are we going?* I want to ask questions, but I can barely swallow with this gag in, let alone talk, drooling could become a problem soon. I try to shift the gag around by clenching and smiling wide trying to stretch the material.

All of a sudden, Jake moves toward me, and I flinch as he reaches out with his hands. It takes me a moment to realise he's loosening the tie at the back of my head.

"Fuck Joey, you did the gag tight enough. We're kidnapping her, not trying to suffocate her." His voice is tight; however, I notice a slight husky tone in his American accent.

With the material loosened, Jake moves back to his seat and my shoulders sag with the relief, my cheeks rejoice from the pressure being released.

"The bitch is feisty. She was kicking and screaming. I had to do it fast, Jake," Joey whines.

Jake grits his teeth and looks to the side, rubbing his hand over his chest once. He runs his fingers through his short hair as he sits back and glances at the ceiling. He closes his eyes and gets comfortable, and that's how he stays for the rest of the ride in the van.

After what feels like half an hour, the van comes to a stop.

A knock comes on the van door and a man yells. "Ready!"

Joey stands and opens the door.

Jake moves toward me with the black cotton bag he caught earlier, and he shoves it over my head and down my face until I am in complete darkness, my hot breath filling the bag, creating heat around my face. Palpitations fill my chest, and my mind races with thoughts of what this could mean.

Hands touch my waist, and immediately, I thrash around and yell, "Let me go!" but it comes out skewed under my gag.

"Stop." Jake's voice is stern. "If you keep squirming, I will have to carry you over my shoulder, and trust me, in your dress you don't want that." I freeze and decide he's probably right.

"I'm taking you into a warehouse where your sister will be, and we will be getting the two of you ready for transport. This will go easier if you don't struggle. There is no escape, but there will be pain if you fight." A whimper slips through my lips. *Transport. Pain.*

He picks me up and carries me like a parent would hold a small child. The first thing I feel is the chilly night air hit my legs as we leave the van. My chest is rising and falling fast, and my breaths are coming in short bursts.

"Calm down," he growls.

This guy is insane if he thinks I can be calm through any of this. However, I try, attempting to concentrate on the future, and any opportunities to get away. Slowly, my heartbeat calms, and I take stock of being in Jake's arms. His heart is beating rapidly; so much so, I can feel the thumps on my right arm.

Suddenly, the cool breeze is gone, and it feels as if we entered a building. Jake stops, kneels and lowers me to the ground. I'm lying on a cold cement floor.

Hands wrap around my shins, and a sticky material is tied around my ankles. I kick out at whoever is holding them, but my legs are easily restrained.

The bag is ripped off my head, and as soon as my head is free, I look around wildly for Sasha. All I see is what looks like a warehouse with aeroplanes and five or six men walking around. I turn my head the other way, and then I see her. She's lying about five metres from me, gagged, her hands and feet tied up the same as mine. Her head is turned toward me, her body shaking, with tears falling from her terror-stricken eyes that stand out from her pale face.

Tears flood my eyes, and a cry escapes me at seeing my

little sister so scared. I try to communicate with my eyes and tell her it's going to be okay, but I'm not sure she understands me. She's too far gone, too afraid.

I see Joey kneeling over Sasha. He has a needle in his hand, and my heart accelerates so fast I think it will explode out of my chest. I start screaming under my gagged mouth when I see him place his hand on Sasha's head and stick the needle into her neck.

I roll to my side trying to crawl to my sister. But I'm pulled back and held down, a hand pushes on my head and I feel a sting. I groan, frustrated, knowing they just did the same to me.

My eyes start to feel heavy, and I try to fight to stay awake, knowing whatever they have just given us is to make us sleep. Through heavy-lidded eyes, I watch a man walk over to Joey. He points to Sasha.

"Take that one with you."

"Will do, Mick," Joey replies.

The man moves his head my way. "This one will come with me. Jake, you go with Joey and make sure everything goes smoothly."

My eyes get heavier with every second that ticks by. I take one last glance at Sasha and see she's already passed out and being carried over Joey's shoulder.

Rolling my head to the side, I taste salty tears on my lips. My head is heavy, and everything is going in slow motion. Consciousness is slowly slipping away from me, but not before I look up and see him, staring back down at me. I slip into a deep sleep while staring into his dark brown eyes.

I wake to a strange smell of musty air-conditioned air, my head throbbing the more I wake up. I want to rub my temple, but my arms feel sore when I try to lift them like I slept in the same position for too long. I freeze, remembering the van, being tied up, the warehouse, Sasha!

My eyes dart open, and I sit up. Looking around the room, my head spins from the quick movement and my stomach rolls at the dizziness. I'm in a tiny room with a double bed and some cupboards to each side. I feel a dip, and grab hold of the bed tighter with my hands. *A plane, oh, God, I'm on a plane.* Holding onto the covers, I realise my hands and ankles are now free.

My eyes start to go glassy, and I look around the tiny room for any signs of Sasha. Shit, where are they taking me? Where's Sasha? A lump forms in my throat as I feel my sanity start to lose its grip on my mind.

With glassy eyes, I get up and pound on the door that sits right in front of the bed. It opens, and a man walks into the room. I step back and fall to the bed when the back of my knees hit it. I remember him. He was at the warehouse. They called him Mick.

He's a tall, large guy, with shoulder-length light brown hair and bushy eyebrows. He smirks at me, and it pisses me off.

"Where's my sister?" I hiss, with shaking hands, sounding braver than I feel.

"Hello, Lily," he says, bringing my licence up to his face.

My stomach drops. He went through my handbag, and

now he has everything; my passport, all our money, our home address.

"Don't worry about your sister. She's safe, for now." His voice is rough and irritating to my ears. "Just like you are. Keep being a good girl, and then nothing will happen to you, on this flight anyway," he finishes with a sly smile.

I narrow my eyes at him and think of every possible way I could maim and kill him. Losing my patience with his games, I scream at the top of my lungs, "Sasha!" I take a big breath in and scream again, "Sasha!" I inhale another big breath when Mick interrupts me.

"That won't do you any good. She isn't on this plane."

My body stills and my throat constricts. My fear is confirmed. They have separated us, not just by rooms but by miles, possibly countries. Oh, my God, shit, what am I going to do? I need to get to my sister.

He must see the panic on my face because he informs me, "Don't worry. You will see her soon. She may be on another plane, but she is headed in the same direction we are."

"And where is that?"

Mick grins. "None of your business, little girl." *Little girl, he can't be much older than me.*

I laugh at his answer, and it comes out strangled. "You think you can just kidnap people. You can't. The hotel will wonder where we are!" I end on a shout.

Mick jumps forward and backhands my face. I fall back to the bed with a scream and curl into my body to protect myself from any more strikes. The right side of my face pulsates with pain as the sheets of the bed rub against my tender skin.

I'm facing the wall when I hear him laugh. A whimper rises to my throat, but I won't let it fall from my lips. I swallow it down and will my tears not to escape. I will not satisfy what he obviously gets off on, and that's seeing women as an object to hurt and demoralise.

"I told you, you would be safe as long as you behaved. That was just a little taste. Now shut your fucking mouth and stop asking questions." He kneels down on the bed and whispers in my ear, "Forget your old life, Lily. You are now owned. You no longer have a say in anything that happens to you. Who knows, a feisty bitch like you might enjoy all the cock you will get."

That is all it takes for my facade to crumble, causing the whimpers to tear from my throat.

Owned

WHAT FEELS LIKE THREE OR FOUR HOURS LATER, THE door to the room opens and rough hands grip my upper arms. "Get up." Mick pulls me from the small bed.

He takes me out of the room, and we walk through a set of seats. I notice the plane is just as long as any normal plane, except the seats are black and luxurious. A man opens the exit door and steps out of the plane with luggage.

Mick stops us at the plane's open exit door, and pain shoots up my arm as his grip on my upper arm forcefully pulls my shoulder on an angle, so I am facing him.

"Don't even think about trying anything when you leave this plane. See that car down there." I look to where he's pointing and see a black shiny limo. "Your sister is in that car waiting for you." I whip my head back to him, ready to get going. "Try to run or struggle, and that car will drive away, and you will never see your precious sister again. Do you understand me?"

I glare at him, sneering my answer, "Yes."

Mick squeezes my arm tighter, and I flinch at the pain. "See now that attitude is going to get you into a lot of trouble, Lily."

I square my shoulders to show him I'm not afraid of him. *I am though. I'm terrified.*

He shakes his head then pulls me down the stairs, leaving the plane.

We reach the bottom of the stairs, and Jake walks up to us, again his gaze penetrates into my eyes and I'm confused as to why the intensity is there.

"Jake, take Lily to the car and make sure she behaves. She's already fallen onto my hand once. Wouldn't want that to happen again," Mick says, wearing a smug look.

Immediately, Jake's eyes roam my face until he stops on my right cheek. He shows no emotion though, just a blank expression. *Bastards, all of them.*

Jake starts pulling me along with him. His steps are twice as big as mine. "I can walk on my own. You don't have to drag me." My voice is low and angry, frustration radiating off me. I try and pull my arm free, but I fail miserably. There is no way I can match his strength.

Jake jerks me into him roughly, and I gasp at the shock of being held so tightly to his chest. He's huge and his hands feel warm on my skin. It feels nice. That thought alone confuses and disgusts me, as if I would ever find comfort in someone like him.

Jake looks over to Mick, who is walking around to the other side of the plane talking to two other men.

His head turns back to me, and I have his attention again. He speaks low and impatiently, "You need to watch your mouth. Trust me. A backhand to your face is nothing to these men. Start realising you are in a different world now, a world where you have been caught and are now owned. You may not respect any of us, but we will demand it from you, or there will be punishments." I find my mouth wide open and clamp it shut. *That word again, owned.*

"There are other men where you're going, and they are just like Mick. If you aren't picked into the collection and become a slave of the house or sold off to God knows where. To those men, you are just an object they are allowed to play with. Don't give them reasons to take it further."

Collection, other girls, slave of the house. Terror rolls through me. This is hell. I have entered hell, and I'm entering it with my little sister. How can I protect her?

He starts walking again and my feet trip over themselves, my mind still stuck on his words. He slows his pace as I whisper, still stunned, "What's with the warnings. I'm sure my sister and I are just pay cheques to you, or are you one of those perverted sickos who actually gets off on seeing girls beaten and raped."

Jake scowls at me, frustration coating his features as he rubs his hand across his head angrily. "Fuck, no, I'm not, this is strictly business for me. Take my advice or leave it. I don't fucking care." His words sound strangled, as if it took great effort to get them out.

I'm about to ask Jake what the collection is when he opens the limo door and puts his hand on my head, more gently than I thought he would, directing me into the car.

As soon as the top half of my body is in the car I search for Sasha, and I see her anxiously waiting for me, obviously having watched me being walked over. I step into the car, and as soon as the door closes, the doors lock. I jump across the seats and hug my little sister. Thankful she is okay and unharmed; we cling to each other.

"Oh, Lily, I was so scared. I had no idea where you were, and no one would tell me anything. I woke up in a small room, and when I tried to get out the door, was locked. I screamed but no one answered until the plane landed. Then they told me you would meet me in this car. I thought they were tricking me, and I didn't know what else to do, but when I saw you walking over, I was so relieved."

I'm about to start answering her when she gasps.

"I'm going to kill them," she seethes.

Sash reaches up and gently touches my cheek. I flinch at the pain.

"Oh, Lil, what happened? Who did that to you?" she demands.

"I'm okay, and a man called Mick did this. Apparently, I was asking too many questions."

"Lily," Sasha's voice quivers, "what are we going to do?" she asks. I can already hear the defeat in her voice.

She knows we're outnumbered and overpowered. Any other time, I would lie and fix whatever situation we were in to protect my little sister, but I can't. I need her to be ready, mentally and physically, for what we might have to go through at the hands of these kidnappers.

My eyes sting with tears that I won't allow to fall. Rage and desperation surge through my blood like a torrent of forceful water, heating my body and clenching my fists. I don't want to do this. I don't want to tell my sister she may get hit, that she may get touched. *Oh, God, someone, please save us.*

"One of the men, Jake, just told me there are other girls where we're going, Sash. Some of the things they've insinuated..." I try to say this as gently as I can. "The men are brutal, and wherever they are taking us, it's going to be bad." I squeeze her hand, staring at her face trying to gauge how she's handling the information I just threw at her.

Tears start to fall from her eyes, and she whispers to me, "I heard men talking on the plane. I placed my ear to the door hoping to hear if you were out there with them, but all I heard were the men talking about you going into something called the collection. I have no idea what that is, and I'm worried what that means for us." She looks to the floor, her face clearly telling me her thoughts have turned to a dark place and the situations we may face soon.

I grab Sash's shoulders and turn her toward me, making sure she's looking me straight in the eyes. I vehemently assure my sister, "Sash, it doesn't matter what it is. We won't be staying there. I will find a way for us to escape."

Sasha's eyes spark with life at my words and she agrees, "Yes, we will find a way out, or we'll find someone to help us."

I come up with an idea. "We need to figure out where we're going. We need to look at what towns we pass. Look for names of any businesses that we could go to for help." At my words, I look out the window and start observing what is around us. Both planes sit on the end of a long landing strip that is surrounded by jungle. I see one large white building where people must wait for their flights and ten or more hangers, but there's no one around, except the men I recognise from the warehouse. I catch sight of Jake walking over to a large black 4WD. *This is an airport. Where is everyone?*

I look back at Sasha, who is also looking around, and I see my strong little sister start to lose it.

"What if it's in the middle of nowhere? What if there are too many guards? What if they kill—" She stops as sobs start to fall from her lips.

I pull her into my arms and rock my sister while she cries. Reassuring her with words that somehow I will find a way to free us.

⬩◆⬩

JAKE

I walk toward my ride when I hear Mick shout, "Jake!" *Great what does the prick want now?* I turn and see him walking over to me.

"Go with the sisters. Make sure they behave. You know

what to do if they don't. Joey's driving. The guys and I will be following, watching for tails."

He hands me the tranquiliser; the same drug we used on the girls in the warehouse. Insurance to get them quietly onto the planes, not wanting to risk people noticing two struggling girls. That's not a problem here though. Marco owns everything. All he had to do was tell them he had a delivery, and the whole fucking town clears out.

I nod and walk over to the black limo. I don't have to take orders from Mick. If it came down to it, it's me who he would have to follow. But I don't give a fuck who gives the orders. At the end of the day, they still have to be done. This life leaves your heart black. The less I'm responsible for, the better.

Before I get into the car, I need to remember why I'm here. I need to turn everything off and remember my end goal. I will not fail because of a girl who the old me may have fallen for years ago. She isn't going to fuck up my plans. She's just one of many, and I can get gorgeous pussy whenever I want. I shake out my arms and loosen up my neck to get in the frame of mind that has helped me all along— Indifference. I don't fucking care about anyone or anything else, except what I want.

I get into the car and sit down, expecting to find two frightened and pissed off girls looking back at me, but instead, what I find sends a jolt to my chest. Lily is cradling her sister while she sobs into her chest. Lily speaks to her in hushed tones, but I can't hear what she's saying.

The car starts, and neither girl shifts or seems to notice we are on the move.

A short time later, it seems Sasha has fallen asleep on Lily. Lily looks up and startles at seeing me. She narrows her eyes and scowls but says nothing.

I'm a sick fuck because I like her anger; it has my dick jumping. Everything she's done for the last two weeks has turned me on, but seeing the fire in her eyes now, that sends me crazy. This woman has so many different alluring versions of herself. She's intriguing. Just to look at her you would see a beautiful pure innocent woman, carefree with a fun-loving nature. But I've seen her turn her back to the world and crumble while she thinks no one's looking. I've seen her break, yet every time, she pulls up all her strength from deep inside, turns around and smiles a big fucking grin. Now there's fire in her eyes, gorgeous fucking fire like a wild animal standing in front of its prey, protecting it. She's addictive to watch. *Shit, stop going there.*

I shake my head to chase away my thoughts and answer her scowl, "Lily." Jesus, I almost moan. Her name on my lips for the first time feels so fucking good. "I already warned you about that attitude when you leave this car."

She ignores me and looks out the window. I see her throat close in, and then expand a second later. Knowing that action is from her holding in her tears and trying to stay strong makes my chest ache again. I rub where the pain is and wish it would stop fucking happening around this woman.

I have plans, and even if I wanted to save them, it's too late now. A lot of men would pay a large amount of money for beautiful, sun-kissed, Australian women with that innocent look. They ooze light, and knowing that light will soon be crushed under the weight of pain and fear, fucks with my head. I've seen it time and time again, but for some reason, looking at Lily, this time it feels different. She's a fighter. I know that. I already know she won't give up easily, not like the others.

The other girls started out strong, but by the time they got off the plane and into the car, they realised what was happening. Usually that's when the begging would start, then hysterical crying. Then I would have to give them the needle to shut them up. I shake my head to stop the memories. There isn't anything I can do for them now, and there definitely wasn't anything I could do for them then.

After an hour on the road and complete silence from Lily, she is still holding a sleeping Sasha. I notice she is concentrating hard on looking out the window, sometimes muttering under her breath. We've passed a few towns and her fingers have risen one by one. Realisation dawns as I figure out what she's doing.

"Lily." My voice is penetrating as I demand her attention, and it works. She turns to listen. "That won't work. Whatever you're trying to do with your fingers and counting the towns, it won't work."

Lily's eyes widen a bit, but not by much. She hides her obvious horror at being caught with a shrug. "I have no idea what you're talking about," she lies, relaxing her fingers, but doesn't put them down completely.

I sigh, feeling compelled to explain how impossible it is to escape. I want to give her some answers in the only way I can, which in this situation is ludicrous. I can't do shit to help her or her sister, and my answers will only back her into a corner and make her feel more trapped, but I still choose to fill her in.

"There are still two more hours before we reach our destination, and we only have one more town to pass, then there will be no more. Where we are going, there is nothing but ocean, highways, and fields. If you try to run and are lucky enough to get away from the fenced and guarded house, you will be walking for days before you even reach the first town. And trust me when I tell you Marco owns every one of these towns we have passed." I point to the outside world we are passing. "You will be found and held until someone comes and picks you up, and then you will be punished for running. And punishments for escaping are brutal." I stress the last part.

Lily's stunning eyes get glassy, but no tears fall. I can see it takes a great deal of her strength to do this. Fuck, am I still sitting here appreciating her courage, her strength to still look me in the eyes, after I just told her there is no hope for her and her sister?

Christ, I need to get away from this woman. She's fucking with my head. I focus all my attention staring out the window and ignore Lily. I need to get the fuck away from her. I can't care about her. I have come too far to lose it now. Four long years I have worked to get where I am now, and I won't let two Australian girls ruin it for me.

Bargains

SASHA WAKES UP, DISORIENTATED AT FIRST, SHE SITS UP and glances around the limo. I watch as she notices Jake. Her face falls, she hugs her middle, and the flicker of memories in her eyes breaks my heart.

Her tense shoulders turn toward me, and she whispers, "How long have I been sleeping?"

Softy, I reply, "I think about three hours, maybe a little less than that."

Sasha tilts her head toward Jake, who is still staring out the window, ignoring us.

I shrug, unsure what to tell Sasha. I don't want to tell her Jake laid it out for me and explained we have no hope of escape.

I start rubbing my temples, feeling a sliver of my sanity leave me, as again I'm left to tell my little sister that we are doomed. I have no idea what to do. I only know what people do in movies and books, but those ideas won't work in real life or would get us killed.

I don't care what happens to me. I just want to get my sister out of this situation.

Sash pulls my hands away from my head. "Lily, it's all right. We will get through this together, okay?"

I nod with a tight-lipped, shaky smile. *My beautiful, brave sister.* I close my eyes and exhale, rebuilding my strength. I will be strong, for Sasha.

I glance over at Jake. He's watching me, his hands clasped, arms resting on his thighs, eyes dilated and narrowed on me. A shiver runs through me as I endure his penetrating gaze. It's as if he's caressing my skin to find a way into my soul. Why does it seem like he sees straight through me? Why do I feel like I need to try harder to fool him? I don't want him or anyone to see the real me, the weak me.

Being the big sister, I will always put my sister first. It's what older siblings do. I can't fail, so I push my insecurities and fears aside, doing what's best for my sister, as I always have.

The car takes a turn, the first turn in a long time. I look out my window to see we're heading up a long cement driveway to a huge, black iron fence with intricate damask designs. The car stops in front of the black iron gate with stone pillars.

My eyes widen, and a tremble goes through my body when I see men dressed all in black, walking along the iron fence.

They are carrying machine guns. Radios are attached to their thermal army jackets on their left shoulder, and all have on black gloves, pants, boots, and ski mask. All you can see are their eyes.

My heart drops to my stomach. *Oh, God, it's a fortress.*

I turn my head, feeling pressure on my hand and realise Sasha is squeezing me tightly, almost painfully. Her face is pale and frozen with panic, mirroring my exact feelings.

Sweat coats my forehead. My stomach rolls, and I cover my mouth with my hand. I slump back into the seat as defeat slams into me and takes hold.

My eyes fall on Jake, and I notice him examining me with a strange look on his face, almost as if he's sorry that he was right.

Our car drives through the gates and veers to the left. We drive around a big circle of beautifully clean-cut green grass. Straight through the circle of grass is the biggest house I have ever seen—no, not a house, a mansion. A massive building made of marble. A large old-fashioned house I've only even seen in movies. We drive all the way around until the car stops in front of the towering manor.

My head shakes back and forth, not wanting to believe what I'm seeing. "What is this?" My voice tremulous. "I need answers. I need to know what we're about to walk into." I direct my question at Jake, my eyes begging him to tell us something.

Jake looks at me with what I guess is pity in his eyes. "Inside that house is a man named Marco." He points to the front door. "He's the boss. He will determine where you both go. Just keep your heads down and shut your mouths, and you'll get your answers. Just remember one thing, you think it can't get any worse; I'm telling you it can. Do. Not. push your luck with him. He's not a man who likes disobedience, at all."

I can't breathe. I'm suffocating, and I need to get out of this car. A door opens and Jake exits the car quickly, and then closes the door. A clicking sound echoes through the car. *Locks?*

I try the door handle, my assumption right. We are locked in the car. "Damn it!" I bend to put my head between my legs trying to breathe.

"Lily, what are we going to do? They have guns. Every single one of them has guns!" Sasha ends on a hysterical yell.

Oh, Jesus, we're both losing it. I focus on the carpet flooring, take four big breaths and sit up. Keeping my voice strong, I say, "I know. Escaping is going to be harder than we thought, but there will be a way. There has to be a way."

Sasha turns her head to the side and bites her lip. I take her hand in mine and attempt to reassure her. "We can do this. We need to be strong, and we need to listen to what they tell us. I don't know what they want with us." My voice wobbles. "The only permanent thing they can do is kill us. Anything else we need to stay strong and endure, until we can escape." My traitorous tears fall from my eyes as I tell my baby sister I can't protect her.

Sasha's eyes soften. "It's okay, Lil." She reaches up and wipes away my tears. "I understand. I'll be strong. As long as you promise, you will be too. I need you."

I drop my chin to my chest, and a sob rips from my mouth as my little sister forces herself to be brave for me. *Why aren't I strong enough to save her?*

The door closest to Sasha opens, and someone grabs her. Our clasped hands are ripped apart. We both scream. My nails scratch down her legs as I try to keep her with me.

All of the sudden, hands are under my arms pulling me backwards. I lose my grip on Sasha. I twist my body to loosen whoever has me. But I'm still easily pulled out of the car.

My hair blows in my face, and goose bumps rise on my skin from the cold breeze. I smell salt and can hear waves crashing; we're close to the ocean. I survey the area around me, and then I see it, the sea. The mansion sits right on a cliff. *Wonderful, another obstacle to getting out of this prison.*

Mick has Sasha and begins walking her toward the house. She glances back at me while trying not to trip over her own feet to keep up with him. A hand grips my upper arm, and I glare at whoever is holding me. Realising it's Jake, my blood boils. "You could have just asked us to get out of the freaking car."

He smirks. *How dare he*!

"And if I had asked you to get out of the car, would you have done that for me?" *No. No, I wouldn't have.* I would have sat there until someone had to rip us out. So what, they still could have asked. I choose not to answer him.

We walk up five marble steps and past four enormous

Sasha, tears silently fall freely down her face. I can see how close she is to losing it.

I look around the room. Seeing Mick first, his expression blank, uncaring. I spy the man in the corner who is still staring at the floor. This time he looks up and sees me watching him, his expression is unreadable, but I'm sure I see pity flash across his features.

"Father," he speaks, "we should be leaving."

Marco nods. "Yes, yes. Jake, Mick, good work, boys."

Marco picks up his briefcase and walks to Jake and me. Only speaking to Jake, he says, "Jake, I'm putting you as Lily's personal guard. She isn't to be out of your sight. The men already know not to touch my collection pieces, so if anyone steps out of line with her, you know what to do."

Jake answers quickly, "Consider it done."

Collection piece, is he fucking kidding?

Jake grips my elbow, obviously sensing my anger. I look down to my clenched hands; my knuckles are white. I need to calm down, *breathe, Lily*.

"Jake, Lily will be your new assignment now. If everything goes smoothly, you will accompany her to my home with the rest of the collection. You've earned your place. I trust you above many others. It's time for you to guard my prized possessions."

Jake tenses at Marco's words, and his hand squeezes my arm hard. I don't think he realises he's doing it.

"Take Lily to her room, third floor, first on the left. It's ready for her. Tell the slave girls to prepare her for a private party tonight. I will have Charles pick her up out the front at six pm."

Marco leans into me, and I don't move away. I'm in shock, trying to process and keep up with everything he is saying. "Lily, see you tonight. I can't wait to show you off." My stomach threatens to empty at his hot, nicotine breath on my face.

Untouchable

MARCO LEAVES BEFORE I CAN EVEN THINK ABOUT WHAT his words mean. Jake looks at me with an apologetic look. The expression disappears quickly, and he recovers with an emotionless face. What is he sorry about? Could it be the party? I need to find out what that is, and fast.

"Come on, girl. Time to go." Mick starts pulling Sasha out of the office. I step forward, but Jake pulls me back and gives me a warning glare. Sasha looks back at me with panic written all over her face.

"Please Jake, can't Sasha stay with me? We'll share a bed. Please, just let us stay together," I beg.

His voice is stern and gives me no room to argue, "I can't do that. She's to be sold, so she is a slave while she's here, and you're not. She goes to the other side of the house and stays with the slave girls."

"Lily!" Sasha screams. "Don't let them take me, please."

My heart explodes at hearing my little sister scream for me. She's thrashing around in Mick's arms. My mind is racing, and I'm acting before I even think about what I'm doing.

I forcefully shake my arm out of Jake's grasp with strength I didn't even know I had. I run to Mick and reach out to him to pull his hands off Sasha. He sees me there and pushes me backwards easily, and I take a few steps to regain my balance. I feel hands whoosh past my waist, but I'm quick, and I grab onto Mick again.

"Let her go!" I scream. "You have no right to do this to us!" I scratch my nails down Mick's arm, hoping that will get his hands off Sasha.

"Fuck, you bitch, you scratched me," he fumes.

I look down and see a small amount of blood drip down his arm. *Shit.*

While Mick is still looking at his arm, I take the opportunity to reach for Sasha. An arm wraps around my waist, and I go flying back into a chest. My breath is pushed out of me from the force of hitting the hard body. When I finally catch my breath and stop the dizziness, I look up to see Mick sneering down at me, raising his fist.

"You will pay for that, bitch." I flinch, ready for the hit, when I'm suddenly pulled around to the back of the body I was forced into. I look up and see the back of a familiar head, Jake.

"Don't even think about it, Mick," Jake growls. "She's part of the collection now, so that means you keep your fucking hands off her. Do you understand?" Jake's voice is loud and clear, with an edge that screams danger if Mick doesn't agree.

I look around Jake to see him and Mick glaring at each other. The air crackles with the furious anger in the room.

Mick growls and grinds his teeth together. "Fine, if I can't touch that bitch, I will just take it out on her sister then."

My heart stops and my breathing comes to a halt. I rush around Jake. "Please, don't hurt my sister." *No, please, don't let him hurt her because of me.*

Suddenly another man walks up behind Sasha, picks her up and throws her over his shoulder. She screams and starts kicking and hitting. "Lily!" she screams.

I try to run toward her, but again, I'm pulled back into Jake's chest. This time I don't need to recover. I see red and a voice I don't recognise shrieks out of me, "Let me go. Let me get to my sister!" I'm twisting and kicking in Jake's arms. "Don't you dare fucking hurt her. I will kill you if you touch her!" I screech to the man walking away with Sasha. My heart slowly dies as I watch my sister be taken further and further away from me. The man disappears down another hall, and Sasha is gone, out of my sight.

Mick just laughs at me.

My body sags in Jake's arms as I realise no matter what I say and do, I can't get us out of here yet. I'm only making it worse for the both of us. Tears continue to pour down my face.

"Please, don't hurt her. I will take whatever you think I deserve. She did nothing to you," I plead.

Vaguely, I'm aware Jake's arms tighten their hold on

me; however, I'm not sure. I feel numb. All of this feels surreal as if I'm watching it all from outside of my body.

Mick again laughs in my face. "I wish, bitch, but for now, you're untouchable. Won't be forever though. Then I'll repay the favour and make you bleed as well," he taunts.

"Fuck off, now, Mick. You've had your fun." Jake's voice is low and threatening.

Mick sneers at me once more before turning his back to us and going down the same hall the other man took Sasha down.

I'm powerless. I grab at Jake's fingers to pry them off from around my waist. I'm hysterical at the thought they will hurt Sasha when it should be me.

Jake lets go for a second, but before I can turn to run down the hall, he grabs hold of my shoulders in a frighteningly tight grip. His voice is low and penetrating. "Lily, I know this is hard for you, to be separated from your sister, but you're only making it worse for her. There is no getting out of here. You are both here in this house, and you're not leaving anytime soon. You need to start accepting that and start following the rules. The less you misbehave, the less they will take it out on Sasha to keep you in line." His voice turns soft as he feels the fight die out of me.

My chest is rising and falling fast. My head feels like it's full of pressure.

"Lily, did you hear me?"

I start pulling at my hair roughly, wanting to wake up from whatever nightmare I'm stuck in. This can't be happening. *No. No, wake up. Wake up!*

Jake grabs my hands and pins them to my sides. I see worry and what looks like concern in his eyes, but I must be mistaken. A man who lives this kind of life can't possibly care about me and my sister. It's just business for him.

My body gives up on resisting his hold. I still. "P-please, let u-us g-go," I beg through my wobbly voice.

Jake shakes his head. "Not happening." He pulls me with him by my arm, and leads me out of the room. I look back at the hallway and promise myself I will find a way to get down there and get Sasha out.

Everything Comes At A Cost

JAKE

I BRING LILY TO THE ROOM MARCO INSTRUCTED SHE STAY IN. He seemed intrigued by her, and I knew he would want her in the collection. From the moment I saw her in New York, she had become the most beautiful woman I had ever seen. Add in her fiery spirit and being from Australia, there was no way Marco wasn't going to keep her. I don't think he's ever had an Australian in his collection before.

I release Lily's arm and look at her devastated and pained face—still the most beautiful woman I have ever seen. She steps back from me and starts inspecting the room. The area is double the size of any standard master bedroom. She walks to the lilac cotton blanket on the luxurious king-size mattress and feels the material. Lily's eyes widen and she covers her mouth in shock at seeing the chandelier hanging in the middle of the room. Her legs move her to the white mirrored dresser. She looks at the perfumes that sit on top but doesn't smell them. She then heads to a set of double doors and opens them, her eyes going wide.

Lily gasps in surprise. She's gaping at the walk-in closet. It's full of shoes, drawers of clothes, and expensive dresses hanging up, plus accessories. Lily shakes her head and closes the doors. Opening a door next to the walk-in closet, she finds the bathroom with toilet and shower. She whips her head around to the windows, as if just remembering she needs to find a way to escape the room. Lily moves quickly to the white curtains and moves them aside. Her shoulders slump at seeing the bars on the windows. She looks to the right and sees in the corner, a small white metal table with two matching chairs. She spins to the door, her lips press tightly together at spotting the dead bolts on the outside of the door.

*Fuc*k. I quickly walk over and close the door. Too busy staring at her, when I should have been securing the room to make sure she can't get out. *Don't fuck this up.* I've worked too hard for the last four years doing dirty, gritty work to get Marco to notice me.

Marco O'Connor, king of the black market when it comes to sex slaves and the infamous collection. Four long-ass years of doing his dirty work to get here. I cannot mess up all that hard work, just for a hot chick. I have bigger plans. This is my one and only chance to get to the top.

Lily sits on the bed. Bringing her hands to her face, she sighs, "Beautiful room with bars on the windows and locks on the doors," she says quietly, muffled by her hands. "A beautiful prison." Soft words, laced with anger.

My eyes grow soft, and my chest aches again. I catch myself and decide I need to keep moving. I decide it's time to get her prepared for tonight. I get out my two-way and radio down to the kitchen.

"Maggi, send up some girls for the new collection piece. She needs to be ready for a private party tonight." Maggi is in charge of the slave girls. She organises their chores and makes sure the girls understand their roles in this house. Maggi isn't a slave. She is paid to be here just as I am. She lives close by with family. When she came to this house, her family were starving and she begged Marco for a job. So Marco gave her the slave girls to command. Maggi struggled with her position for months, but when you join Marco's empire, there is no getting out.

Maggi replies quickly, "Yes, sir."

Returning the two-way into my back pocket, I seek Lily out with my eyes and find her studying me. Probably trying to work out how I turned out to be such an evil bastard. *Join the club.* I have no idea when that happened either.

Lily glances away when I notice she is looking at my two-way. She starts biting her bottom lip and focuses on the carpet. She seems to be lost in her thoughts. If I had to guess, I'd say she is figuring out if these girls who are coming up can help her. I turn my back to her, as I can't hold back the grin that appears on my face. She's definitely not giving up anytime soon. A beautiful fighter, and fuck me if I don't want her to keep fighting, and hopefully find her way out of this hellhole.

"You were right. This place is a fortress. Getting out of here isn't going to be easy," Lily announces.

I turn to face her, my expression blank. "You will never escape, but I see you haven't given up yet."

She narrows her eyes at me. "Never say never."

My dick jumps. Fuck. I'm staring at her with an intensity I'm not used to, and it's just... Not. Fucking. On.

I turn away quickly and head over to the walk-in closet. Pulling out a few long dresses, I put them on the bed for her to choose from later on.

"There are rules for tonight and things you need to know," I explain, and Lily sits up on the bed waiting for me to keep talking.

"You will wear one of those dresses." I point to them. "I don't care which one, no jewellery, no—" Lily interrupts me when she starts laughing.

"Where the hell am I going to get jewellery from? As you can see," she points down to her day old blue dress, "I only came with what I was wearing when I got kidnapped off the side of the road," she hisses.

I raise an eyebrow at her and find I'm grinning, again. *Christ, I can't help it.* Lily is gorgeous when she's sarcastic and angry. The fire in her eyes could almost spark out and burn the fucking room down.

I walk into the closet. I sense Lily close behind me watching what I'm doing. I stop at a set of drawers and open the top drawer. Lily gasps, and I know why. The draw is full of millions of dollars' worth of diamonds, necklaces, bracelets, earrings, and rings. Everything a woman could only ever dream of owning.

"What on Earth is all this?" Her first reaction is to touch them; she gently strokes them with her fingers.

"You're in the collection now. That means you will receive jewellery, expensive clothing, shoes, the best of everything. Marco treats the collection like priceless jewels. You will never want for anything, ever again. But that comes at a cost."

"The Parties," she mutters, while still staring down at the diamonds.

"Yes," I answer quietly.

"Lily," I say sternly, making sure I have her full attention.

She raises her eyes to mine and holds my stare. "Always make sure to call him Sir. You don't want to know what he does to the women who call him by his name. Only the men are permitted to do that. He may keep you in jewels, designer clothes, and luxurious houses, but hear me when I say that does not mean he will not hurt or belittle you. It's what this is all about, his control over you."

Lily's eyes shine with unspilled tears. She walks out of the closet and I follow close behind. She walks to the middle of the room and gestures to the bedroom door with her arm. Still facing the door, she changes the subject, "Do you think my sister is being hurt right now? Do you think she is okay? Would anyone tell me if she got hurt?"

I sigh. I need her to focus on the party right now. "No, I don't think she is being hurt."

Lily's eyes swing back to me. She breathes out an enormous breath, like the weight of the world just lifted off her shoulders.

I continue, "Not physically anyway. She will be sold. The men know they can't damage the goods. And no, no one will tell you now or in the future if she gets hurt. You're likely not going to see her again. She will be with the rest of the slaves and made to work away from this side of the house until Marco finds a buyer for her. She will be dressed up at one point, and they will photograph her. Her picture will be sent out to possible buyers."

I do feel for her, and I understand her concern for her sister, but I won't help her. If Lily and Sasha had come a year or two ago, I may have cracked and helped them, but not now. I've come too far. I'm too close to getting what I want. I'm taken from my thoughts as Lily moves to sit on a chair at the small table. She hangs her head then pierces me with her eyes.

"I don't know nor do I care what made you into this horrible person, but I hope you and every other sick asshole in this house dies a horrible, painful death, hopefully in a burning fire, from a match stick that I light."

A smile touches my lips. I can't help but hope for the same thing. That's what all the men in this house deserve, including me.

I decide to change the topic. "The girls will be here soon. They won't speak to you. They have been instructed not to talk to men, or the women of the collection. Some have learned the hard way what happens if they disobey, so don't think you can get them to help you. If you still intend on trying, remember if they get punished, that will land on your shoulders. Do you have any questions?"

Lily's eyes flare with anger. "That's disgusting. Those poor girls."

I nod, not wanting to get into this with her. "Questions, Lily," I firmly state to keep her focused.

Her eyes go wide and she scoffs at me, "Are you kidding. I have hundreds. What is this private party? What happens there? Who will be there?"

I had hoped she would stick with the topic of the slave girls. The weight of those questions suddenly drains the energy from my body. I grab a chair from next to the window and straddle it. "I can't answer any of those for you. You will get told at the party." I could tell her, but we have learned in the past telling them too early made for an ugly fight getting them to the car. After hearing what happens, none of them want to go, not that I blame them.

Thank fuck I won't be there when Lily is told. Her horror-filled expression would fuck with my head even more. There's no way I wouldn't want to storm out of the place with her over my shoulder. My body is screaming at me to drag Lily out of this house right now. I clench my hands to stop myself from actually doing it. *Fuck, conscience, this is not the time to make a fucking appearance.* I have my orders, and I will follow them.

Lily lets out a cute huff. "How convenient. When I'm there and won't be able to leave." Ah, she's too smart for her own good. I shake my head, trying to keep the laugh to myself again.

A soft knock comes from the door. I go over and unlock the bolts with my keys. Three slave girls are there. I open the door wide in invitation for them to come in. They stand to the side and wait. I turn to Lily and see her observing the girls.

She turns to me as I speak in a serious voice, "Remember what I said, Lily. They won't talk to you, and if they do," I turn my head to the slave girls, "they will be punished." They all nod to me.

"Jake?"

I'm walking out when I'm surprised by Lily saying my name. I turn around and look at her anxious expression. "Will you be coming with me to the party?" The question throws me for a moment. Why would she want me to be there?

"No, Lily. A private party is for Marco to show you off so it will only be you there tonight. A party means you and the rest of the collection and their guards will attend. And only the top guards attend the parties. If I make it as a collection guard and come with you to Marco's house, then I will be attending the parties with you."

The thought of arriving at Marco's house sends adrenalin pumping to my chest. *Fuck, it can't come fast enough.* Lily nods to me, and I exit the room, locking the deadbolts. I sit on a chair in the hallway and wait for the girls to knock to let me know they are finished, and Lily is ready to leave for the party.

I sit forward and place my hands on my head. This shit is too much sometimes. Why is she affecting me so much?

I give myself a hit to the head. *Stop thinking about her, you dick.*

Soon, very soon, thanks to Lily, I will be going to the secret location of the biggest sex slave empire in the world, guarding the world's most sought after women. Then I will have it all.

Chapter 7

I'm So Fucking Sorry

AS SOON AS JAKE SETS THE DEAD BOLT, THE THREE WOMEN start talking to each other. They discuss who will choose my outfit, and do my hair and makeup. While they talk about me as if I'm not even here, I take the opportunity to study their appearance. All three young women have brown hair, varying from mousey brown to dark. Their hair is the same, tied back in a tight bun. A plain white sundress with thin straps covers their far too skinny bodies.

I take a step toward them, and they all turn to me. I decide to take a small chance, hoping this won't put them in harm's way. "I know you can't talk to me. But if you could just nod or shake your head. Can you please tell me if my sister is okay? I need to know. I think one of the guards, Mick, I think he might hurt her." My eyes dart to each of them, not wanting to miss any potential nods or shakes of the head. All I see are sad expressions. My heart starts beating a million miles an hour wondering what that means. *Argh.* "Please, please," I choke out. "We can call it a favour, and if you ever need one, I will repay it to you." I look at them, hoping this will convince them.

The girl standing in the middle turns her back to me and pulls up her dress to her knees. I gasp at seeing long white scars on the back of her calves. She drops her dress and turns quickly after my shocked response.

Tears fall from my eyes at thinking of what that must have been like for her. I hope to God Sasha doesn't go through that.

"I understand. I'm sorry for asking."

She steps forward, grabs my hand and squeezes. My tears slow then stop.

After a few moments, they all scatter around the room. One into the bathroom and one pulls out a long table in the back of the walk-in closet. It looks like one of those tables you lie on in a beauty salon. Another woman goes to the dresses on the bed.

Two hours after being waxed, prodded, pulled, and dressed, I'm standing in front of a massive mirror in the walk-in closet. I can't believe my eyes. The girls have worked magic on me. Pity I can't smile and thank them like I would have in any other situation. No, now I've grown angry.

Angry that there are people in this room, right now, who probably know what is happening to my little sister. People in this room who know what I will be walking into and they can't tell me anything. I want to scream and shake them until they tell me. But their scars flash through my mind, and I remember to bite my tongue. I remind myself, Sasha and I are not the only women being held captive here.

I distract myself by examining my reflection and see the beautiful black dress I'm wearing. Lace overlay, open back, princess neckline, three-quarter sleeves. A miniskirt underlay that sits mid-thigh, with lace falling to my feet. My hair is in a braid that hangs over my left shoulder. It's beautiful with a few strands hanging down just near my ears. After my shower, the girls pointed to the long table for me to lie down. One of the girls did my makeup, and she was fairly quick. When I study myself in the mirror, I see she went with a natural look. I'm thankful. I never wear makeup. It always looks wrong on me. Probably from my inability to know how to use all those confusing products.

After she had finished my makeup, I was sprayed with some perfume. One girl gave me a manicure then pulled me to the mirror where I got the shock of my life at my reflection. I was stunning, more stunning than I had ever seen myself.

Gazing at myself in the mirror, I can't help letting my mind wander to imagine myself getting ready for a date, a ball with a handsome prince. But reality is quick to snap me out of those thoughts as the girl who showed me her scars comes and stands next to me in the mirror, me in my gown and her in her dirty white dress looking underweight. I look to her, and she has a small smile on her face. I smile back with the same sad smile. She then leads me to the door, and one of the other girls knocks twice. We wait only a moment before I hear the deadbolt unlock.

Jake enters the room. His eyes hit me and go wide. His body freezes. *Do I not look okay?* My confidence wanes for a moment until I see the heat in his eyes. They dilate, and he licks his lips.

Jake clears his throat and runs his hands through his hair. He strides over to me while muttering something under his breath. I think it's a curse that hits my ears, but his voice is too soft to be able to tell for sure.

God, he is handsome. Why couldn't I get ugly scrawny Joey as my guard? I can see the guilt and indecision all over Jake's face. I wonder if he realises he lets his emotions show at times, or maybe he doesn't realise his walls fall down every so often.. When we were talking to Marco, Jake was completely blank. I couldn't see one flicker of emotion until Marco had left the room.

I wonder what made him who he is today. Did he have a bad childhood? No love from his parents? Is he as caught in this life as I am? His body screams power, but his eyes show me how lost he is, and as crazy as it sounds, I feel sorry for him.

I look away and laugh inside my head. How crazy is that? The man is holding me trapped, and I feel sorry for him. *He's the bad guy, Lily.* Maybe I'm going crazy. Maybe all this is too much for me and I'm starting to lose it.

Jake steps up to me. "You look beautiful, Lily," he announces softly. I'm amazed at his words. He thinks I'm beautiful? No, just a beautiful piece in the collection, to possess and control. Not a human being, a girl with a beating heart.

I take a step away from him. He doesn't care for me. He only cares for himself. He flinches as I distance myself from him. Again, he shows me a piece of himself I don't think he would show others.

Jake composes himself, and with his blank expression back, he grips the top of my arm tightly but not painfully, and pulls me to the bedroom door.

"Charles is downstairs waiting." His tone is stern and absolute.

His words paralyse my heart, and I feel myself suffocating. Fear is pulling me under to a full-blown panic attack. *Breathe. Inhale, exhale.*

We stop just outside the door and Jake twists his head toward the girls. "Girls, clean this room and have it ready for when Lily returns."

They all nod at the same time and start moving around the room.

Jake guides me down the hallway to the staircase, and I'm more alert now than when I climbed the stairs the first time. The walls are white with beautiful paintings strategically placed. There are tables against the walls with flowers, also chairs and sofas, all of them white or cream. This house screams sterile. Everything is clean, white and expensive.

We descend the staircase, and a thought enters my head. "While I was getting ready, did you see my sister?"

Jake answers, his voice toneless and uncaring. "No, I

sat in the hallway the whole time." My heart plummets. I need to find out something, anything, soon.

We step down from the stairs, and in a rash decision, I decide to make a run for it. My heart thumps hard against my chest. I clench my hands and bend at the knees ready to use all my strength to pull my arm out of Jake's grasp and surprise him. My legs spring into a run and Jake's hand slips off my arm. I'm starting down the hallway I saw Sasha dragged down. My mission, my aim is to get to her. Unfortunately, I'm not quick enough, and Jake has me by both my shoulders only a few steps away from where I started.

"Lily," he growls in warning.

My body sags in disappointment, knowing I can't match his strength. I give up, for now.

We exit out of the front door, and the same shiny black car that brought Sasha and me to this horrible place is parked right up at the front door. Jake walks me down the marble steps to the car. As he's reaching for the door, I feel him pause for a moment; however, he comes out of his moment and opens the door.

"Please, Jake," I say gently, resting my hand on his arm. "I can see you wavering. I can see you struggling with sending me off to God only knows what is waiting for me. Please help my sister and me. Marco isn't here. Just get my sister and let us run. All you have to do is watch us leave, nothing else," I implore.

Jake is silent for a few seconds, and for just a moment, my hope soars as I see him thinking it over. Jake shakes my hand off his arm, and my hope crashes and burns.

"I'm sorry." His voice is hoarse. "Fuck." He pauses again. "No, get in the car, Lily. There is no getting out of this. There's nothing I can do."

Jake pushes me gently into the car, and I go willingly, realising he may be fighting a war within himself, but there is no changing his mind. He wants something else more. Something more important to him than saving two trapped women will ever be. I'm numb as I sit and buckle myself in.

Jake leans into the car, his face expressionless but his eyes shine with misery. "I'm so fucking sorry." His whispered voice radiates conviction and honesty.

He steps back from the car. The door closes, and the locks fall. The car drives down the driveway and I look out my window and watch Jake following the car with his eyes until we turn, and I can no longer see him. I only see black iron gates, men with guns, and my little sister locked inside.

The Collection

I'M DRIVEN FOR ABOUT TWENTY-FIVE MINUTES BEFORE I FEEL the car come to a stop. Nothing happens for a moment, so I unbuckle and try the door handle; however, it's still locked. I hit the door hard with my fist.

"Shit." Maybe I could just break the window with something, climb out, and run. But I have no idea where the mansion is, where Sasha is.

I'm pulled from my thoughts as the car door suddenly opens, and I'm yanked out by ice-cold hands. A huge man in a black suit, white shirt, black tie, and bald round head has hold of my upper arms while I try to twist and squirm out of his grasp. Breathless and feeling a burning sensation on my arms from trying to get free, I give up. I look up and see the unimpressed expression on his face, as if he's seen a hundred trapped women, and he has no time for my hysterics. I'm nothing but a tiny annoying fly to this guy.

I decide to examine what is around me. I see an orange and white villa in front of me. It has archways that go the whole way around the front of the house. It's much smaller than the mansion but still substantial. It sits near the ocean. I hear the waves and spot the start of a sandy beach just to the right of the villa.

The massive man starts walking and I have to jog to keep up. Usually, I would tell him to slow the hell down, but this man does not seem like someone I want to upset. We walk under an archway and through an already open glass door. He takes me down a hallway. I look to my right and see a sitting area. The room looks like your average home by the beach. Painted blue and white, with pictures of boats and the ocean on the walls. I try to look to my left, but I miss my chance as Hulk moves us quickly down the hall.

He pulls me further into the villa, and then stops at a set of double wooden doors. I rub my fingers over my clammy palms as I watch him enter a code into the metal keypad on the door. He swings the door open, presses his cold hand to my bare back, and shoves me inside the room.

I yelp as I trip over my dress. Recovering, I turn quickly to grab the door, and it shuts in my face. I shake the handle and pound on the door. "Dammit!"

"It's no use. They won't open the door now until the party is ready for us." I spin around at lightning speed, whipping myself with my braid, at hearing someone's voice, a woman's voice.

Too concerned with getting out, I didn't look around to see I wasn't alone.

I come face to face with a stunning brunette. Her skin is fair, and her hair is dark brown with caramel highlights and big curls falling down just below her elbows. She's wearing a gorgeous, one-shouldered dark blue dress.

The woman holds her hand out to me. This time she speaks in a firm, businesslike manner. "My name is Emily."

I take her hand, shake it, and introduce myself confidently. "Lily."

She drops my hand and walks over to the lounge area where I see another four women, standing, staring at me.

Emily's hand indicates to one of the women, my eyes find a Chinese woman. She is stunning with the bluest blue eyes I have ever seen, olive skin, and short jet-black hair to her chin. Her dress is bright pink with lace embroidery and a mermaid fish tail, a Chinese-style dress.

She smiles at me and says, "Nin hao."

I'm at a loss at what she is saying to me; however, Emily saves me and explains, "She is saying hello. Her name is Cho."

I smile and softly say, "Hello, Cho." She nods her head and moves back to sit on the lounge.

Emily keeps going, "And this is Natalia."

Natalia has tanned skin and stunning wavy, brilliant red hair. Her hazel eyes sparkle accented by her sequined princess-cut top that attaches to a long light green flowing skirt.

"Hello," I say.

"Hola," she replies with a small smile. I know by that accent she's Colombian.

"Natalia says hello as well," Emily informs me.

A woman comes forward from behind Natalia and reaches her hand out to me. "Hi, my name is Megan." She grabs my hand, squeezes and gives me a bright smile. It's friendly and reassuring.

"Hi, Megan." I smile back just as wide, finding her friendly personality contagious. Megan has light brown eyes matching her curly light brown hair that reaches just below her shoulders. She wears a red sleeveless gown.

I let go of Megan's hand and turn to the last woman.

This time, Megan introduces us, "This is Adanya,"

Adanya stands and hugs me. Her leopard print V-neck dress feels like silk under my hands. Her hug is hard and tight, as if she will never let me go. She pulls back, and I see a tear slide down her face.

"Jambo," she says almost below a whisper. I think she is from Africa. She's stunning with long black braids in her hair and dark soft skin.

I reply, "Jambo, Adanya."

She gives me a sad smile and embraces me again. I hug her tightly back finally feeling like someone else understands what I am going through.

I release Adanya wanting to get answers from these women. My mouth drops open as it finally dawns on me as I look around the room.

Holy shit. Marco's collection, it's women from all over the world.

Emily sees my shocked expression and asks, "You're Australian, right? Your accent is strong."

I nod. "My sister and I were traveling in New York when we were taken from the side of the road and shoved into separate vans."

Emily nods, and then starts talking, "Adanya only arrived a month ago. She will understand what you're going through."

I glance over at Adanya, who is following our conversation. Emily speaks again but softer this time, "For some of us, having been here a long time, we have become somewhat de-sensitised."

I swallow past a hard lump in my throat. "A long time," I repeat. "How long?" I inquire.

Emily responds, devoid of any emotion. "Well, I have been with Marco for five years."

My eyes go wide. "Five years," I shout out, shocked.

Emily's head shoots up at my high-pitched words. Pain flickers in her eyes. "It does sound like a long time, doesn't it," she ends on a whisper.

After a moment of silence in the room, she regroups and continues, "Cho has been with Marco for four years. Megan and Natalia three, and as I said, Adanya joined us a month ago. There have been others but..." Emily stops mid-sentence with a strangled voice. She turns away and seems to get lost looking out the window. I sense she is fighting back unwanted memories.

I face the other four women and ask, "What happened to the other women?"

Megan answers. "They didn't behave, so Marco had

them removed from the collection. We don't know what that means. We just know we never see them again."

"What does not behaving mean?" I bite my nails knowing I don't want to hear this.

"Take your pick. Anything that isn't what those bastards tell you to do." She points to the door angrily.

"Megan," Emily sternly scolds.

Megan narrows her eyes on Emily. "Just because you are the queen at turning off your emotions, Emily, doesn't mean the rest of us are," Megan snaps.

"You're going to scare her," Emily almost yells.

Megan raises her eyebrows. "You don't think she should be afraid, of what she is going to endure tonight?" Megan yells, clearly stunned by Emily's words.

Aggressively, I run my hands through my braided hair and shake my head. "Excuse me, I am in the room." Both women's eyes swing to me. I take a deep breath and try to stay calm. "I am sick of my questions going unanswered by cryptic conversations. Can someone please just spell it out for me? Because I need to know what the hell is going on." My voices edges on anger but I manage to stay somewhat calm.

"A party is where Marco auctions our bodies off to the highest bidder," Emily answers, her voice dead of any emotion but her eyes show concern for how I may react. I'm too stunned. Her words roll over in my mind again and again until I can make sense of what she's telling me.

Emily continues, "Tonight was supposed to be a private party, a private party is where you get shown off but no one can buy you, yet. However Marco is unpredictable at the best of times and decided he wanted a full collection party tonight instead." Emily gestures to the door. "Out there in the party, we will be standing on a short runway. Surrounded by men, your skin will crawl. Your stomach will want to empty, but you won't be able to move. There will be five white circles on the stage, you must stand in one of them and you are not allowed to step outside of the circle or turn away from the men." Her words start to sink in and my sight wavers. I grow lightheaded. Grabbing hold of the lounge to help myself stay upright, Emily continues in a robotic tone, "The men will talk amongst themselves and eat appetisers as if you aren't even there. They will openly say which one of us they want to fuck tonight, and some even explain how they will do it." Tears start cascading down my face, but I don't move. I keep listening. "The men write down a price, and then put in a secret ballot. At the end of the evening, one of the guards will come and take you to a room where you will meet the man who paid the highest amount of money for your body."

Emily pauses, noticing my struggle to stay on my feet. I inhale a big breath, praying I don't vomit at the same time.

"The highest bidder is allowed to do whatever he wants with you, except leave marks on your body."

My mouth fills with saliva, and bile rises to my throat. I sink to my knees, still hanging onto the side of the lounge. After all the cryptic words from Marco and Jake, this is what I was expecting, wasn't it? To be taken against my will? Oh, god, raped. *Hold it together, Lily.* I can get through this. I have to get through this to get back to

Sasha.

Megan comes to me, sits on the floor, her hand rubbing my back in circular motions, attempting to soothe me.. I stare at the carpet. For how long, I'm not sure. Emily's words repeat in my mind.

Slowly, I swallow my saliva down my dry throat and look up to see Emily watching me with worried eyes. I have the attention of all the women in the room.

Megan's soft voice pulls my attention to her, "Lily, to get through this life in the collection, you will need to find a way to turn your emotions off and go numb. We are nothing but toys for them to play with, and they don't have a care in the world about what they do to us. They pretty us up, just to make us feel like dirt under their shoes. This is how they get their kicks, taking away our control and playing with your emotions. They want to see you cry. They want to see you powerless."

Megan wipes away the tears under my eyes, and with a penetrating voice, she announces, "Holding in your emotions, not letting them see you at your weakest is how you have the power. Choose a happy place now. Go there and stay there until it's over."

The door opens and four guards walk in. They separate, two on each side as Marco walks through the centre, still wearing his expensive looking suit and a smug grin on his face.

Megan pulls me up by the elbow quickly, and all the women stand in a line and lower their heads. Standing next to Megan, I look around the room in confusion and fear. Do I do the same thing? Lower my head? My heart twists at submitting to this monster.

"My jewels," Marco's croaky voice booms around the room, "have you all meet the new addition to your collection?"

Emily speaks up while keeping her head lowered, "Yes, sir, we have all introduced ourselves. Lily is a beautiful addition to our collection."

I gape at Emily. She speaks quietly, her tone obedient, keeping her head lowered.

"Wonderful. Lily, you seem confused," Marco says as he walks to stand in front of me. I tear my eyes away from Emily and glare up at Marco.

"When I enter a room you bow your head and wait for instructions to speak. Do you understand?"

My eyes go wide at his words and anger radiates through me. His voice bears no argument, but this is me. My mouth speaks before my brain thinks. "I'm not a dog. I will speak when I have something I want to say."

I notice Megan tense beside me and Marco narrows his eyes and moves in closer to me.

"That's all right, my girl. This is how all the girls started out, strong, sarcastic. I'm going to enjoy watching you struggle to hold on to that piece of yourself." An evil grin spreads out on his lips. "The men will pay the most for you. I hope to have a good year of your fighting spirit filling my pockets."

I pale at his words.

"Fair warning though, Lily, I may look forward to the men thinking you will be a challenge and paying handsomely for you." His eyes narrow and his face contorts in anger. "But when it comes to me, you will obey me!" he roars at me.

Instinctively from his loud and violent voice, my body tenses and I bow my head immediately.

"If you persist to be a disobedient cunt, it will be your sister who will suffer. Understood?" His low and sinister words are like a slap across my face. I nod quickly, letting him know I understand.

"Good girl," he says. His voice returns to normal with a hint of smugness. He pats my head and my dignity shatters to the ground. Silent, angry tears stream down my face.

"Emily, does Lily know the rules for tonight?" Marco demands.

"Yes, she does, Sir," Emily answers.

I watch Marco's legs step further into my space. He places a finger under my chin and lifts my head. I come face to face with him. In a quiet voice, he says, "If you follow the rules, Lily, you won't regret it. I will give you everything you've ever dreamed of; a luxurious house, all the clothes and diamonds you could ever wish for." My heart feels like a jackhammer against my chest. A tremble runs through my body, and I nod.

Marco smiles. "Excellent, Lily. I knew you were going to be perfect. I have to say you just might be the most beautiful and exquisite woman I have ever had in my collection."

He claps his hands and all the women raise their heads and look to him.

"All right, the party is almost ready for you. Ten

minutes and the guards will come and collect you. I can't wait to see my beautiful jewels all together on the stage."

Marco walks out of the room with the four guards and I hear the door lock.

All the women look at me with astonishment in their eyes. Cho points to me shouting in her language.

Emily nods to Cho and placates her with her hand as if saying 'I know'.

"Oh, my God, Lily. Do you know how lucky you just were?" Emily fumes. The first real emotion I've seen from her.

"I have seen Marco beat a woman for less than just talking back to him. You need to be more careful."

I close my eyes and start deep breathing, just needing a second to calm my heart. "I understand that was stupid of me. I'm just having trouble bending to his will. It's not built into me to take this from a man, from anyone," I explain.

Natalia, Cho, and Emily walk over to Megan and me and we all form a small circle holding hands.

"This isn't built into any of us, Lily," Megan states and continues, "This was physically and emotionally beaten into us until we realised there is no getting away. Don't make our mistakes. Learn from us and save yourself the pain."

I look at them all and nod, understanding they truly do care about what happens to me.

"You're one of us now. We will look out for you as best we can," Emily adds.

"Thank you," I say to them all.

Highest Bidder

NOT LONG LATER, WE ARE BEING ESCORTED OUT OF THE room in a line. Emily leads and the other women follow, falling into line, clearly showing they have done this many times before. There is a guard in front of Emily, one follows behind, and two guards in the middle and one on each side. They make a circle around us, no touching, just ushering us in a certain direction.

We are led into a dark room where a large black curtain hangs down, and lights shine through the middle where there is an opening.

Emily is the first to disappear through the black curtain, followed by Adanya, Natalia, Megan then Cho.

As each woman disappears, my hands start to shake, and I start backing away. I bump into one of the guards and yelp as I jump away from him. It's Hulk, and he looks at me with the same unimpressed expression.

He grabs my arm and pulls me through the black curtain. I shake my head while trying to pull away from him. *I'm not ready*.

I have to shield my eyes from the bright lights. I squint and see a spotlight over each woman. I glance around the room. It's dark. Men are mingling with each other near the bar and runway. All the women are standing in their circles looking out into the crowd of men. Except Adanya, she turns side on and stares at me, our eyes lock and I witness tears falling from her eyes. The men below her are lapping up her crumbling appearance.

Hulk easily pulls me down the runway as I watch what is going on around me. We pass Emily, Natalia, Cho, and I am placed between Megan and Adanya. I look down and see the white circle. Hulk puts me into the circle, and then leaves the stage just as quickly as he got me here.

The stage is long, but it isn't high. It only comes off the ground about two feet. There are women and men walking around in white uniforms carrying platters of food. My stomach grumbles. I haven't eaten since Sasha's and my last meal in our room before leaving for the rave.

I scan the room and the men in it. They're all dressed in suits and every one of them looks refined and respectable. How is it they can do this?

I'm wiping my sweaty hands down my dress when a man stands in front of me and stares. He's so close; he could reach out and touch me. I feel vulnerable and cornered so I narrow my eyes at him, hoping my foul mood will deter him. The man gives me a full smile.

Marco's words about my fiery spirit getting him many buyers rushes through my mind and I chastise myself for doing exactly what he wants me to.

We stand in our circles for what feels like hours. The man who was staring at me is not the last. Many men stand in front of me staring, talking, eating, and pointing. No acknowledgement is made that I am a human being. The men intimidate and scare me. Their leers and sleazy smiles send chills down my spine. My first instinct is to step away from them and walk off; however, Marco's warning about Sash suffering for my actions has me rooted to the ground.

During the night, I hear men state who they have already had, who they thought was the best and who they wanted for tonight. Silent tears fall from my eyes as I hear one man talk about Emily. "Oh, she struggled all right. I tied her to the bed, strangled her until she turned pale, and then let her breathe again. I then did it again, over and over until I decided she was close to death. Then I fucked the shit out of her, and left her naked and passed out. Marco sent Joseph around to me the next day. He beat the shit out of me for marking her, and that beating bloody hurt." He licks his lips and looks to Emily. "It was fucking worth it though."

I now understand Emily's businesslike manner. After five years of this hell, she isn't numb. She is dead inside.

Late into the night, a guard collects Emily, and she follows him off the stage. A few minutes later, Natalia is taken and then Cho. Cho looks back at us all, her face blank, no emotion at all. Another guard for Megan, and then another comes for Adanya. All the women leave with the same unemotional numb look on their face. I am the only one left on the stage and the room is still full of men talking and drinking.

I palm my hands together roughly while my eyes dart around wildly, waiting for a guard to come collect me and take me to my horrifying fate. Minutes later, I spot a guard walking toward me. He grabs my upper arm and steers me to the back of the stage.

We walk through the back room and down the same hallway we passed through to get to the stage. My body begins to shake with panic. *I can do this.* This is just like another one-night stand. That's how I will look at this. Unwanted one-night stand, but I need to rationalise this to get through it. Hysteria sits on the edge of my mind just waiting for me to realise I'm not convincing myself.

The guard swings a door open to my left. The first thing I see is a man's back. He is facing toward a bed that sits against white walls. The bed is adorned with black sheets. How fitting, black for what my heart will turn to after tonight. There's nothing else in the room, just one big bed.

The man turns quickly at our arrival and smiles at me. I don't smile back. I don't remember ever seeing him in the room. He's looks like all the others, dressed in an expensive suit, dark hair combed back with a face any woman would think she can trust.

The guard addresses the man, "Mr Smith."

Mr Smith nods but doesn't take his eyes off me.

A cold breeze whips up my back and I spin around just

as the door is being closed, and I hear the unmistakable sound of another door locking. Another locked room, but this time with a stranger who bought me for sex.

Mr Smith walks toward me. Each step he takes, I take the same amount backwards until I hit the door.

"Don't be frightened. I won't hurt you." His honeyed voice and smug smile shows his assurance is insincere.

Tears sting the back of my eyes.

"Lily, right?" Mr Smith arches an eyebrow with his question.

"Yes," my strangled voice says while my throat muscles tighten with incredible force. I don't want to appear weak; however, fear now has a tight hold over my vocal cords.

"You are the most stunning woman I have ever laid eyes on. Do you know that?" His eyes pass over my body from head to foot. His eyes show me his shameless want.

I remain quiet and still, watching his every move.

He takes two more steps toward me and I'm forced to tilt my head back to meet his eyes. He presses his body against mine and his hands grip my waist roughly. Bile rises to my throat as I feel his erection dig into my stomach. I raise a shaky hand to push him off me, but he grabs my wrist painfully tight, and slams it against the door above my head. A whimper escapes, and every muscle in my body screams at me to fight. But I stay frozen.

Thoughts race through my mind of how I can get out of this situation. But I can't. I need to do this, to survive and to get back to Sasha. I already did something stupid today that may have gotten Sasha hurt, and I can't let that happen again. The fight leaves my body as I realise I have no choices. This is going to happen.

Feeling my body lose it's fight, Mr Smith calms, and he encircles me in his arms. My body tenses.

"God, you smell amazing. I can't wait to fuck you." Whimpers fall from my lips as tears fall from his words.

Mr Smith pulls back and grabs my face, angrily wiping at my tears. "No crying," he orders sternly. "Walk to the bed."

On unsteady legs, I walk over to one side of the bed. I peer down at the covers and try to get lost in the patterns.

His cold hand runs along my collarbone. He clamps his hand down hard on the back of my neck so I can't move and starts unzipping the back of my dress. My spirit splinters as he drags my sleeves down my arms, and my dress falls to the floor.

Cries fall from my mouth as I feel his hands touch the inside of my thighs. Slowly, his fingers drag my underwear to my ankles. I'm standing bare, stripped of my self-worth. My chest constricts, and my mind begins to build walls, protecting itself.

He turns me around, and I hear him draw in a deep breath. I keep my eyes on his neck. He roughly grabs my breasts and starts squeezing, and I hiss at the pain.

"You know you love it," he whispers in my ear. I turn my head away from him and his ignorant words. He grabs my chin and forces me to face him. "Don't turn away from me," he shouts, his voice laced with anger.

I steady my feet and raise my chin to look him in the eyes. All I find is an evil, disgusting excuse of a man, who's eyes are gleaming with excitement.

"Lay down on the bed," he instructs.

I do as I'm told and crawl up onto the bed and lay down on my back, my head to the pillow. I cross my legs and place my hands over my chest to cover my breasts.

Mr Smith starts removing his clothes, and even though I know what's about to happen next, my heart hammers hard inside my chest. Mr Smith holds up his belt to me, and then he places it at the end of the bed.

"I will leave that there, just in case I have to tie you down," he says.

My body is now shaking violently. My fear is spiralling out of control. My breathing is coming quick and heavy.

I watch Mr Smith take off his pants. He begins to stroke himself and my stomach rolls. I put my hand to my mouth, fearful I'm about to vomit all over the bed.

I hear foil rip and watch him put a condom on. Tears fall quickly. One small mercy today, he's going to wear a condom.

He kneels on the bed and climbs on top of me. I can't control my tears now. Even if he threatened me with my life, I don't think I could stop them.

"Why are you crying? I haven't hurt you." He tries to wipe them away. His gentle touch catches me by surprise.

"I don't want this," I whisper on a sob.

"It's okay. I will make you feel good," he says as he starts kissing my neck. I arch away and groan angrily at how powerless I feel.

My instincts are to push up and try to escape, and that's what I do. But his arms shoot out and grab hold of my wrists, holding them down above my head.

I twist and turn to free myself from under him, but the weight of his body is too much for me. I'm not strong enough. Breathless, I look up and glare at him with glassy eyes.

He huffs out a laugh. "Marco was right. You are definitely worth every cent."

He uses his other hand and starts prying my legs apart. I tense my legs and hold my feet together by my ankles with all my strength.

He digs his fingers into my thighs and manages to part them. He falls between my legs, and I feel his repulsive hardness at my entrance.

"Please, please don't do this." I taste the salt of my tears with every plea that falls from my mouth.

His body rumbles with laughter.

I arch my head as far away from him as I possibly can. Sobs rip from my throat as I know what's about to happen.

Choose a happy place now. You will need it for later. I start searching my memories for something I can use.

Abruptly, he forces himself into me, hard. I scream at the burn and the roughness behind his push. He pushes in and out and I can't get myself out of this moment. I'm feeling too much pain. He grunts above me. His grip on my wrists gets tighter and tighter with every forced push inside of me.

He slows and kisses my neck and jaw. A sensation of bugs crawling all over my body takes hold. He moves his lips up toward my mouth, and as soon as I feel him there, I scream and wildly fling my head around, trying anything to get him away from my lips. While preparing myself to bite him if he tries again, I hear him laugh. He then returns to my neck.

He grunts loudly, and then his pushes become ferocious. The room echoes with the slapping of our bodies and his heavy breathing. My chest thumps painfully with the unfairness of what's happening to me.

He groans low and deep before his body falls limp on mine. Tears burn their way down my face, searing my skin as I feel his heavy unwanted body on mine, and the burn between my legs. At that moment, I beg God to end this, to end my life.

Breathing heavily, he rolls off me. My mind shuts down, and my body goes numb. I turn to my side and put my back to him, staring at a wall. I sense him move off the bed. There is silence for a few moments before he walks around to me.

Fully dressed, he bends to my height and pulls my chin down to see his face. He's smiling.

"Perfection, Lily. I can't wait for the next party." He stands and walks away.

I continue to stare at the wall. I crawl into the dark corners of my mind, darkness where I can be untouchable. Numbness is my best friend, and I hope it never leaves me.

◆◆◆

I'm not sure how long I've been laying here staring at the wall. When I hear two knocks, the door unlocks and opens.

There is silence for a moment, and then a man's gruff voice speaks. "You have ten minutes to get dressed and then you will be taken to the car and back to the house. If you aren't ready in ten minutes, I will walk you to the car naked." The door slams.

Still staring at the wall, I wonder how all the evil men in the world found each other. Not wanting to be further humiliated tonight, I sit up and lift off the bed, wincing from the pain between my legs. I look down and see blood. *Rough, bastard.*

I stand and reach for my dress and undies. I dress slowly and struggle with the zipper at the back of my dress. My wrists are too sore to push the zipper up, and I end up having to leave it half-undone. Better than naked.

The door opens again, and Hulk walks in with the same callous expression. He stands at the door and waits for me to exit. As I do, he grabs the top of my arm and leads me down the hallway and out of the villa.

It's pitch black and all I can hear are the waves crashing on the beach nearby. We get to the car and Hulk opens the door. I sit down and buckle up. My door shuts and the car takes off. I don't look back. I never want to see that house again.

I lean my head on the window, close my eyes and return back to the dark corner in my mind and hope that I can stay there forever.

There's No Place Like Home

I FEEL THE CAR STOP, AND AS SOON AS I HEAR THE LOCKS, I step out quickly, not wanting any more hands touching me. A guard I haven't seen before is waiting as I exit the car. I walk to the front door. The guard says nothing, only follows closely behind.

As I reach the stairs, I stop with one hand on the railing and look toward where Sasha is being kept. It feels like days ago I saw my sister being dragged down that hallway, screaming for me to help her.

"Up the stairs," the guard orders.

Exhausted and sore, I decide right now is not the time to attempt anything. I take the stairs slowly and head to the room I was in earlier. The door sits slightly ajar. I push it open further and step inside. I peer around the dark room and find Jake sitting on a chair in the corner. His head bowed and cupped in his hands, he is silent and unmoving.

The door shuts behind me and the deadbolt locks into place.

Jake's head whips up. His eyes find me straight away.

"I hope you have a key to get out because I do not want to be stuck in here with you," I state honestly, walking past him and into the bathroom. I feel his gaze follow me until I close the door.

Standing in the bathroom, I stare at my reflection in the mirror. It's me, but it's a look I've never seen before, one of great sadness. And for the first time in my life, I'm wondering when I will die, when this life of mine that has gone so tragically wrong, will end. My heart is lifeless. It beats slowly. Would it just stop if I willed it to?

How could Emily do this for five years? I would rather die than keep reliving this horrible night. *Sasha.* That's what would keep me going for five years or until I can get her out of here and on her way home.

I start undoing my braid. I want to go to sleep and wake up from this nightmare. I drop the dress from my body and enter the large shower. I pull the white curtain all the way along to block out the rest of the enormous bathroom. A luxury I have now earned, according to Marco. I make sure the water is scolding when I step under, and I hiss as it hits my skin. I find a washcloth hanging on the side of the shower. I take it, rub soap into the cloth and scrub my skin. I clean the blood off from between my legs scrubbing hard and fast, again and again, harder and faster, not wanting to leave a trace of that man anywhere on my body.

After a while, the bathroom door opens. "Lily," Jake shouts. "You've been in here for over an hour. Are you okay?" At his words, I notice the water is now cold.

"Get out, Jake," I growl back at him. I don't hear the door close, and my blood starts to boil. Can I have nothing anymore? No time to myself, no time to recover and lick my wounds?

Angry and not thinking straight, I step out of the shower. Jake's standing in the middle of the bathroom staring at the shower with indecision in his eyes. My guess is he's deciding whether he should go or stay.

As soon as he notices me, his eyes grow wide.

"Is this what you want? You want a look too, to have a go of me as well?" My voice is thick with emotion but controlled by my anger.

With wide eyes, Jake quickly swings his head to the side; however, he ends up facing the mirror and my reflection is still there, naked for him to see.

All of a sudden, his jaw hardens and starts ticking. He swings his head back to me and his eyes bore holes into the washcloth in my hands.

I look down to see what he's staring at, and I notice the blood from between my legs has turned the cloth pink. A heavy weight lands on my chest. It's as if at that moment, everything, comes crashing down. Being taken, having my sister ripped away from me, locked away and having someone forced on me. *It's too much.* And now, standing here before another man, naked... What am I doing? I drop the cloth to the ground, and openly sob.

Suddenly, something soft hits my body and I look up to find Jake wrapping me in a white cotton robe. He picks me up and takes me in his arms. They are warm and comforting. *Why? Why does he feel warm and safe to me?* Am I so far gone, so far fucked-up that I will take comfort from anyone right now? I answer my own question by burying my face in his neck and grabbing a tight hold of his shirt and crying into his chest.

He carries me out of the bathroom and gently places me in the bed. He pulls the covers over me, and tucks me in. My sobs slow from feeling warm and safe. I hiccup as he gently removes my wet hair from my face and lightly kisses my head. The action is way out of line, but I can't help but treasure the gesture in my moment of vulnerability. He leaves me and goes back into the bathroom. Instantly, I feel deprived of his attention.

I hear the shower turn off. Minutes pass, then all of a sudden I hear a thundering man's roar and glass breaking. Silence again.

My eyes start closing and I wrap myself further into the blankets. Repeating in my mind until I fall asleep... *There's no place like home. There's no place like home. There's no place like home.*

◆◆◆

I wake with a start, my mind forcefully reminding me of things I wished I could forget. I glance around the room and find Jake asleep on the other side of the bed. On top of the covers, his feet to my head, facing toward me. No shirt on just a pair of jeans. He's lying on his arm as it rests stretched out under his head. I can see cuts on his knuckles, so I assume he must have punched the mirror. *Why?* Is this his first time kidnapping someone, and he can't handle it?

There's bad men and there's good men, but Jake keeps swinging like a pendulum between the two, and I can't fit him into a category where I feel he belongs.

My eyes find his chest; it's masculine, defined, and tanned with a small amount of hair. He has tattoos over his arms and chest, a cemetery tattoo covers his entire right arm and up over his right pectoral. I see tombstones with men's names on them; Phillip, James, Alex.

I creep out of the blankets and lean down closer to his chest. I move on to another tattoo and freeze. The tattoo on his left pectoral has a world globe with a ship's anchor and an eagle sitting on top of the globe. My eyes go wide when I read, *U.S. Marines,* at the bottom of the tattoo. Jake's in or been in the US Marines? My mind is reeling from all the possibilities. Can he help me? Why is he working in human trafficking?

Suddenly, my wrist is pulled back roughly. I didn't even realise I was touching him.

Jake rolls off the bed and pulls his shirt on quickly without even looking at me once. "You're a marine," I whisper, looking at the back of his head, begging him to turn around and talk to me. After a moment, he turns. I can see him thinking over what answer to give me.

"I was. I'm not now," he clips out.

"The names on the tombstones, were they soldiers?" I say softly. Jake closes his eyes tightly, and I see pain cross his features. He shakes his head and looks at me. My eyes soften, and I feel sympathy for him, but at that moment, his face darkens and shuts down.

"And what makes you think they aren't men I've killed." His tone is icy. "I put them on my skin to remind other assholes if they get in my way, they will pay with their lives," he growls.

"Lie," I think and say at the same time. The lie is written all over his pained expression.

Jake looks at me shocked as if he's surprised I just called him out on it. Damn my big mouth. Jake makes an angry laugh. I can see his veins in his neck straining from his anger. "You think you know me, from one tattoo?" He smacks his chest angrily where the tattoo sits.

"No," I answer softly, treading carefully, realising he's right. I don't know him at all. But of course, my mouth is ahead of my thoughts, and I say, "But I do know all of this." I swing my arms around. "This life you lead is hard for you. You try not to let it show, but you care. You care about the horrible things these men are doing," I end with a raised voice.

Jake's stare is firm and unwavering. I feel like I need to get out of the way of a fireball he's about to launch at me. His chest is rising heavily, and he starts pacing angrily, shoving his hands through his hair. Then he turns to me, red in the face like he is about to explode, and he does.

"Because I don't fucking care!" He roars at me. "Fuck," he yells to the ceiling.

He swings his head back at me with wild eyes and heavy breathing. He looks like a cornered animal ready to strike. He pinches his nose and closes his eyes trying to calm himself, his chest is still rising and falling rapidly.

"I didn't fucking care about any of it," he mutters so softly; I can barely hear him. He points a finger at me. "Until you."

My eyes grow wide and my mouth drops open from his revelation.

"There's something about you, Lily, and for the life of me, I can't get you out of my head. You're not the first woman I've seen go through this place and be destroyed. No, there have been many, and it's fucking hard to watch."

I tense as he takes purposeful strides toward me. He sweeps me up into his arms, and he whispers into my neck, "But fuck, watching you in pain, watching this ugly world destroy you, it's not just hard, it's crippling."

My hands gently rest on his biceps not knowing what to do. My emotions are begging me to hold him, but my mind is telling me he is the enemy.

"I don't know you at all, but shit, I care what is happening to you, and I hate that." He sounds so lost. We stay for a moment in this position, frozen in time.

And then all of a sudden, Jake drops me from his arms and steps back. "But I have my own plans and my own goals. I'm not going to let you or my feelings get in the way of them."

He storms across the room and pauses, breathing deeply. He turns and looks back at me with a hard stare. "I may care, but it will never be enough to take my eyes off the prize. And that is getting to Marco's house, getting to the top of the ladder, and to the top of this empire."

My heart squeezes at his words. Still, I dare to ask the question I need to know. "So you could save me and my sister?"

Jake closes his eyes tightly, and then opens them, nailing me with a penetrating stare. "I could, but I won't. I won't save you, or anyone else." His tone is stern and absolute.

"This doesn't make any sense," I say, shaking my head. "Why do you need a human trafficking empire at all?" I ask, struggling not to cry.

He stands frozen staring at me, again surprised that I keep questioning him. "None of your goddamn fucking business," he snaps back angrily. "Now, get dressed." He heads for the door.

The blood running through my veins bubbles with anger.

He could save us, but he won't. Bastard.

I want to go feral and scratch his eyes out. I want to smash everything in this cage they call a room. I may be physically weak, but I'm still a fighter.

"You sick bastard," I hiss at his back as he tries to leave the room. He stops in his tracks and turns back to me. He gives me a blank expression, uncaring to my growing anger.

"Glad you finally figured out who I really am."

"Oh, I know who you are. You're as bad as those men who raped me and the other women from the collection last night." I stop to catch my breath and find I'm panting heavily.

Jake's whole body freezes. Deceptively soft, he asks.

"What did you just say?" I should feel terrified by his tone, but I was too angry to care.

"You heard me arsehole," I reply.

The room goes eerily quiet. Then I feel it. The anger and the ferocious tension in the air. Jake looks like he's paralysed, his eyes black, his hands fisted causing his knuckles to go white. The only thing moving on his body is his ticking jaw.

Losing some of my anger at realising just how angry Jake is, I swallow and take a step back.

"The Collection was there?" Jake's asks. Still frozen in one spot, his voice is low and taut.

I nod, too scared to talk right now.

"Who?" he demands and finally moves by taking one step toward me. "Who the fuck was there, Lily. Did you see them? Did you talk to them?"

Panicking, I answer, "Y- Y- Yes I met them and got their names. There was Natalia, Cho," I shut my eyes tightly, trying to steady my heart and remember all the women's names. "Emily, Adanya and Megan," I quickly finish.

"How many guards were there?" Guards? Where is he going with this?

"I think four. Four walked us to the stage, maybe five. There was another guard who walked me to and from the villa."

Jake sits on the end of the bed with his hands clasped in front of him, muttering to himself under his breath.

I walk over to stand in front of him. I should have more thought for my safety, but curiosity wins out. "Jake," I say to him. He looks up at me as if only just realising I'm still in the room. "What am I missing here? Why do you care who was there and how many guards there were?"

Jake narrows his eyes at me then stands. I think he's going to just walk out of the room, but he doesn't. "I need to know how many women are in the collection to know how many guards there are. I need to know there is still a spot for me when you arrive there."

My mouth flies open at his words. He's only worried about himself. Am I that desperate to want the man who cared for me last night to have some redeeming qualities, that I am now making them up in my head?

He smirks at me. "Oh, Lily, don't go making me the good guy. You will be disappointed."

Jake moves away from me and leaves the room.

Well, if Jake refuses to see me as a person worth saving, I'm just going to have to change his mind.

Let the games begin.

Chapter 11

If Only She Knew

JAKE

IT'S DAY SIX OF LILY BEING AT THE MANSION AND I'M walking out of my room this morning with a huge fucking annoying smile on my face. For the last four days, Lily has tried every trick in the book to get to me. However, I see straight through her actions. I see her plan. She wants me to care for her, to see her as a person so my conscience will get the better of me, and I will save her and her sister. I'm wondering what new strategy Lily will try today. This damn smile, I can't get rid of it. So far, she's told me jokes which I laughed at, but only because they were so bad.

"Hey, Jake, what do Eskimos get from sitting on ice for too long?" I'm silent, looking at her with my usual blank

expression knowing she will pop out with the answer soon.

"Polaroids." Her eyes sparkle with laughter, and her expression shows her eagerness for me to react to the joke.

I bark out a laugh, shocked at how much the stupid joke makes me laugh and her cute determination to get a reaction out of me. Damn, this woman will be my downfall.

Then Lily moved on to tell me stories about Sasha and herself as children. I listened intently, eagerly wanting to learn anything new about her. Lily explained that her and Sasha would talk for hours in their favourite childhood tree.

"When Sasha was seven, she wanted to take over the world by making an addictive chocolate so she could control everyone. However, after we talked to our mum, she informed us that, number one, people were already addicted to chocolate and that plan would only work on women. So we went back to the drawing board."

I would try to cough or cover my mouth to cover my chuckle, but Lily would spot me and jump head first into her next story.

She broached the subject about her ex-boyfriends, which made me grunt and walk out of the room. I didn't leave because of the topic. No, I left because that just happened to be when I'd had enough of her playing this game. *Lie.*

I went back to her room hours later to install a new bathroom mirror for her since I punched the other one. Luckily this place is so huge I could just take one from another bedroom that's never been used. Lily followed me into the bathroom, sat in the bathtub and changed her tactic to telling me about her family's farm, a farm that has been in her family for four generations. Every memory reignited the light in her eyes. The room lit up with her beautiful smile. You could tell she had a wonderful childhood surrounded by family who loved her very much. Her childhood reminds me of my own, filled with laughter, love and big family get-togethers.

Day four when I returned after taking her lunch away, her locked door handle was rattling, and I laughed aloud realising she was trying to pick the lock. As soon as I laughed, the rattling stopped. I opened the door, peeked into her room, and she was casually sitting on the bed reading a book... upside down.

I examined her and found nothing. When I asked her what she was using, she just shrugged, and said she had no idea what I was talking about. I wanted to throw her across the bed and rip her clothes off at that very moment. The sneaky minx was fucking hot when she was defiant. I searched her room and found a metal spoon with a bent handle hiding under the bed.

I've since talked to the slave girls about all Lily's cutlery now being plastic, Lily was not impressed at dinnertime that night. Her response was a lot of muttering and cursing me under her breath. Fuck, my cheeks are starting to hurt from grinning so much. I shouldn't be having this much fun with her, but I am.

Day five, I could see as soon as I entered her room she was agitated, narrowing her eyes at me. She had given up on talking about herself and had started confronting me with questions about me.

"Why are you pretending to be someone you're not? I can see you're trying to show me the big bad man you think you are, but too many times you slip and I see a gentle, caring man."

This woman, she constantly shocks me with her defiance. She has no defences yet she doesn't give up her fight. Why isn't she scared of me? I'm not saving her. Her stories of home and family will do nothing to deter me from what I want.

"It's complicated and not something I will discuss with anyone. I am off limits. If you try to dig too deep, I will walk out of this room and not return until we leave for Marco's house. That could be weeks, months. Do you want to be alone that whole time?" I'm a liar, not even King Kong could hold me back from being around Lily now.

I see her flinch at thinking about having no human contact except for the parties for that long. She walks away from me and into the bathroom, slamming the door closed. I smile at her attitude, and again look to the heavens and pray I can hold on to my sanity when it comes to her. If God had created a woman to truly test me, that woman would be Lily Morgan.

Lily's plan is working though. She is getting to me. Every moment we have together and every story she shares with me is slowly breaking me down. When I feel myself losing my fight, I leave the room to remind myself of why I'm here, and why Lily is staying here too. If Lily was suddenly able to leave this house, it would probably devastate me. Her smile is the only bright thing in my life right now. I'm desperate for her to know the real me, to choose me, even if all she will ever have is my dark side.

No matter what Lily does, I'm intrigued. I want to know more about her. I want her to show me how much further she's willing to try to test me. I'm a sick bastard, but I'm getting off on it. I've never needed to get myself off since I was a teenager. In the past I've headed into town taking whatever woman is willing. I had a fucking fantastic time, but in between those times, I've never felt the need to take care of myself, but I've never had a fucking gorgeous Lily Morgan wrapping me around her finger before either. Now, every night I go back to my room with a rock hard cock and the need to relieve myself, so I don't crash tackle her to the bed the next day.

Stroking myself, one hand to the wall, the other imagining it's Lily's defiant mouth licking and sucking me up and down, slowly. All it takes is remembering her strength, resilience and each time she tried to out manoeuvre me or get to me. I let out a roar of ecstasy as my cum spurts onto my hand. I fall against the shower wall breathing heavily.

If only she knew what she did to me. It would probably disgust her.

My now hardening dick brings me back to the present. As I turn from my door, which is only one room away from Lily's, my cell phone rings. I take it out of my pocket. It's Marco. Could this be the day we leave for his private house.

I answer quickly. "Jake," I clip out.

"Ah, Jake, how is everything?" Marco asks in his horrible croaky voice.

"Everything is fine, Marco. What can I do for you?"

"Dr Kingsley will give Lily a full check-up today. Make sure Lily is compliant." A doctor's appointment, that's all, damn.

"Will do, Marco, anything else?" I'm hoping he might give me some information on our moving date.

"No, just keep watching my precious piece. I've had a lot of intrigued men wanting to know when my next party is thanks to Lily. Nothing can happen to her. Do you understand, Jake?" Marco demands.

My stomach feels like it's churning up sharp nails as I reply, "Understood." Marco hangs up.

I head to Lily's room, needing to get her ready for the doctor.

All the slave girls have gone through the same check-up. The doctor is a woman. She sees the girls when they arrive and for any other medical treatment. I know Doctor Kingsley is unhappy about what she does. She's not here just for a job. She's here because she feels she has to be.

I unlock Lily's door and enter as she's exiting the bathroom, showered and dressed in a pair of denim shorts and a white t-shirt. Her style is casual and comfortable, yet she looks like a goddess, her dark blonde hair flowing over her shoulders and her curves begging me to caress them with my hands.

Our eyes meet, and my dick instantly goes from semi-hard to rock hard. *Fuck.* Every time I see her, her eyes always knock me on my ass. I will never forget the way they sparkle and how they make me feel. It's as if they pierce me right through the heart. They will haunt me every day for the rest of my life. They entrap me. I force myself to look away, feeling like I've just stripped her naked with my bare hands.

I clear my throat and look back at Lily. She's still standing, staring at me, her look now inquisitive.

"Marco sent a doctor here this morning to see you. She will be waiting for us in a cottage out the back of the house," I explain. Lily's face goes from furious to quietly angry. She calms as soon as I mentioned the doctor is a woman.

"It's standard. She will test for diseases and illnesses, but you will need to strip for her. I will wait outside the cottage until you're done."

Lily ignores me, goes into the walk-in closet and pulls out a pair of sandals. She sits on the floor and starts putting them on without a word to me and what I've just told her, so today must be 'ignore Jake day'. That could work for me.

She stands, finished with her shoes. Lily walks to the door and waits, fidgeting with her hands and staring at the ground. She looks lost in her thoughts. *Is she planning again?*

"Lily, you should know, the doctor is on Marco's payroll. Telling her anything won't help you." Lily's head shoots up to me, and after a moment, she scoffs and rolls her eyes at my comments.

"Christ," I curse under my breath, while massaging the aggravation out of my neck. She was going to talk to the Doctor.

I take Lily's upper arm like I always do and we walk

through the hall and down the stairs. I lead Lily toward the back of the house. She tenses as she realises we will be walking down the hallway where Lily last saw Sasha. I glance down at Lily and see the hope on her face.

"I can't promise you will see her." I can't stand seeing the anticipation on her face when my job is to keep them apart.

Lily looks up at me. Her face is hopeful and sad at the same time. "That's better than nothing," she says softly and the ache in my chest returns.

I lead Lily down the hallway, into a huge kitchen area, and then out the door to the backyard. I hear her sharp inhale as she feels the sun on her for the first time in six days. Her eyes explore the lush green grass of the massive backyard. The grounds stretch out until it hits the cliff, and all you can see is the deep blue sea that goes on forever.

Lily looks to her left and sees the rows of veggie gardens. Behind them are fruit trees—apples, oranges, and bananas. Part of the slave's jobs is to maintain and collect the fruit and vegetables. Marco believes if they are kept busy, then there is less chance of them trying to escape. Crazy enough, the man doesn't think the public beatings are enough to sway the girls from trying.

Marco has twenty-five guards who guard this mansion and twenty slave girls who work it. This house is where he has the auctions for the girls he kidnaps. Three times a year, he sends out hunters to pick up girls, just like we did for Lily, but when we search for a collection piece, Marco has a particular type of girl he wants, and he doesn't care where she comes from. Usually, he instructs us to pick up homeless girls, or women who look like they are alone at college, or just moved to a new city. The hunters do an assignment for about two months making sure the girl won't be missed. Then the girls are picked up, brought here, and work until their auctions. Marco does the auctions through a video message. The buyers look over all the slaves and they put in bids—highest bidder wins. Highest bidder always wins. Marco only ever does anything to make more money and have more power for himself. His obsession is power. He has as much as one person probably could ever have, but he never stops striving for more.

I keep us walking down a path to my right, seeing the cottage just five metres from us. I'm focusing on the steps that are coming up when I feel Lily use all her strength to twist and yank her arm from my grasp. "Lily!" I quietly shout to her. My hand slips from her arm, and I try to grab her with my other hand but only lightly brush her skin as she makes a run for it.

She sprints to the left, and I quickly peer around her, searching for where she's headed. I spot a brown-haired girl kneeling on the ground picking tomatoes. Sasha—Lily spotted her. I could quickly catch up to Lily, but I delay my reaction and then start chasing after her.

Auction

I'M SPRINTING, MY PULSE BEATING HEAVILY AGAINST MY SKIN. I see her, my sister. Nothing is going to stop me from reaching her. Finally, she's in my sights again. Kneeling on the ground with her head down, she's touching plants in front of her. I look around, and I see a lot of women kneeling around the plants, their heads down in concentration as they work.

I come to a stop behind Sasha—her hair looks ratty, and she's wearing a filthy white dress that looks like it has never been washed.

I bend down and gently touch her shoulder. She flinches at my touch. I pull my hand back and softly speak, "Sash?"

She spins around and my eyes widen. *No.* Her lip is severely cut and her right cheek has a purple bruise. Oh,

God, what have they done to her? I grab my sister and hug her tightly hoping to fuse us together so no one else can hurt her, and Sasha hugs me back just as furiously. I feel her tears hit my skin, but I hear no sobs coming from her, and I gently rock Sash, hoping to soothe her.

"You can't be here." I hear a rough voice say behind me.

"What the fuck happened to the girl, Mick?" I hear Jake demand.

"I have no idea. Maybe she slipped and fell over," Mick responds with a sly tone. My body stills, and my hands curl into fists at his response.

"Bullshit, you know the rules, Mick. You don't touch the face when they are punished. Sasha is up for sale in a few days. If Marco finds out, there will be hell to pay."

"Fuck off, Jake, she'll heal and be fine for the auction. Marco never needs to know," Mick spits at Jake.

My blood runs cold. *Sale, Auction.* Sasha tenses in my arms.

As Jake and Mick argue in the background, I hold Sasha's face in my hands, careful not to hurt her bruises. I wipe away her tears and look into her eyes. She looks defeated and lost.

"I will find a way out before then. Please trust me. Do what they say until then, okay?" Her eyes are shining, and her lip quivers. "I know this is the hardest thing you have ever had to do, but please hang on just a little bit longer for me," I beg.

More tears fall from my baby sister's eyes, and I feel some of my own as she nods.

She puts her arms back around me again with so much

strength I can't breathe properly, but I don't care. I never want to let go of her again.

"I love you, Lily. Please, always remember that," Sasha fiercely whispers to me. A sob rips from my chest, and I nod into her hair, praying to God too. *Please get us out of here.*

Jake's warm hand tugs on my shoulder. My first instinct is to push away from him, but now more than ever, I understand I need to behave.

I kiss Sash's forehead, stand and leave with Jake. Walking away, I keep my eyes on Sash. She watches me until I see Mick say something to her, and she cowers and starts working on the garden again.

I stop dead on the spot and throw as many spears from my eyes at Mick as I can.

"Lily," Jake warns, "you will only cause more trouble for her. Leave it alone."

I remember her beaten face. "He hurt her," I whisper.

"Be thankful that's all that happened to her." Jake's tone is gentle.

I reluctantly let Jake pull me toward the cottage. "You knew she was going up for auction soon, and you didn't tell me," I say furious.

"Yes, I knew you would go ballistic. I didn't know how to tell you and then have to try to contain you." His eyes tell me he is telling the truth.

Jake stops us near the entrance of the cottage and turns me purposely toward him. "You need to think about the possibility that Sasha could go somewhere better than here. There are people who go to these auctions to save those who are trapped."

Hope blooms in my chest. "Do you honestly think that could happen?"

Jake looks back to the house and then back to me. "Yes, I do think that is possible. Plus a lot of places would be better than here."

"And what if someone like Marco buys her? What if someone like—" I can't finish my sentence remembering the party. "I can't take that chance, Jake. What if some sick asshole gets to her, and I have no idea where he takes her. It could take me years if ever to find her. And that is when or if I ever get away from here." Frustration coats my words.

"Sometimes you just have to have faith, Lily. Plus there is nothing you can do right now."

"Ha! Really? If you had a sister or brother, could you do the same? Just hope that everything turns out okay?" I growl.

"Yes, Lily, that is exactly what I would have to do since there is no way to escape. Now, come on. The doctor's waiting."

Jake cuts off our conversation and begins walking into the cottage as I whisper, "I said could you, not would have to."

Jake shows me which room I need to go into. I enter and leave him behind. I fumble with the back pockets of my shorts as my nerves play havoc with my mind.

The room is straight out of a hospital. White walls, long

bed, machines, and blue curtains going around the bed.

A tall, gorgeous woman with shiny black hair steps out from behind the curtain, wearing a doctor's white jacket over a black dress with black high heels. She smiles and extends her hand to me.

"Hello, I'm Dr Alexa Kingsley," she states in a friendly and sweet voice.

I just stand there motionless and stare. She actually expects me to shake her hand? I don't return her smile either. As far as I'm concerned, she is betraying the whole female race and should hand in her female card and get a sick and twisted bitch one back. Yeah, I'm angry. Angry there are people all around me, and no one is willing to help me.

Her smile dies when she notices my scowl. She hurriedly gets to work, not looking me in the face again, only giving instructions on what to do. Her voice is emotionless now, but I can still hear the soft, friendly tone she has. She sounds just as unhappy to be here as I am. She takes my blood, checks my weight, height, and does an internal exam, which is uncomfortable, but at least a woman is doing it.

As she sits me up and starts writing in her folder, Marco's son, Joseph, enters the room. He steps to the back of the room, leans against the wall and crosses his legs. He's wearing another expensive suit. If he weren't the devil's son, I would admit to myself that he is gorgeous.

My attention is pulled away when Dr Alexa drops her folder and pen to the ground. She attempts to pick it up but fumbles. She seems nervous all of sudden. I look back at Joseph and see him smiling down at her. Hmm, what do we have here? She manages to gather the folder up and hastily fills her bag with all of her instruments and my blood, and then she leaves the room without a word. I watch as Joseph follows behind her.

Watching them leave, I see Jake walk into the room. I cross my arms over my chest and zero in on him with a sneer. He laughs at me, and I am most definitely not in the mood for laughing. I narrow my eyes to show him I am not mucking around, and he holds his hands up in surrender, motioning for me to stand and come with him. Having spent the past five days with Jake, we have formed a sort of friendship. The friendship has boundaries, but he is the only person in my world right now, and when I look hard, I find he's someone I do want to be around. Until we crash into our boundaries, and then I hate him again. He's standing there waiting for me to get up, I want to be a pain and stay here, make him ask me to get up, but realising I may pass Sash again has me jumping off the bed and out of the cottage fast.

Outside in the distance, I can see Alexa and Joseph in a heated discussion. I peer at them. It seems Joseph is trying to talk to her; however, her body language and expression would suggest she is telling him to get lost. *Hmm, maybe she isn't so bad after all.*

"Was she gentle?" I'm stunned at Jake's question. I also notice he isn't holding my arm. We're just walking next to each other, like two normal people would. I shrug as my answer. I'm not sure why he would even ask. Would he really care if she hurt me?

Jake blows out a breath and shakes his head frustrated. His frustration irks me. What does he have to be frustrated about? He didn't just give blood to God knows who for God knows what.

We're passing the gardens, and all my focus is on seeing Sasha, but no one is there, not a single person.

Seeing my disappointment, Jake informs me, "She's in the laundry room now."

"Are you telling me my sister is the one who has been washing my clothes?" I ask, astonished.

"Yes, the slave girls do everything around here; cook, clean, work the vegetable gardens, pick the fruit and feed the animals."

Jake and I make our way into the house, toward my room. "So that's all they do here? That's why they were kidnapped, to cook, clean, and work?"

"No, first and foremost, they are here for the men. Marco rewards us with a lot of money, and women whenever we want them."

I inhale harshly, "Sasha."

"No," he says quickly. "Marco wants to sell her, so that means she is off limits to the guards, unless she's in trouble and then she will be punished. Most buyers want women who have hardly been used, so Marco makes sure to sell them without being touched by his guards. The other girls you see in the house are Marco's. Sasha is the only one here at the moment who goes to auction."

I look to the floor and shake my head, trying to understand this world and all the vile people in it. My stomach hurts at the thought of Jake touching or hurting one of the slave girls. Have I been wrong about him? Is he truly as horrible as the other men here?

We arrive back at my room. Jake shuts the door behind him, and I spin around and ask what has been going through my mind, "So you sleep with those girls? You, you rape them?" My voice comes out strangled as I pass the ugly words across my lips.

Jake flinches at my words and he answers quickly, "Never. And I never will. I've done many things in my life I can never take back, but I do have boundaries that I will never cross."

My body surprises me by relaxing immediately at his words, making me aware of just how much his answer mattered to me. Imagining Jake hurting a woman churns my stomach. It would mean he really is the bad guy. But imaging Jake with another woman, willingly, sends a stab of jealousy to my stomach. *Whoa, no, no way am I jealous.* I shake my head at the ridiculous thoughts.

Jake gets comfortable in his normal chair in the corner and looks up at me, his eyes always assessing, staring. I sense he can see right through me, and worse of all, I like it.

A thought comes to my mind. I start pacing the room as the idea starts coming to life. "Could I bargain with Marco? Get Sasha clean clothes, medical help for her face? Not money this time. I know now he has more than enough, but something else. Something else he would want from me?" I stop and stare at Jake as I end on a whisper, fidgeting with my fingers.

Understanding flashes across Jake's face, and he sits

forward in his chair, elbows on his thighs, hands clasped out front, "No. Forget it. Not ever going to happen," he says sternly.

"Can't you just ask, Jake? I need to try something, and that seems like the only thing I can actually bargain with here," I plead and swing my arms out to elaborate my meaning.

He stands and hisses at me, "Are you crazy, Lily. You're willing to be with him, fuck him, for some material things for your sister?" His reaction both surprises and pisses me off.

"I'm willing to do anything for her," I declare. When will he get it through his head that I won't stop until she is safe and away from here.

I pace around the room more, tapping my hands on my legs, and thinking of all the things I could do to help Sasha.

"I could also request to get her away from Mick," I say, uncaring that Jake is fuming in the corner.

Jake laughs. The tone is condescending and a sliver of his anger creeps in. "Lily, you can request those things from Marco, and if he does take your body, he will never give you anything in return. You have no power here. If Marco wanted you that way, he would have already had you. The collection pieces are off limits to everyone. Even Marco doesn't touch them. He is only in it for the money and the power," Jake states.

An invisible hand wraps around my throat and squeezes tighter and tighter the more Jake explains just how powerless I am. I'm frustrated and angry at his words. This feeling of being defenceless is emotionally and physically painful.

My face heats as the anger grows within me. Uncontainable, I blow and Jake is in my firing line. "The collection pieces?" I repeat deceptively soft, contempt dripping from my words. "We have names," I snap. "You're just like them," I yell. I want to hit him, scratch him, and make him bleed. Something to show me he is human.

Jake blinks, stunned at my outburst. He walks to the door, and I start to grow angrier that he can just leave this room whenever he pleases. Something else I can't do, something else that makes me weak.

"Go on, leave, you coward. You can't handle the truth!" I shout to his back.

He turns and charges at me so rapidly that I stumble over my feet walking backwards, hitting the wall. Jake grabs hold of my shoulders, his brown eyes piercing into my wide ones. "I'm nothing like them," he roars at me.

I'm shaking and my heart is racing. I'm scared. I have no idea how far I have just pushed him.

He lets me go and steps back. His hand rubs his chest over his heart, like he is in pain, and then he speaks softly, "You just keep pushing and pushing, Lily. There is only so much I can take."

I open my mouth to say something, and then close it quickly when I realise I have no idea what he means.

Jake looks to the ceiling and growls, "Fuccckkkk." His eyes shoot straight back to mine. They show the storm of emotions he's fighting inside.

Desire, need, and resentment. A shiver races through

me. My body wants him.

A pained moan escapes Jake, and he grabs my face roughly and kisses me. I tense up at his touch. His hold becomes gentle. His warm, soft lips start to graze mine. Within seconds, my body relaxes, and I start kissing him back. His tongue slides across my lips begging for entry. I open slowly, making him work for it.

His hands grasp my arse and he picks me up. My arms go around his neck and my legs wrap around his waist. He pushes our bodies together against the wall. With one hand on my arse, he brings the other around and up my shirt. Speedily, he pushes my bra up and my breasts fall out of the cups. He scoops up my right breast and gently squeezes, and then does the same to the other, showing both the same amount of attention. His rough, calloused hands feel like heaven on my sensitive nipples.

Our kiss is interrupted by Jake groaning. He kisses me along my jaw and neck. "You have no idea how much I have wanted to do this, Lil. Fuck, your skin feels like silk and your tits are so heavy in my hand. I could blow just from touching you."

Hot sensations run through my body, and I moan as his cock begins rubbing up and down on my clit.

Jake lifts me higher up the wall and starts lifting my shirt up. God, yes, the thought of his soft warm lips on my breasts is intoxicating.

His eyes peer up at me. His focus clears, and he suddenly stops. Seconds pass with his eyes boring into mine, our heavy breathing in sync, and it's a tune I never want to forget. Jake swiftly places me on the ground and steps back.

"Shit," he says breathlessly.

My chest is rising and falling fast. I lean on the wall for balance. We just stare into each other's eyes for a moment, need screaming from both of us. I'm sure if I made the slightest move toward him, he would pin me to the wall in a heartbeat. But before I can make that move, Jake turns and swiftly walks out of the room.

I hear the lock. My body sags against the wall and I sink to my arse with my hands holding my head, thinking I must be crazy. Yep, I'm losing it. I am falling for Jake. The man who keeps me trapped, who plans to keep me caged forever.

Possibilities

THE MORNING AFTER MY KISS WITH JAKE, I'M SITTING ON the bed reading. I hear the door handle being unlocked. Jake opens the door wide, and he stands with the handle still in his grip.

A slave girl walks past him with a table cart and a tray on the top, my breakfast. The girl leaves the cart at the end of my bed with a small smile.

Jake follows her out, not one glance my way. Jake hasn't returned since our kiss. Avoiding me seems to be his way of dealing with what happened between us. The locks click into place yet again. I'm sure that sound will follow me forever in my nightmares.

I look under the tray seeing a ham salad sandwich, an apple, and ice tea. I look over the table cart and see an apron on the second level. I pick it up to check it out. It has food on it and smells like what you would think a big restaurant kitchen would smell like. I feel something in the front pocket of the apron, so I pull it out and find a lead pencil. I wonder why the slave girls have them. Could they use them to communicate with each other when they are around Marco, the guards or the collection? I search the apron for a note-pad or anything they may write on, but I find nothing.

An idea comes to me. I place the pencil under my pillow and put the apron back in the cart. I sit down and start eating my lunch, eating half of the ham sandwich, a few bites of the apple, and some sips of the ice tea. I then go to the door and knock. "Yes," Jake talks through the door.

My God, he isn't even opening it to talk to me anymore!

I compose my growing anger and answer, "I've finished my lunch,"

The door opens, and Jake walks past me to the tray. "That was quick, Lily," Jake says as he reaches the cart.

What is he doing?

"You didn't eat it all. Are you sure you don't want to leave it a bit, in case you want more?" His voice is soft and husky. My mind instantly jumps back to yesterday up against the wall, remembering his expert hands and dick. *Focus, Lil!* I shake off the thoughts, wanting to get on with my plan.

"No, I'm sure. I'm stuffed," I say, walking over to the table cart.

I grab hold of it as Jake starts pulling it. "What are you doing? The slave girls usually come and get it."

Jake looks down to my hands holding the cart then his eyes find mine. "I can get it out of here for you and leave it in the hallway for them."

He begins pulling it again, and I hang on with a death grip for a second, and then let go when I notice Jake's eyes assessing the way I'm acting. Damn.

"Well, can you please send a girl in for me soon? I need something done," I say while walking back to my book, trying to remain calm.

"What do you need done?" *Crap, think, Lily, think.* "Umm, just some girly stuff," I say, waving my hands around in the air. Oh, God, lucky Jake doesn't know me, because if he did, he would know that I'm lying, as my hands tend to get very vocal. It's my tell.

I cross my fingers to stop my hands from talking with me and to hope Jake believes my fake calm appearance. Jake narrows his eyes at me for a moment, and I panic he is about to call me out and search my room. He's become very good at finding my hiding places, but then again in a room, it's easy to run out of hiding places.

Jake nods and leaves. *Phew!* I quickly walk to my bedside table and pickup one of the books I have already read. I rip a page right out of the back of the book, silently saying sorry to the book gods. I place the paper under my pillow with the pencil and wait for the girl to arrive, wondering which one it will be.

A few minutes later, I hear the door unlock, and Jake pops his head in again and spots me on the bed. I smile at him, which is probably the wrong thing to do as he narrows his eyes and then starts looking around the room. I wipe the smile away and scowl at him. He narrows his eyes further. Then after a moment, he motions with his arm and the girl walks in. It's the same girl who showed me her scars. Jake takes another look around the room, then back at me. This time, I look exasperated by his presence. That seems to do it, and he finally shuts the door. I let out a big breath.

The girl begins to walk over to me, and I quickly get the paper and pencil from under my pillow. I motion for her to take them, she gasps and shakes her head at me. Her arms fly out crossing each other in a no gesture. Her eyes wide with fear, she refuses to touch the paper and pencil. "Please, please, you won't be talking to me. You will be writing to me. I just have some quick questions," I beg.

She sighs as she takes the pencil and paper from me and leads me into the bathroom, shutting the door behind us. She motions me with her hands to start quickly asking my questions.

"My sister Sasha, is she okay? Are the men hurting her?" She begins to write. I peek down, unable to wait patiently, bouncing on my heels.

Your sister is safe as long as she behaves, but she is a fighter, and it has gotten her into some trouble. I believe she has learned and will do fine now.

A Fighter. I smile. However, remembering her bruised face, I hope she behaves as well. "I don't want her to be sold. Is there any way I can get her out?" My voice is pleading, the girl studies me for a moment, and I can see her struggle with how to answer this question.

If you try, the consequences are deadly. You would be

risking your lives.

Anticipation vibrates through me as I realise she didn't say no. "Is there a way?" I ask quickly. She starts writing again.

There might be. Are you really willing to die, to leave?

"Can you honestly tell me she would be better being sold to a stranger than trying to escape this place?

I can't tell you that. I know of too many evil men who would be at the auction to buy someone like your sister.

"I would need to make sure the plan was solid before going ahead. I need certainty when it comes to my sister. In the end, it will be up to Sasha." I need her gone and safe. "And as for myself, I don't care what happens to me. I need to get my sister out and safe before she goes to auction next week. I'm not even sure what day it will be."

There can be no promises. If she goes ahead with this, it will be up to her to carry it out.

"What do you mean? How will she get out?" I ask, and she begins to write before I have even finished my question. This time she takes a while to write.

A plan is in the works at the moment. Another slave girl, Maria, is planning an escape next week. It is planned and prepared. Dr Kingsley and I are helping her. I am allowed to go into town once a week for supplies. Dr Kingsley sometimes escorts me. One guard still comes along. We travel to the nearest town to get our supplies from the grocery store. Maria will sneak into the trunk of the car earlier in the day. She will hold it down so it doesn't lock. While Dr Kingsley, the guard and I are in the grocery store, she will leave the trunk and head to a house Dr Kingsley has close by. There will be a map in the trunk with the address and details on how to get there from the store. I will need to speak with Maria and Dr Kingsley before I can promise Sasha's place in the escape plan.

Reading Dr Kingsley's name and finding out she is helping these women escape, shocks me, perhaps I judged her too soon. However my focus is on the fact that, this plan could work. It's tricky but they could really get away. Hope soars in my chest and I smile at the girl. Curiosity crosses my mind and I ask, "Why haven't you tried this before, with yourself? With any of the other slave girls?"

Many people have tried to escape and failed. Most of us are too scared to attempt it. We would rather live in hell than die here. I will need to return to the house, so I am not suspected. Understand, if Sasha and Maria are caught, I will say I didn't know. I will say they did it without my knowledge. This will fall only on their shoulders.

"I understand," I state. And I do understand why she would do that. She already has enough scars on her body.

I hear Jake yelling through the bedroom door, asking, "Are you finished doing girly shit?"

I open the bathroom door and yell back. "In a minute!" I giggle in my mind for a second at how normal that short conversation just sounded. If we were anywhere else in the world, people would think we are a couple.

I step back into the bathroom. The girl pushes the paper and pencil back in my hands, her expression terrified. "It's okay. I won't let anyone know about this." I hold her stare, so she knows I'm serious.

"Can I know your name?" She bites her lip and glances

around the bathroom before taking the pencil and paper back from me.

Beth

I smile at Beth. “That’s a beautiful name.” Her faces brightens, and she smiles the biggest smile I’ve seen from her.

I rip the paper up into small pieces and wet them in the bathroom sink then flush them down the toilet.

I look at Beth and smile. “See, no one will ever know. I promise.” We exit the bathroom, and I place the pencil back under my pillow.

“I will ask for you again tomorrow. We can discuss more then.” She nods and walks to the door. She knocks on the door. Jake opens it and lets her walk past him.

I lean against the bed trying to look bored. He looks over to me, and then scans the room. Having not found anything out of place, he leaves and locks the door.

I look around the room wanting to scream and shout that I may have found a way out for Sasha. I calm myself and go to the window, looking through the bars to the green field and deep blue sea. I send up a silent prayer that this will work, and I will get my baby sister on her way home and away from this evil world.

◆

Hours after Beth leaves, I see the door open, and Jake walks into the room and locks the door. I lay the book I’m reading down on my lap and watch him walk over to the bed. He looks nervous, and I could almost giggle at how fidgety he is.

He looks to the ground and rubs the back of his neck. After a second, Jake looks up at me and goes to talk, but no words are spoken. He shuts his mouth. He tries again, but nothing comes out. He breathes out heavily, sits on the bed and puts his head in his hands.

Oh, he is gorgeous like this. Maybe I should put him out of his misery. "Jake, is this about the kiss?" He blows out another heavy breath and turns around to me.

"I'm sorry I did that, Lily. I was out of line. I was angry, and fuck, you look so hot when you're all fired up. I went too far, and I'm sorry for that." His voice is soft and full of remorse.

"I'm not sorry," I bravely say, not sure why or how I feel. But I'm sure of one thing. I don't regret that kiss. I would never regret that kiss.

Jake eyes widen at my words. "You should be. I was rough, and out of line."

"It was the best kiss of my life," I say quickly, regretting my words as soon as they are out of my mouth. *Oh, my God, how embarrassing.*

Jake stares down at my lips. His stare makes my mouth go dry, and I lick my lips. "Fuck," he growls. He gets up and takes purposeful strides to the door. Then he suddenly pivots and pounces on the bed. I let out a squeal as my book is thrown from the bed, and his hands go to my waist. In no time, I'm flat on my back with Jake's lips on mine again. *Oh, heaven.* I kiss him back right away, arching my spine, moaning into his mouth at how wonderful his lips feel on mine.

I grab hold of his shirt and pull him further into me,

never wanting to let him go. Nothing is going through my mind except the need to feel this man all over me and inside of me. I feel his erection press into my tummy, and heat floods to all the right places.

Jake kisses my neck and jaw. As soon as I feel his erection hit my clit, I start grinding shamelessly against him.

Jake moves slightly to the side, and I whine, vibration from his chuckle sends waves of pleasure to my pussy. His hand gently slides down the front of my shorts and panties. I arch my back and moan in ecstasy as he strokes my clit and fingers me at the same time. The feeling is euphoric. My legs quiver and sweat builds behind my knees. Heat slowly rises up my legs and swirls at my clit. The impending explosion promising to be orgasmic.

His lips glide across to my ear. "Fuck, Lily, what you do to me. I need you." His voice is low and husky.

I'm riding the best high of my life, and I'm so close to the edge. "Jake, please don't stop. Oh, God, I'm, I'm com—" Jake covers my mouth quickly with a kiss and swallows my scream. Feeling only ecstasy, I fall off the cliff, lost in the most intense sensation of my life.

When I come to, I hear deep growling, and my body starts heating up all over again as I watch Jake close his eyes and suck on the fingers that were just inside me. His eyes open. They swirl with passion and desire.

Jake pulls me into his arms and hugs me tenderly for a long moment. He loosens his grip and looks down at me. "Lil, I will never forget what you just gave to me. In this sinister world, you gave me something beautiful and I will hold that memory close to me forever." Then he lets me go and steps back from the bed. Rejection spreads through me like wildfire.

I'm Begging You

JAKE

I MESSED UP BIG TIME, BUT IMAGINING LILY'S DELICIOUS taste in my mouth and watching her come undone from my touch was too much of a temptation. It's hard to believe what just happened was a mistake. But it was, and it can't happen again.

"Jake," she whispers.

I swear my heart cracks at hearing the sting of rejection in her voice. "Lily, that shouldn't have happened. I keep crossing the line with you, and it has to stop. If Marco found out what we just did, I would have blown my chances of being your guard for here and Marco's house. I can't do that." I'm starting to fucking forget why I'm here. I can't let anything get in the way.

"I'm an idiot," she mutters to herself as she sits up on the bed and pulls a pillow in front of her, putting a barrier between us. That small movement wrecks me.

"Shit, my head gets so messed up around you, Lil. I can't fucking think straight." And now I need to shut my mouth. Spouting all this bullshit is not going to help.

"No, I get it, Jake. Nothing matters to you except getting to Marco's house and being one of the top guards of a sex slave empire."

I take a step back, noticing her temper rising. Number one reason is that she is fucking hot when she's angry, and I can't risk jumping her again. The other reason, she's unpredictable, and there is a lamp right near her that I don't want thrown at my head.

"What, are you trying to take over? Be the one to inherit all this evil shit when Marco dies," she hisses.

I can't fault her for thinking that, but I want so much more. I want it all. "Yes, Lily, and nothing is going to get in my way, not even my feelings for you." I walk to the door realising I just admitted to having feelings for her. *Stupid, Jake.*

"You have feelings? Wow, let me know when you find them so I can shove them up your arse, and they can join all the other shit you speak," she snaps at me. Fuck, that attitude just makes me want her more. I smile on the inside, knowing right now is not the time to show her how much I love her temper.

I'm hurting her. I know that, but I'm also saving her. How the hell she could want anything to do with me is just fucked up. Lily deserves so much better, and one day she will have it. I walk out of the room and don't look back.

LILY

I'M A FOOL. ***WHAT DID YOU THINK WAS GOING TO HAPPEN,*** *Lily*? I don't even know what I expected from him after that. I just couldn't stop what was happening. I didn't want to. My body comes alive like it never has around Jake. I betray myself by wanting him, but who will stop me if I can't stop myself?

He didn't even relieve himself. I don't understand how someone so gentle and caring can switch off his emotions so effortlessly and want this evil, disgusting life. But why would he want me, when he said he had no trouble getting women? He can have both: his sick need to reach the top and beautiful women.

Is this all mind games for him? I fell for my captor, and now I feel foolish. I decide to hide my shame under the blankets for the next few hours; however, after a few minutes with my body relaxed from Jake's expert hands, my eyes grow heavy and I drift off to sleep.

I wake sometime later in the dark to the smell of hot food. My stomach rumbles, and I push the covers off me. I spot something move in the corner of my eye, I jump back and squeal. But see it's only Jake sitting on his chair in the corner.

"Sorry, Lil," he states gently. "I was coming in to let you know your dinner was here. Only I couldn't wake you. You looked so peaceful."

Memories of Jake's hands and mouth on me race through my mind. The shame and rejection fill my veins. "It's Lil...ly," I draw out my name, "to you, and thank you. I'm awake now. I'll knock when I finish," I dismiss him, shift to the end of the bed and lift my tray to find lamb and vegetables for dinner tonight. I'm surprised to see I have my steel cutlery privileges back. I lift them in the air and raise an eyebrow to Jake.

He shrugs and says, "I think we both know you proved they were of no use to you anyway."

I ignore him and start eating, waiting for Jake to leave. However, he doesn't move, so I decide to keep eating as if he's not even there. Soon enough, he gets up and leaves the room. My shoulders sag. Being a bitch is hard work.

I devour my dinner, starving from rushing through my lunch today and not eating much of it. I remember my talk with Beth and can't help but smile at the prospect of getting Sasha back home.

I go to the drawers and get some pyjamas out; peach silk boxers and matching silk singlet. I knock on the door, letting Jake know I'm finished with dinner and rush to the bathroom before he can enter the room. I shut and lock the bathroom door.

I put my ear to the door and listen to Jake enter the room, hear the cart being rolled out, and the door close again. I lean against the door, wishing so many things could be different. I wish Jake thought I was worth saving.

I shower, and as soon as I'm dressed and my hair is dry, I turn the lights out and get under the covers. I find it hard to sleep tonight. My fingers touch my lips softly, and the memory of Jake's rough, passionate kisses sends a shiver through me. However much he hurt me, I will never regret what happened between us. Jake shows me a side of him I don't think he lets other's see, and for that, I will always cherish our moment.

My back is to the door when I hear it open. I know it will be Jake checking on me for the last time before he goes back to his room. I close my eyes and feign sleep. Hearing footsteps coming closer to the bed, I hold my breath, and then there is nothing for a few moments. A warm, soft hand brushes my hair behind my ear, and a soft kiss is placed on my temple.

"Sweet dreams, Lil," Jake whisper's quietly. I stay still, hear him walk out of the room, and the lock click into place.

Tears form in my eyes; confusion and anger pound at my heart. I don't understand him, and I don't want to. I want nothing to do with this new world of mine.

But tomorrow will bring new plans with Beth. I need to stay focused on getting my sister out of Hell.

All morning I have been sitting at the window watching the outside world. The clouds still move across the sky. The breeze still moves on to the next gust of wind that picks it up. The ocean waves keep crashing against the cliff. But me, I stay here and just wait. I can't move on.

Inside my head, I'm screaming and crashing through walls to get out of here, but on the outside, I am calm and silent.

I have gone to knock on the door too many times to count to ask Jake to send up the same slave girl, Beth. I'm still trying to think of a reason I would need her for. I need to find out what is happening, but I can't tell Jake that. I have never been a patient person, and this is too much for me.

I stand to actually knock this time when my door opens, Beth walks in carrying a bucket and cleaning products. She closes my door, and I can't hide my smile that she came back.

Beth walks straight to the bathroom. I dash to my pillow for the pencil and take another page out of a different book. As soon as I enter, Beth closes and locks the door. My heart is beating rapidly, dying to know what news she has for me.

She takes the pencil and paper and starts writing.

I don't have long. Your guard thinks your bathroom needs to be cleaned. Maria and Dr Kingsley have agreed to help your sister. We go in three days, which will be this Wednesday; we usually leave around eleven am. Sasha is intended to go to auction Wednesday night. They have already told her she will need to be ready by five pm. I have talked to your sister about our plans; however, she is reluctant to leave without you.

I quickly reassure Beth, "Don't worry about Sasha. She will do this. Somehow, I will find a way to get in contact with her and reassure her I will be fine."

I don't know if I can see you again before Wednesday. If

you feel you have to talk to me, ask for someone, and I will try to make sure it's me they send up.

Beth pauses in her writing, looks up to me, and then begins writing again.

I can see how much your sister means to you. I promise to try my hardest to get her out of here.

Silent tears fall down my face, and I grab Beth's hands and hold them. "Thank you," I reply with every ounce of sincerity I have in my heart.

Beth and I do a quick clean of the bathroom in silence and then she leaves.

I pace the room trying to think of a way to see Sasha. I have only two days to see her and say goodbye. And most importantly, convince her I will be fine. She needs to take this opportunity.

Breakfast and a shower later, I still have no idea how I will see Sasha. While I'm going through the closet searching for some clothes to wear, I decide to talk to Jake, feel him out, and see if he will let me have another run-in with her. I dress in a black tank top and a pair of skinny jeans that look very expensive.

I knock softly, and the door opens. Jake's dressed in his usual black cargo pants, grey t-shirt, and army boots. He licks his lips while his eyes roam over my body, and a shiver runs through me. He finds my eyes and arches an eyebrow, waiting for me to speak like he didn't just eye fuck the hell out of me. He must see the desire in my eyes because he crosses his arms against his chest and takes a step back. Goddamn, those arms, when he crosses them, they bulge to massive. *Focus!*

Finally, I remember why I knocked and say, "I would like to see my sister again." I stare into his eyes, so he knows how serious I am. "I want to make sure she is okay. Can we walk past wherever she will be today?"

Jake's arms drop from his powerful stance. "Lil, you know I can't do that. Sasha is on the other side of the house. There is no reason for us to be there. Questions will be asked and I can't risk that." I know Jake is genuinely sorry, but I won't take no for an answer.

"Jake, I'm begging you. I *need*," I stress the word need, "to see Sasha before she goes to auction. I have to say goodbye to my sister. And to make sure her face is healing, and that she is okay. If I don't, I will go mad."

Jake's face shows signs he's struggling with how to handle this situation. He seems torn, and I hate making him feel that way, but this is too important. I decide to try another tactic to get what I want.

"If you don't help me, I will scream this place to the ground. I will kick and hit the walls. I will smash everything in this room and tear up all those very expensive dresses," I say as I motion my arms toward the closet worth millions of dollars. "I'm sure Marco wouldn't like that, now, would he? He might think you're incompetent to watch over me." I know it's a low blow, but I'm desperate. Jake has his goals, and I have mine.

Jake looks to the ceiling. "Fuck, woman, you are going to get me killed."

He lowers his eyes to mine, blows out a big breath, and smirks, "Well played, Lil. I will see what I can find out, but I can't promise you I can make it happen."

"That's enough, thank you," I say with a huge grin on my face. Jake glances down to my mouth, and then mutters words I can't hear as he leaves the room. I'm left waiting for him to return with an answer.

An hour passes since Jake left, and my sanity is hanging on by a thread. I am so close to making this plan a reality that every minute that passes and Jake doesn't come is torture.

My door opens, and I spin around to find Jake closing my door. "Well," I say impatiently.

"Tomorrow morning after breakfast, she will be in the wine cellar doing stocktake. The guards don't usually guard them too closely down there as there is no exit. There will be only one guard at the entry to the cellar. I will tell them you are choosing a gift for Marco, so be prepared to find a wine for him as well."

I squeal and jump into Jake's arms and hug him tightly. "Thank you. Thank you so much, Jake. You have no idea how much this means to me."

His arms encircle me. My body relaxes in his warmth and safety. We hold each other for a moment. Jake places a soft kiss to my neck, lets me go and walks out.

The day passes excruciatingly slowly. I try to read. I take a few showers to pass the time, but nothing helps. The anticipation and excitement I have inside me, has me feeling like I will explode before I even get to my sister.

Finally, dinner comes, and this time, Jake comes with his own food and eats with me. We sit at the small table in comfortable silence eating spaghetti bolognese until Jake speaks, "I checked on you a few times today. You were either staring out the window or in the shower. I counted four showers. Is everything okay?" he asks as he fills his mouth full of spaghetti.

I shrug and explain, "I'm excited to see Sasha tomorrow, and I'm bored. There's nothing to do to pass the time. Reading isn't holding my attention at the moment. There's too much on my mind." Jake nods and keeps eating.

"So tell me, why we are waiting to be moved to Marco's house?" I inquire. I need more information about Marco and where I will be going. Because as soon as Sasha is safe, I need to start planning my own escape.

"It shouldn't be long now. Marco is very careful about moving the collection around. He has a lot of enemies who would love to find even just one of his collection pieces. You were outed at the party, so moving you to his home is going to be secretive. He can't have anyone knowing where he lives or have anyone follow us. He needs to let the dust settle, and then he will move you."

Jake scoops up a big forkful of spaghetti. He sucks in the strands that don't make it in his mouth. *Lucky spaghetti*. Staring at his lips, I notice he starts talking again. "From what I have heard, all the other girls are moved to a secret location after a party, and then one by one, he will have them secretly taken back to his home. That's where you will stay most of your time. It is guarded and only known to Marco and the collection's guards."

"Why does he have enemies?" I ask.

"Marco has been known to tape the men with the collection pieces, and he uses those tapes to bribe politicians and the mob to get what he wants. Bend the law, it's how he has been able to stay out of jail. A lot of them want to see him, and his collection wiped out. But he also has a lot of supporters such as the men who attend the parties."

The mention of the men from the parties has me losing my appetite.

"So does Marco only throw a party a month?" I ask Jake quietly, unsure if I want an answer or not.

Jake looks at me with guilt in his eyes. "Honestly, I'm not sure."

We finish our dinner in silence, and Jake looks lost in his thoughts. I don't think even a drumming band could get his attention. I stay silent and watch as numerous emotions pass over his face. His forehead creases a few times, and he clenches his eyes closed once. I wish I knew what he was battling. If only he would just come clean, maybe we could help each other.

Jake comes back to the present and looks at me with an intensity I'm seeing more and more from him lately. "Lily, I know this might be hard to believe, but I am not going to let you get hurt again. You don't need to know how or why. Just know that I'm going to protect you from now on."

I stare at Jake stunned. "How can you promise that?"

"I can't." His eyes examine my face. "But I will try my hardest to keep you from any more parties. We'll say you're not well...something. I will come up with a plan." His voice is strong and reassuring.

"I don't understand you at all, Jake. I'm afraid you're

playing me, but something in me trusts you," I end on a whisper, looking away, feeling vulnerable that I just let him see a piece of me.

My eyes swing back to Jake as he speaks, "I'm not playing you, Lil. I'm just as trapped as you are, because I need to stay. I don't want to, but I have to. And being this close to you, having feelings for you, could hurt you more than you ever know, but I know enough now that I'm not going to stay away from you. There is something between us that goes beyond what we both think we should feel. Now it's my turn to have faith that everything is going to turn out the way I want it to. God, no, the way I need it to." His eyes penetrate mine. I can see the conflict he's battling within himself to open up to me.

Jake walks around the table to me. His hand cups my left cheek and he kisses me on my lips. The kiss is slow and gentle; the sweetest kiss I've ever had. He pulls back and kisses my forehead. "Sweet dreams, baby." Then he takes the cart and leaves the room.

I fall back on the chair, gazing at the ceiling with a giant smile on my face. My mind tells me I'm crazy for considering this man an ally. However, my heart won't let me pull away; it wants him. I don't know how long my mind will rule my heart. For every moment I spend with him, my heart grows stronger than my mind.

This Is Goodbye, For Now

IT'S MORNING AND THE DAY I GET TO SEE SASHA. I'VE BEEN mentally preparing myself to stay strong. Saying goodbye will be hard, but it's only for a little while.

I'm just pulling on some sandals when Jake comes in with my breakfast. I'm on the floor in a short red halter summer dress. It's beautiful, something I would wear back home around the farm on a warm day. Jake's gaze goes straight for my breasts, and he licks his lips. I instantly want to rub my thighs together to ease the vibrating need between my legs.

Jake shakes his head and says, "Eat quickly, Lil, and we'll head straight down to the wine cellar." Those words are like ice water hitting me, and I jump up and start eating.

While eating, I glance at Jake. He's leaning against the

wall, arms crossed and watching me eat. "Jake, I have some questions about last night, about...us."

Jake's eyes soften when he answers, "I don't have answers for you, Lil. We can only take this one day at a time."

"And if I don't want this," I point between the two of us. I do want this, desperately. Which makes me insane to wish for anything with him, but I've never been one to fight what I know I want, and Jake is something my body craves.

Jake smirks as if he can read my thoughts. "Oh, baby, then you should have hidden that fiery temper from me. Now I've seen it, there will be no getting away from me." He winks, walks over, grabs my waist and looks into my eyes. "And you know you want it too, Lil. I can see it in your eyes and feel it in the trembles that travel through your body when I touch you. But until I work out some details, this stays between us. If Marco finds out I've touched you, we'll pay the price with our lives. So out of this room, we mean nothing to each other, understood?" His tone is firm.

I nod, understanding and agreeing with him. "This is insane," I mutter.

Jake laughs. "God, you have no idea. We're just asking for trouble." He kisses my hair. "You ready?"

"Definitely," I reply.

Jake smiles down at me and my heart thumps hard against my chest. He makes me weak at the knees just from a lift of his lips. I clear my head of naughty Jake thoughts as we head down toward the cellar.

We don't pass any guards until we hit the kitchen. Four are at a bench having breakfast, and none even turn our way as we pass through the room.

We exit the kitchen and Jake leads me down two hallways before I see a guard sitting on a chair looking down at his phone.

He peers up at us and lifts his chin at Jake.

"Phil," Jake addresses the man.

"Hey, Jake, what's going on?" The guard takes me in, then turns back to Jake.

"Lily needs a gift for Marco," Jake confidently replies.

Jake gestures to the door. "Slave down there?" I tense at him calling Sasha a slave. I know it's not real, but it still hurts to hear her referred to that way.

"Yeah, but she's quiet. You'll be fine."

Jake lifts his chin, and then opens the door for me to enter first as the guard goes back to his phone.

I take slow steps until I hear the door shut behind us. Then I start running down the steps. The walls are made out of rough-edged stones. A metal gate greets us at the bottom of the steps, and it's already open. I race through and view a vast room with five rows of shelves with thousands of bottles on each shelf.

I start searching down every row. On the third one, I see Sasha standing, looking toward the shelves with a folder in her hands.

I run toward her, and she twists at the sound of my feet hitting the concrete floor. She spots me and smiles. She begins to run to me, but I get to her faster, and we crash into each other. Our arms squeeze each other firmly.

"Lil, I've missed you so much," she whispers into my neck.

"I've missed you like crazy too, Sash."

Jake coughs behind us, and we both jump at the sound. "We can't be long, Lily. I will wait over there." He points to the first row of shelves.

I nod and turn back to Sasha. Her face is healing nicely. Her bruise has turned yellow, and the swelling is gone. Her lip still has a cut, but it's much smaller now. I check her arms, legs and look down her dress. Sasha giggles. Relief floods through my body that she is healing, and she doesn't have any new marks on her. I glance back and see Jake is far away from us.

"Sash, has Beth talked to you?" I question.

"Yes, she told me everything, but what about you, Lily? I can't leave you here," she announces.

"Yes, you can, and you will, Sash. I have a nice room. I'm fed and I can shower. I am and will be just fine. You need to get back home to Australia. Tell the police. They will help me." I speak with absolute confidence. Sasha just has to get home and tell them what happened to us. Thoughts of what would happen to Jake flutter through my mind, but I quickly push them away to think about another time.

"But—" Sasha starts to speak but stops. I see her struggling with what she wants to say. "I've heard about the parties. What happens there? Did someone hurt you?"

Oh, God, if I tell her the truth, there is no way she will leave me behind, so I do the only thing I can right now.

I shake my head, begging my eyes not to betray me. I

stare straight at Sasha and I lie, "No, no one hurt me." My voice comes out stronger than I thought it would.

"What's the collection then, Lil? There has to be a reason to keep you."

I need to get Sasha to focus on her. "Sasha, don't worry about me. You get home and safe first. Then you can help me, okay?"

Tears spill from Sash's glistening blue eyes as a sob escapes her lips. "What aren't you telling me? I don't want to leave you here all alone."

Oh, my beautiful Sash is so worried about me. I'm so proud to have such an amazing sister.

"I know you don't, Sash. But I'm okay. Look at me. I'm healthy, clean, and protected." I point back to Jake. "He's good to me," I whisper.

She examines Jake, and then smirks, "Lily Morgan, no boy could interest you back home and then you go and find one when we get kidnapped. Are you kidding me?" She laughs. I have missed that sound. It's music to my ears.

"It's not even funny, Sash. He's a kidnapper," I say in a high-pitched whisper. "But he cares. He helped me get down here to see you. There's so much more to him. I just haven't figured it out yet, and I may never."

"Go with your heart, Lil. That's what Mum would say." My heart squeezes as I remember many times our mother saying that to the both of us when we were unsure about something.

I nod, trying hard to keep my tears back. "So the plan is ready?" I ask, just getting the words past the lump in my throat.

"Yes, Beth filled me in on everything. She's going to unlock the trunk for Maria and me, and then we will sneak in right before they leave so no one notices us gone."

Okay, that sounds like a good idea. "How will you get to the car?" I want to know everything.

"We move freely around the front rooms on this side of the house. We clean them regularly, so they don't bother us when we're working. Beth said if we need help, she will have Sally ask the guard for something, and we will quickly slip out and into the boot." *Sally,* another faceless girl who is risking her life for my sister.

As Sasha's explains the plans to me, her hands begin to shake.

"You can do this," I declare, my voice firm and resolute.

Sasha's head bobs yes, as if she's trying to convince herself. "I know I can. I have to. I can't get sold, Lil. Some of the stories the other girls have told me..." Trembles violently shake her body. "I would rather die than be sold to those monsters."

"That won't happen. You will get out and be on your way home this time tomorrow." I smile, trying to show her the positives of this plan.

She smiles back at me. "I'm actually looking forward to driving the combine." I laugh out loud at Sasha's words. The combine is a massive machine we use to harvest the wheat. Sash hates driving it and being stuck in it for hours at a time. She would whine about it all the time when we were home. What I would give to go back to those days. I guess now we will appreciate everything more, appreciate our freedom so much more.

I glance to Jake. He's patiently waiting, but I know we need to go soon. I examine my sister before I let her go. I want to remember every freckle, every strand of hair and her glistening blue eyes that have been with me in all the significant moments in my life.

A silent tear escapes my eye. "I have to go, Sash, so this is goodbye for now." My tears fall faster as I take in Sash's crumbling face. I wipe them away as my sight starts to blur. "I'll see you soon." I hug her. "Be careful. I love you," I say as I squeeze her tighter.

Sasha clings to me with a death grip. "Lil," she whispers.

"Yeah?" I reply.

"I want you to know, that I love you and that Mum and Dad would be so proud of you. You're the best big sister any little sister could ask for."

My chest squeezes painfully at hearing Sasha talk about our parents, and my silent tears turn into whimpers. Our hug becomes impossibly tighter. Both of us refusing to let the other go. She feels like home.

I hear boots and twist my head around. Jake approaches us, his expression filled with sadness. "Lily, this is all the time I can give you two. We have to go."

I turn back to Sash and wink as I mouth, "See you soon, sis." She smiles at me and nods.

Jake has Sasha's full attention and then she speaks, "Jake, thank you for looking out for my sister." She gives him a small smile. God, I love her.

Jake's face softens and he only nods as he gently pulls

me by my arm, somehow knowing I can't physically remove myself from my sister's presence.

Walking toward the stairs, I look back at Sasha. She picks up her folder and continues counting wine bottles, but this time, with a smile on her face.

We walk up the stairs and open the door to where the guard is sitting. My heart comes close to exploding for a second when I realise we have no wine with us, but then Jake holds up a bottle to the guard.

"Got it. Catch you around, Phil." My heart starts to calm, but still beats wildly. Phil lifts his chin to Jake, and we continue through the house toward my room.

Jake closes the door to my room, and I collapse on the bed with a heavy exhale. "I totally forgot about the wine. Thank God, you remembered."

Jake puts the wine on my dresser and asks, "What was your sister thanking me for?"

"She was questioning the parties and the collection." I shrug. "So I pretty much told her nothing happened to me, and you were protecting me. I don't want her to worry about me while she is trapped as well."

"You would have told her that, whether it was the truth or not, wouldn't you?"

"Yes," I answer honestly, and I notice Jake rubbing at his chest again. "You're a good sister, Lily."

"I'm doing what anybody would do for someone they love," I reply.

"Yeah, you are." Jake's voice sounds far away and he faces the window and gets lost for a moment.

Whatever thoughts are haunting him, he shakes them

off and says, "Her face looks better."

"She does look better and thank goodness there are no new bruises or cuts."

"The two of you looked to be having an intense conversation. Also you both seemed happier than two sisters should be, saying goodbye before one goes off to an auction."

Damn, he's suspicious. I feign a shocked expression, "So there's a manual I should read on how to say goodbye to my sister? Anyway, it's not goodbye. I will see her again, and that's what I told Sasha. I kept our time together light and happy," I lie.

"You're not telling me everything, Lily. I can see it, and you suck at lying," Jake states. His eyes are boring holes into me.

I hold his stare as long as I can, and then I head to my messy bed and start pushing the covers up to make the bed up.

"Lily," he growls at me.

"Leave it alone, Jake," I say, trying to stay calm,

"Fuck, Lily, what have you done?" His voice is firm.

"Nothing that concerns you, Jake. You made it very clear you wouldn't help Sasha and me get out of here." I continue to make the bed, trying to ignore the storm building behind me.

"I understand you want to help your sister, but trying to get her out is going to get her killed. I know what's happened to her so far isn't nice—"

I cut Jake off, my anger growing every second he keeps talking. "Isn't nice?" I whisper. "What you and these men do here is evil, and I will do whatever it takes to get my sister away from this," I end on a growl.

Jake freezes and stares straight at me. Guilt and remorse flash in his eyes. "Whatever has or is happening to Sasha, Lily, at least she is still alive," he stresses to me.

"You think after being sold to someone who will do God knows what to her, who will probably beat and rape her, that she will be alive? No, if I don't get her out soon, she will be a fucking shell of who she is now. And I will have no idea how to find her. I will not let her be sold."

"Whatever plans you have, Lily, let them go, please," Jake pleads.

"I can't. You need to understand if Sash gets sold, if that happens, it will kill me," I say calmly, trying to make Jake accept what I can't live with.

"Fuck," Jake shouts to the roof. "I know, Lily. I know." He breathes out. "I hope whatever plans you have fail, Lil, because the alternative could be so much worse than being sold." Jake turns and storms out of the room.

I look out through the barred windows to the deep blue ocean, hoping I'm not making a huge mistake, and sending my sister off to a worse fate than the one we are already headed toward.

Bang!

I BARELY SLEPT AT ALL LAST NIGHT, TOO ANXIOUS AND excited about Sasha escaping today. I shower early and get dressed in jeans and a deep blue lace tank top.

I'm not sure what time it is. The only way I can tell around here is when I get my breakfast, lunch, and dinner. I try to read but can't focus on the story.

I'm looking out the window when the door opens. Jake walks in with the table cart and wheels in my breakfast. There's no way I can stomach food this morning; I feel like butterflies are killing each other in my tummy. However, I need to. I can't let Jake see there is anything different about today.

He sits and watches me while I eat, and it makes me slightly uncomfortable because I'm hiding something. Any other time, I love it. Usually, it's like he's trying to peel back layers to see my soul, like my physical being sometimes isn't enough for him, and he wants more. It's intoxicating to know just how much I intrigue him.

"Lily, there's something you need to know." I stare up at Jake, waiting for him to finish. "Sasha's auction is this afternoon at five pm." Jake's face is soft as he tells me, apprehension flashes through his warm brown eyes.

I blink a few times and leave my expression blank for a moment thinking how I should react. Jake knows I'm planning something, but not when. If he knows it's before the auction, will he try to stop it? I trust Jake, but that trust hasn't been tested yet, and Sasha is too important to me to test if Jake is being honest with me. So I decide to lie, nothing is more important than Sash.

"What?" I whisper, pretending to be shocked. I jump from my seat. "So soon, that's too soon. I thought her face had to heal completely first?" I challenge loudly, continuing to surprise myself with my acting skills.

Jake stands with me, stretching his arms out to touch me, but I back away. "I'm sorry, Lily. I know this is going to be hard for you."

I walk over to the window, finding it difficult to keep looking at Jake as I lie. "Can you please leave me alone? I don't want to talk to anyone right now."

I sense Jake come up behind me, and he softly touches my waist. "Knock if you need me." His voice is thick and full of understanding.

I give a slight nod, and then hear the door close.

I blow out a breath and pray. *Please, God, let this work. Take my sister home safely.*

I grow more anxious as time progresses and it's showing. I'm fidgety and I start biting my nails until I'm sure it must be eleven am or just after. I'm mentally exhausted, and my emotions are all over the place.

A knock comes at my door. It opens, and I spin around with wide eyes. I'm on the edge, feeling that at any moment my life could implode.

A slave girl brings in my lunch cart. She shuts the door and motions her head toward the bathroom. *Oh, my God, she wants to talk to me.*

I race to my pillow and grab the pencil, then pick up the closest book to me and tear out the back page. I hurry into the bathroom and close the door, not bothering to lock it.

Instantly, I ask, "Is everything okay?" I push the paper and pencil at her, and she starts writing.

Beth asked me to see you after they departed, to ease your worry and let you know they left the house without any problems.

My whole body sags against the bathroom door. I finally feel like I can breathe again. After her words sink in, a massive smile erupts on my face, and I grab the girl and hug her tightly; she lets out a squeak at the shock of it.

"Thank you, thank you, thank you!" My heart is soaring, nothing could bring me down from this high.

I let the girl go, and she begins to write again.

Myself or Beth will come and see you later to let you know how the rest of the trip went.

I nod, still smiling brightly. "What's your name?"

Sally

"Well, thank you for letting me know, Sally. This news means the world to me." My smile seems to be contagious because Sally's lips spread to a grin as she leaves the bathroom and heads out of my room in a hurry.

I turn to the mirror and see my sister's smile. Maybe some people were right and we do look alike.

I hear the door open and step out of the bathroom, attempting to put a blank expression on my face, obviously failing as Jake narrows his eyes when he sees me.

"I thought being cooped up in this room all day might have been too much for you." He lifts an eyebrow in question as to why I might be trying to hide a smile, but I stay silent, and he continues speaking, "I thought you might like to go down to the cliffs, get some fresh air and enjoy the wide open space."

"That sounds perfect," I say, hopefully not too cheerful.

Jake tilts his head the side, and it's easy to see he's trying hard to decipher my mood today. Apparently, I failed at blank.

"I'll go get ready," I say as I walk to the closet and get some sandals.

Jake leads me through the house and down to the cliffs, about one and half acres from the house. It's beautiful down here. The fresh sea air with the sun shining down warms me from the cold breeze. The view is stunning: giant cliffs with clear blue water crashing against them.

Jake is over to my left, sitting against a tree, watching

me closely. A small part of me loves that he's trying to distract me from what he thinks will be Sasha's auction day, but another part of me is angry he has anything to do with this in the first place. I want to know how he got here. He's compassionate and gentle. How can he stand to live like this? There has to be so much more than what I'm seeing.

I close my eyes and breathe in the fresh ocean air. My mind goes to Sasha and Maria. By now, they would have arrived at the grocery store. They would have made their escape from the trunk of the car and be on their way to Dr Kingsley's house. Then she will be on her way home. Finally, my sister is free and safe. Keeping my eyes closed, I take a big breath in, and I laugh as a memory of Sasha comes to my thoughts.

"Lily!" I hear Sasha yelling for me.

"In the kitchen, Sash," I shout back.

Sasha enters the kitchen like a bull seeing a red flag, feet apart and her nostrils flaring.

"You were right. That asshole Jimmy was seeing that whore behind my back." Oh no. I didn't want to be right about that.

"I'm sorry, Sash. Are you okay?" Her chest is rising and falling rapidly. She is pissed.

"Oh, I will be. Where is that bat Dad kept in the house for when we had dates?" Shit, she's furious.

"Umm...I'm not sure I want to tell you. What do you plan on doing with said bat?"

She gives me an evil Cruella de Vil smile. Uh oh.

"Sasha Morgan, you touch his car and he will go

ballistic."

She walks out of the kitchen still talking to me as I follow her through the house, and she starts her search.

"He should have thought about that before he cheated on me," she seethes.

She did eventually find that bat. However, Jimmy's car didn't get a beating, Jimmy did. He loved that car so much, he took every swing she aimed at that car.

I open my eyes and giggle, remembering him walking around town with a black eye and his arm in a sling for weeks. Looking over the blue sea, it feels like my home is worlds away from here. I just have to wait now, because I know Sasha will go straight to the police as soon as she can. I just have to hope I don't get moved before then or figure out a way to prolong it as long as I can. Thinking about leaving already has me missing Jake, which is strange. I've only known him for a short time and already I miss him before we are even separated.

My ears pick up a piercing sound coming from somewhere. I still my body to hear it again or see if it's just in my head. I hear it again. It's a scream. It's coming from somewhere around me.

I whip my head around and peer up at the house. Another scream hits my ears. It's coming from the side of the house. The screams are blood curdling; someone is in a lot of pain.

I turn my whole body around toward the house, glimpsing at Jake, who is also staring up at the house, confused.

I put my hand over my eyes, squinting, trying to

identify what I'm hearing. Another scream, louder this time.

My blood runs cold. *No!* Sasha.

Instantly, my legs start pounding the ground. I'm running faster than I ever have in my life. I hear another scream. My heart pushes at me to run faster. My legs and arms are pumping ferociously. My ankles twist on the ground as I hit small holes and rocks in the earth, but I keep going, not feeling the pain. I vaguely hear someone running after me, but I don't stop or look behind me. I hear another scream and my heart threatens to burst from my chest at hearing my little sister in so much pain.

I finally get close enough to see her. Her hands are tied above her head to a wooden pole on a concrete slab. The back of her white dress is soaked in blood. *Oh, my God, there's so much blood.*

I push myself harder and faster. I see a lash from a whip come down on Sasha's back. She doesn't move.

I screech, "STOP!" No one notices me.

I keep sprinting toward her while screaming at them to stop. Another lash hits Sasha's back. She's still not moving. God, no, this is not happening. I'm so close I can hear the sound of the whip as it's retracting.

I approach the area, my throat burning from my shrieks. I head straight for Sasha. My only thoughts are to protect her.

Reaching out with my arms, I fall on top of her, and cover Sasha with my body. A second later, I take a hit with the whip across my neck. The pain is excruciating, and a piercing scream rips from my throat.

There's loud angry yelling in the background. "Fucking stop! She's in the collection." Immediately, I pull at Sasha's ropes and stumble trying to untie her hands.

"Sasha? Sasha, can you move?" No answer. My heart constricts painfully. I pull Sasha's hands loose and bring her arms down. I haul her into my body and turn her over as I sit back on my calves. I inhale sharply at what I see and tears pool in my eyes. With shaking hands, I gently touch her face. Her once beautiful face is now bruised and bloody. She's been severely beaten. She makes no movement at my touch.

"Sasha!" I shake her shoulders and shout in her face. Nothing. No response.

I look around me wildly and scream, "Someone help her, please!" No one moves.

I look back to Sasha. *Think, Lily. What do I do?* I look to her swollen eyes and see a sliver of her beautiful blue irises. If she were dead, her eyes wouldn't shine so bright would they? *She's awake!* Hope blooms instantly and then fades away just as quickly as I notice they aren't moving. My eyes slip to her chest. It isn't rising or falling. I put my ear to her mouth and feel no warm breath coming from her. *No, No! This isn't happening!*

I shake Sasha mercilessly. "Wake up! Don't do this. Don't you dare leave me!" I beg. A sob explodes out of my mouth. "Please, don't leave me here. Take me with you," I plead softly.

Tears are now pouring down my face, raining onto Sasha's chest where a red pool builds. I twist back to the guards, imploring them with my eyes to help me. My sight is blurry. I attempt to wipe the tears with my shoulders but more just keep falling.

Jake is standing closer to me than anyone else. I lift Sasha up to him, begging him to take her, to help her. But I'm too weak to hold her up while Jake stands frozen. The only movement is his glassy eyes hitting mine: agonised pain reflecting my own. A high pitched cry violently rips from my chest as he stays frozen just staring at me, while I hold my dead sister in my arms.

I stare back down to Sasha and put my hand to her chest, trying to feel for my little sister's heartbeat, but I find nothing... stillness.

I lift my hand to her head and cup her cheek. Blood smears her face. Shaking, I kiss her temple. "I love you," I say, barely above a whisper. "I will see you soon, sis."

Another screaming cry forces its way out of my lips as I can't stop myself from staring down at my little sister, laying lifeless in my arms, her dead swollen eyes staring back at me. My mind desperately calls me to the dark corner, to be as far away from here as possible.

I twist my neck as my head grows heavy on my shoulders, my eyes stinging. I gently place my baby sister on the dirt and blood below me. My body feels lifeless and weak; sobs keep crawling from my mouth.

I want to lie down next to her and beg God to take me too.

Movement has me turning my head to the guards standing around me. Some with wide eyes, and others, their expressions blank, not caring that they have torn my world apart.

I catch sight of a gun sitting on a chair to my right. I blink twice, clearing the tears from my eyes.

Vengeance! Roars through my mind.

I understand what I have to do without even thinking, I'm up and running. I can vaguely hear yells, orders. I'm not sure; all my focus is on getting to that gun. I'm almost there and fall to the hard cement ground, feeling my jeans rip, and my skin peel as I slide to the chair.

I grab the gun and twist the top half of my body around. As soon as I look up, my eyes find Mick with the whip in his hands. I let out a deep guttural scream I don't recognise as my own; it rips its self from my throat, but I know it's me from the shaking in my arms and the rumbling in my chest. This is something ugly inside of me. It's madness. I've been standing on the edge of a cliff and I was just pushed, and all the rage building inside of me from the first day I arrived in Hell is thirsting for revenge, for blood to be spilled.

Bang!

I pull the trigger as Mick drops the whip and heads toward me. I watch as he's forced back by the bullet, and he falls to the ground. I'm shocked by the force of the gun as my arm knocks back from the recoil.

Hazily, I hear Jake in the background yelling not to shoot me, but I can't be sure. There's too much noise in my ears, a roaring sound telling me to avenge my sister and kill these monsters.

I aim the gun at another guard and shoot without a second thought. I'm ready for the recoil this time and adjust to aim at the next guard quicker. Then the next guard. I feel a pain slash through one of my thighs, but nothing matters more than killing them. Kill. Them. All.

Bang! Bang! Bang! Bang!

Suddenly, I hear a clicking sound, but my arm isn't forced to brace, and I realise the gun is out of bullets.

The haze clears, and I focus on what's in front of me. Five dead men lying on the ground, blood seeping from their wounds. Four dead guards and Jake, dead. Blood spills from his neck and chest. I drop the gun immediately and cover my mouth as a cry escapes. *Jake.*

I hear yelling from faraway and boots crunching on gravel running toward me, but they aren't here yet.

A gun is haphazardly lying on the ground between me and a dead guard.

I pick it up and put it to my temple. I close my eyes and drift off into the darkness, thinking only of seeing my sister soon.

Bang!

Abruptly, I'm taken out of my thoughts by a guard picking up the gun sitting on the chair. I look up and see all four guards and Jake still alive and staring at me. I shake my head, trying to clear my mind of what is real and what I wish I could do.

Someone picks me up under my arms, and I start thrashing around and screeching, "I'll kill you! I will kill you all for what you have done!

Numb

JAKE

LILY'S LYING ON THE BED, STARING AT THE WALL. SHE sleeps, wakes, cries, and stares at the wall. The same thing, constantly on repeat.

I walk to the bed and kneel between Lily and the surface she has been staring at for the past two days. Her haunted green eyes sweep over me, but there's nothing there. No recognition, no change to the lifeless body lying here.

"I'm so sorry, Lil." My words come out strangled and thick.

I drop my head to the bed and feel my eyes glass over. I don't know what to do, how to help her. I grab her hand, place it to my mouth and kiss her hard and long. Praying she can make it out of this, fight her way out of the dark and come back to me.

I observe her beautiful face: her eyes, still lifeless, her fiery spirit gone. Watching her like this is fucking killing me. The pain radiating from her body is like soundwaves knocking me back. It's excruciating.

I get up and head for the door. Halfway there, she finally speaks to me, and I freeze. "You let them hurt her. Never touch me again." Her voice is dead of all emotion.

Those words may as well be bullets straight through my chest. They send me to my knees, and I hang my head. I've lost her, before I ever really had her.

LILY

DARKNESS ENGULFS ME, NOTHINGNESS.

I feel something warm and soft on my hand. It pulls me from my dark numb corner. I don't want to come out, but the warmth spreads to my chest.

My eyes shift to the offending existence that dares to bring me out where I know all the pain awaits me.

Jake.

Anger overpowers the warmth and entwines itself through my heart, barbed wire choking and slicing my insides. I know what comes next, memories and agony. No, go back into the dark corner where I can feel oblivion once more.

First, I want to hurt him.

"You let them hurt her. Never touch me again." I hear

the words but don't feel them come out of my mouth.

Crawling back into my dark place, numbness curls around me like a warm blanket. Nothingness.

There You Are

STAYING IN THE DARKNESS ISN'T AS EASY AS I WISH IT COULD be. The pain and memories slowly slip through. I try to shove them back; however, I hear a voice, smell some food or feel the need to use the toilet. I don't want to do normal things. If Sasha can't, I don't want to.

Sometimes I think I can hear her, telling me to get up, fight. She sounds irritated at me. But that can't be possible, just the memory of her lifeless body in my arms sends me crawling back into my dark corner, begging the agony to leave me. I can't continue. My heart won't take it. I always knew my parents would die with a broken heart if they had to live without the other. I didn't realise I would do the same without my little sister.

I hear his voice again. *Argh*, I wish he would just shut up. He keeps bringing me back. I don't want to come back.

I want to stay here forever. I want to wither away to nothing and see my family. I have nothing left to live for. What's in my future worth fighting for anymore? The darkness is the only place I want to be.

"Lily, it's just you and me now."

We're sitting in the front pews of the church, shoulder to shoulder, leaning on each other's heads, having just said goodbye to our parents. Everyone else has left. Thankfully, giving us some time alone.

"Yeah, Sash, I can see Mum up there now, trying to tell us things, such as, don't use the expensive china. Don't press the power button on the dishwasher too many times; you'll break it." We both laugh at remembering our mother's words.

"I hope we die together. I would hate to be the last one left," Sasha says softly.

"Sash, that won't happen for a long time, and then we will have families of our own. We won't be alone," I assure her.

"Well, if it ever happens, Lil, I want you still to have a happy life. That's what Mum and Dad would want for us, and that's what I would want for you," she insists.

"I would want that for you too, Sash, but enough with this. You will be with me when we're old and grey, and we have a hundred grandchildren running around our farm, through our green fields and wrecking our favourite tree." We softly laugh together.

"Come on." I pull my sister up to walk out of the church. We hold hands along the way. I feel something wet and look down to our joined fingers, blood, all over our hands.

My eyes flash to Sasha's face, it's bruised and swollen. "Lily," she whispers shocked. She then falls into my arms and I scream.

I hear screaming. My eyes are stinging and there are hands on me.

My eyes open and my throat hurts. All at once, I realise it's me. Jake is hugging my body, rubbing his hand up and down my back.

"Shh, baby, it's okay," he tries to soothe me.

I'm confused. The dream I just had comes back to me: Sasha dead in my arms. My heart splits open all over again. Every time I wake up with the same pain, my heart smashes open, the sharp edges cutting through my chest, and it's too much. I'm so tired. I just want it to end.

Jake's arms around me bring warmth and safety. I feel protected and hatred for him all at the same time. He awakens me to my life, this life with too much pain for my weak body to handle. However, just this once, I need him to give me some peace. I'm so tired of the pain. I want him to make me forget.

I've stopped screaming. Instead, I'm clinging to Jake's shirt with strength that would rival Superman's. No one is taking me from this peaceful moment. I just need a minute to believe, whether it's real or not, that I will be all right.

Jake tightens his hold on me, and we lay in silence for a while. When he pulls back slightly, he examines me. His expression is tormented. A wave of guilt and longing sears through me.

With glassy eyes, he says, "There you are. I thought when I met you, I had seen the most stunning green eyes in the world. I was wrong. Right now, seeing them spark with life after seeing nothing in them for the past three days, they are the most beautiful eyes I have ever seen."

I act without thinking. I kiss him. He pauses for a second before he's kissing me back, hard and possessively. God, he feels so good, and now I know what Hell feels like, I can honestly say Jake's mouth and hands on me are Heaven.

I start to lift his shirt over his head, but he pulls back, his eyes staring into mine. "Lily, you're hurting. We can't do this right now." Jakes voice is clear and confident but his dilated dark brown eyes show me just how much he wants this.

I capture his face between my hands. "Please, Jake," I beg. "I want to feel something, anything, other than the pain."

Jake blows out a big breath. "Fuck, Lil, I want this, so fucking bad, but—" I can see the concern for my state of mind and the indecision on his face, so I cut him off.

"Jake," I say with a firm, controlled voice. "I will not regret this. I want this." And I do. I want anything other than the pain I know will return once my mind has time to think. I do want Jake, but I push those thoughts to the back of my mind unable to process what that might mean and what Jake's role in this house of horrors really is.

Jake surprises me by giving in and swooping down, kissing me hard, passionately. I lift his shirt again and this time he helps. He releases my lips and whips the shirt straight off his body. His chest and arms are tanned, defined, and filled with incredible artwork. He's magnificent.

Jake reaches for my top, and I realise I'm in my silk top and boxers. For a moment, I wonder how I got changed, but I'm too desperate to have Jake inside me to care. He does away with my top and slowly pulls down my boxers and panties. With each inch he lowers them, he kisses my thighs, knees, shins, and ankles. A delicious shiver spreads through my body, subduing the heartache, just for a moment. The pain will return with force, but for this moment all I want to feel is Jake.

Jake discards my clothes and sits back on his haunches. He sweeps his gaze up my body, slowly and greedily, until he reaches my eyes. "You are so fucking beautiful," he breathes out.

His gaze darts down to my breasts as he lowers himself and takes one nipple into his mouth. I arch my back at the welcome feeling. Warmth spreads to my pussy, and I grow wet from his addictive licks and sucks. I twist my hands through Jake's hair and force him down harder on my nipples. I want him to bite them and suck harder. He groans and obliges. My breathing accelerates with every thrilling lick and an electrifying shock shoots to my pussy as Jake bites down hard on the side of my breast. I moan and fist the sheets.

Jake kisses his way up my neck and jaw. He pushes up until he is kneeling above me. He releases his erection from his zipped pants and holds his cock. One white bead spills over, and he rubs his cum covered head on my clit in circular motions, slowly. I moan in pleasure, my legs quivering from the intense orgasm that's building.

Jake cups my cheek with his other hand and rubs his thumb over my lips. I slowly close my eyelids at his beautiful, intimate touch. My eyes open to see Jake's heavy-lidded eyes staring down into mine.

"This is your last chance to stop this, Lil. If we go any further, I won't be able to stop myself." He looks down my body and licks his lips. "Tell me now, baby, are you sure you want this? Because when I've finally had you, you are mine." Jake pauses for a second, before he continues with a thick voice, "You've turned my world inside out, baby. There will be no going back." Jake continues to circle my clit with his cock.

Even if I thought I wanted to stop this, there is no way my body would let me. I shake my head and plead, "Please, Jake, don't stop."

He slows his movements and his cock glides around my clit again. My hips spasm with need.

"Baby, I want to hear the words. Do you understand what this will mean? You will be mine, now and forever."

For this moment, I am done pretending I don't want to be his. "Yes, yes, I understand," I breathe out, grinding my hips harder on his cock.

Jake stops his movements on my clit, devastation and need fills my veins. I glare up at him only to find a smirk on his face.

He reaches down to his pants and pulls a condom out of his wallet. With a quick tear, it's open. I lick my lips as the condom stretches to breaking point trying to fit over his cock.

Jake looks down to my slick wet folds and groans.

"Fuck, I can't wait to be inside you, Lil."

Jake covers me with his body, one hand slips into my hair, and he brings my mouth to his. His kiss is aggressive. I love it. Holding onto Jake's neck, I kiss him back just as roughly, biting his lower lip. His other hand pinches my nipples and my orgasm starts to rebuild.

He breaks the kiss and brings his cock to my entrance. "Jesus, Lily, you're so wet, and it's all for me," he growls.

Jake's possessive gaze pins me, keeping me hostage as he slowly slides the head of his thick cock inside me. I moan as liquid heat runs through me. He pulls out and does the same again, and it's agony. I just want him inside, stretching me.

He grabs hold of my waist and rolls us, pulling me on top of him. "Hold on to the bedframe, baby."

I follow Jake's instructions and hold tight to the metal bars.

"Take me at your own speed." I stare down at Jake and understand what he's doing. He's giving me control, and even though I trust him, he's giving me choices. He's giving me back a piece of myself that was stolen.

I slowly lower myself. My head flies back and I arch as I moan from the exquisite feeling of Jake filling me.

"Damn, Lily, you're perfect for me, so tight around my cock."

Slowly, I slide up and down his girth, before building to faster, harder, faster, harder.

Jake's eyes are transfixed, watching our connection as I rise and slam down onto him again and again. "Jake," I moan, his actions getting me off just as much as having his cock inside of me.

"Shit, baby, you feel fucking amazing." His voice is thick and hoarse.

My legs start to tremble. I'm seconds from falling into ecstasy.

"Hold tightly to the bars, Lil." I tighten my hold and Jake grips my waist and thrusts up into me powerfully, surging into me again and again. I clench around his thrusting cock, and I moan, lost in the intoxicating bliss. I'm about to fall into the best orgasm I've ever had.

"Eyes on me, Lil," Jake growls. "I want to watch my woman's eyes go off when I make you come."

My eyes find his and I scream, "Jake!"

He groans, "There's my fiery girl. That spark breathes life into me, baby." His voice is husky and strained from the powerful pounding he's giving me.

I watch in a hypnotic state as he clenches his eyes closed and shouts out, "Fuuuuck!" His thrusts grow more powerful with every stroke in and out. Jake's whole body tenses as he finds his release.

His hands loosen on my waist. Sitting up, he encircles me in his arms and buries his head in my neck, breathing heavily.

Jake grasps my arse and lifts me, gliding me slowly up and down his softening cock, then he gently lifts me off and lays me onto the bed.

He walks to the bathroom, probably to get rid of the condom. My eyes start to close, sated and exhausted, and I start to drift off to sleep.

My eyes open as one of my legs lifts up into the air, and

I feel a warm washcloth between my legs. My heart trips over itself at this intimate gesture.

Finishing, he heads back to the bathroom, and then he strolls back over to the bed, naked and glorious, slipping into the bed behind me, hugging me to his front.

My body grows heavy, recognising the feeling of safety. Finally, I relax. Jake's lips kiss my neck and my eyes close, and for the first time in days, I get a restful, full night's sleep.

She Was Everything To Me, My Whole World

I LAY IN BED SNUGGLED UP TO JAKE FOR A WHILE BEFORE I decide it's time to open my eyes. The memories and the pain are still poking and piercing at my heart; however, for some reason this morning, in Jake's arms, I feel better able to hold it together.

Guilt is burning through my blood like fire. Guilt that I am letting a man, a man who is part of this evil place comfort me, help heal me. Have I lost my mind so far that I find peace in what I should hate the most? In the back of my mind, I know Jake is the exception in this house of horrors. Last night was incredible. Something shifted between us, but I don't want to acknowledge it. I can only handle one thing at a time, and right now, pain is the dominating factor. It spreads through my body like wildfire wanting vengeance.

Jake kisses my shoulder and I tense at the intimate gesture. "You're awake." His breath warms my neck. I push away, now uncomfortable with our position.

"Lily," he warns, rolling me over and pinning me with the weight of his body. Jake's hands gently cup my cheeks. I have nowhere to look, except into his warm, compassionate eyes. I do not want his sympathy.

"What?" I hiss. "Trapping me in this house isn't enough for you? Now I'm to be trapped beneath you." I have so much anger in my soul that I don't care who I'm directing it at.

"That look right there, Lil, the hatred I see you have for me, it kills me."

My eyes go wide at his words, *Hatred.*

"That's not hatred, Jake. That's rage. I want everyone in this Godforsaken world to pay for what happened to my sister." I want someone to burn for taking my sister away, and right now, Jake is in my firing line. I don't hate him, but someone must pay.

Jake hangs his head and sighs.

"Get off me," I demand.

Jake shakes his head. "We need to talk, Lil."

"Stop calling me that. She called me that," I scream at his face.

Jake flinches at my outburst. "I can see you dying on the inside," he whispers, his face one of pure agony. "Please come back to me, Lily. I don't want to continue this without you."

"Continue," I repeat his words in a whisper. "Continue what, Jake? This isn't a fucking holiday," I hiss.

"Continue to fight," he yells. Jake's expression screams at me to understand him. He softly continues, "I need you to hang on. You need to trust me, Lily. I know that's asking the impossible, but you can feel it. I know you can. I see the way you look at me. You feel safe with me, just as my heart knows you are mine. It's instinctive and unexplainable, but we're connected. We have been from the very beginning."

He's asking too much of me. "You want my heart, Jake?" I snap at him.

"Fuck, yes," he snaps back.

My eyes fill with tears, and I whisper, "The remaining parts of my heart are broken pieces of glass with sharp edges, and I dare anyone to come near it. I will make sure it cuts them." My voices breaks at the end.

He lays his hand over my dead chest. "I will piece it back together, and I would take a million cuts before I would ever consider giving up." Jake lifts my chin to make me look him in the eyes. "I'll show you. Your heart will begin to beat again, in time, and I will be here waiting to catch the first new beat it makes. Then and for always it will be mine."

His tender words stop my anger in its tracks, a wall I built in my dark corner crumbles. Pain, longing and guilt spreads through my veins.

"I will do everything in my power to get you home. I just can't stop the hurt in the meantime."

Get home. Those words rock around in my head. At every turn I'm reminded of what I have lost. "Get home to what? I have no one left," I whimper. "She was everything to me, my whole world." He doesn't understand, no one understands.

I look up at Jake, but he's just staring at me so lost. "You have me, Lily. You may not want me, but you have me," he says softly.

My heart flickers with excitement, the smallest pulse letting me know it may not be dead after all.

A thought crosses my mind and my body stills. Why hadn't I thought to ask this before. "Why, Jake? Why did they do that to her?" My voice wobbles.

Jake lies down next to me, and we turn, facing each other. "Are you ready to hear this, Lil? I don't want you to retreat again."

I nod. "I need to know, Jake."

Jake drags his hand through his hair and sighs. "They captured Sasha escaping with another girl. A guard from here was in town getting a few things, and he saw them get out of the trunk. He caught up to Sasha and called in for backup to find the other girl. It was the worst luck they could have had."

Jake blows out a big breath, his gaze penetrating into mine. The air grows thick. "A doctor has seen Sasha, Lily." Jake now has my full attention. "He concluded she died from bleeding in the brain from a hard hit to the head."

My chest clenches hard. "Who was the one who beat her?" I know the answer before Jake speaks.

"Mick," Jake growls.

"And the other girl?" Jake's eyes shift away, and suddenly I'm scared to hear his answer.

"She was caught only a few streets away from where

Sasha was picked up. She resisted and put up one hell of a fight; but, the guard shot and killed her."

My hand shoots up to my mouth in shock as a sob erupts. *Maria.*

"What about Dr Alexa and Beth?"

Jake raises his eyebrow and shakes his head. I see a small smile grace his lips. "I should have known you would get the girls to talk. Even I can't say no to you. They didn't stand a chance."

"They didn't talk to me. They wrote to me. I found a pencil and begged them to tell me if Sasha was okay, and that's how the plan started," I quickly answer, and then ask impatiently, "Well, what about Alexa and Beth?"

"Dr Kingsley, a slave girl, and a guard who escorted them to the grocery store were beaten at the same time as Sasha to find out what happened. They wanted to know how she and the other girl got into the trunk of the car. The guard said he knew nothing. None of the women talked. They told Sasha to tell them who helped her, but she refused to talk."

I can't fathom how people can do these things to human beings. "And how are they now?"

"Alexa and Beth will be okay in time. They were severely beaten but are recovering. I've seen the tapes from the cameras in the house. Sasha and Maria snuck out and hid in the trunk. There was no one there helping them, so Beth and Alexa will be spared. If it had showed Alexa helping them escape, I think there would have been a war between father and son. Joseph is on his way here now. He's going to draw blood on the guard who lifted a hand to Alexa. She is off limits just as much as the collection is."

So Joseph does care for her.

I realise we're both still naked from our night together. "Can you let me go so I can put some clothes on?"

Jake sweeps his gaze down my body. Nodding, he gets off me, climbing off the bed. I watch as his naked body moves in mighty strides. His build is proudly on display, and I can't take my eyes off his perfect muscular arse.

I hear a groan and sweep my eyes up his body to his face, his pupils dilated and desire radiating from his body. "Keep looking at me like that, Lil, and I will keep you naked all day, underneath me."

I'm annoyed he caught me staring, wanting him so badly, again. I start dressing in my silk top and boxers, forgoing my panties as they will get drenched as soon as I put them on after Jake's words.

I turn to Jake as he walks around the bed to me, dressed in his jeans, black t-shirt and boots. "What's the deal with Joseph and Alexa? He cares for her, yet she seemed angry with him when I saw them together after my appointment, and she went against him and his father to free a slave girl. Evidently she doesn't agree with what they are doing here."

Jake sighs and sits back on the bed. "I don't know what is going on between them, but Joseph is not who you think he is. He has gone up against his father in the past regarding his business and lost. He's just as trapped as you are." Interesting.

"Sasha..." He pauses. "If Sasha had given Alexa and

Beth up, she might have been spared the beating."

I shake my head. "She would never do that. My sister would never do that." A sob falls from my mouth. "As much as I could live with her doing that, so she could be alive, she wouldn't be able to live with herself." Sasha was too selfless and brave. "No, this is my fault," I say, my breathing escalating, my head spinning. "You warned me, and all of this is my fault."

"No!" Jake growls. He moves to me and grabs my shoulders, pinning me with an intense stare. "Keep your eyes on me, Lily. I want you to see how serious I am when I say this," he demands, my eyes obey. "You did what anyone would have done for their family. You tried to save her. You tried to protect her. THIS. IS. NOT. your fault."

I know to some extent what Jake is saying is right, but I was so stubborn. All I could think about was getting Sasha home. Not what would happen if she were caught. I felt boxed into a corner and took the first opportunity offered to me. A sob rips from my chest. *How could I have not thought of everything?*

Jake pulls me into his warm embrace. "You have to pull it together, Lily. If you don't, Marco will decide not to keep you in the collection."

I look at Jake shocked and livid at his words. "That's all you care about, keeping Marco happy and still getting what you want," I hiss, pushing Jake away from me and putting my back to him for a second. With rage fuelling my thoughts I turn my body and sear Jake with a pissed off stare, "I should tell Marco you touched me, see how you like it when you lose something you badly want."

Jake heads toward me at lightning speed. He grasps my arms in a tight hold.

"Fuck, baby, I know you're angry at the world right now, but you do that and we will both be sorry, and I don't mean just dealing with Marco's consequences."

I laugh. It's high pitched and crazy sounding. "More cryptic words, Jake. How original of you."

"There is more at stake than what you can see in front of you, Lil," he pleads.

"All I see, Jake, is my dead sister in my arms," I hiss.

"Then fight to get out, for her, to make sure justice gets served for her death." His voice is close to shouting but he controls himself. "Survive, thrive and get the fuck out of this nightmare, and have your justice."

"You're asking me to fight, but to do nothing. You're asking me to thrive, but I am trapped. I. DO. NOT. UNDERSTAND!"

Jake moves his hands from my arms and cups my cheeks. "I know, Lil. This is where you need to trust me."

I do trust Jake with my life. It's a feeling I have that I can't grasp yet, or don't want to acknowledge. But, I still want him to pay for being a part of this place, and that means making him work for my trust even if I do want to give it to him on a silver platter. I need him to earn it.

I take a step back from him. "You're right. Trusting you is impossible," I lie. Jake's eyes clench closed. "But," his eyelids fly up, "I have no other choice, but to trust you to get me out of here."

"Thank you." He pulls me to him. I relax into his body.

He calms me so easily; however, I'm not stupid enough to think this connection we have will go anywhere. I know in the end, there's too much for us to overcome. And if Jake still wants to take over this empire, then I will run to the ends of the Earth to escape him. God will have given me a man I may one day love, but could never be with.

"This trust starts today, Lily. Marco is going to be here today to see you and find out what happened. Marco will be heartless. He will only care about losing money out of Sasha. I need you to ignore his comments and be strong. He is a loose cannon. There is no telling what he will do, and I'm worried he will assume you helped Sasha."

I want to tell Marco I helped her. Have him know I got my sister outside his beautiful cage. But I'm through playing by his rules. I have a lifeline, Jake, and I will do everything I can to stay alive and get away.

"Today will be a big day, Lily. It could go either way. Marco will punish someone, and if he goes for you, I won't be able to stop myself from protecting you, and then we will both be in a world of pain."

My body tenses. The thought of Jake in pain or losing him like I lost Sasha is unbearable. "Don't do that, Jake. Don't risk yourself for me."

"I would never be able to stop myself," he says, staring into my eyes. "My chest has burned since the first day I met you, Lil. The only time I get any rest from the ache is when you're in my arms and I know you're safe."

I stare at him stunned for a moment, before walking over to the window. I don't want to go there. I don't want to admit anything to myself or Jake. I'm nowhere near ready to feel anything but hatred for this place and everyone in it, so I change the subject.

"When does Marco get here?"

Jake exhales loudly, but doesn't call me on it. He answers my question. "I'm about to go find out. I'll be back soon to let you know. Pick something nice from the closet, something a collection piece would wear. The way to win Marco over is to look like you will make him money." Jake wraps me in his arms and kisses my temple long and hard. "I won't be long," he says into my hair. Letting me go, he leaves the room.

As soon as the door closes, the room grows quiet, cold, and I instantly feel crippled by the pain of remembering my sister is no longer in this world with me. I tell myself I have things to do. I need to keep busy, so I go to the closet and begin choosing a dress that will say, 'please buy me and spend a lot of money on me.' *Awesome.*

As much as I want to fall back into bed and hide away from the world, I'm not going to give Marco or anyone else the power to destroy me. It's my time to be brave. I might still cry and I might still fall, but at the end of all of this, I will be free and I *will* bring them all to their knees.

Karma Is My Bitch

I FIND A BLACK LACE DRESS, PERFECT FOR MY MOOD. IT'S ONE shouldered with a thick lace strap that goes over my right shoulder. I shower and blow out my hair in the bathroom. In the process, I discover the cut on my neck from the whip; I hadn't even remembered I was hit until I looked in the mirror. A swollen red line goes from the bottom of my hairline to my shoulder blades. *Sasha*, a sharp pain pierces my heart. No, keep moving, keep focused.

Finished with my hair, I put it up in a tight bun, the only classy hair style I know how to do. The dress falls straight down, stopping tight at my thighs, close fitting to my chest, waist, and butt. Just like all the others: skin tight but beautiful and classy, no jewellery, natural makeup, and a pair of black stilettos.

The thick shoulder strap hides my cut. I don't want to show it off. I won't let them think they hurt me.

Jake isn't gone long. I hear the door open and turn to see him rushing in, but he stops dead when he sees me. His eyes sweep up and down my body, and his gaze telling me he wants me. I shiver and goose bumps rise on my skin. I can see the fight he's having with himself not to pick me up and rip the dress off my body. I smirk at the thought. I'm surprised I have any happy facial expressions left in me.

Jake walks over to me and softly kisses my temple. "Beautiful as always, Lil."

Argh, I turn away frustrated. I asked him not to call me that and he keeps doing it.

Jake takes my hand and turns me back to him. "I'm sorry, Lily. Calling you that is as natural to me as breathing." Damn him and his sweet words. Can't he see I want to hate him? That I need to hate him?

I say nothing and just stare at him. Jake looks at me, but he soon gives up on an answer from me and says, "Marco is almost here. We need to go down to the office and await his arrival. He isn't staying long. He's having trouble with people following one of the collection pieces."

I gasp, "Who? Which woman is it?"

"I don't know, Lily. Until we're at Marco's home, all of the collections' business is kept secret." Jake changes the topic. "How do you think it will go if Mick is present at the meeting?"

Not well at all, I know that much. "First I will need to

find a knife, then some ropes. Do you think they have any ropes in the kitchen?" I ask Jake, not even looking at him, too busy thinking of how many different ways I can kill and torture the bastard who took my sister from me.

"Lily," Jake says tenderly, standing right behind me. "As much as I want to let you at him, I can't, not yet anyway. However, I promise you, he will pay for what he has done. But today is about surviving this meeting with Marco. Focus on that." I stay silent because I can't promise if I see Mick, I won't try to tear him to shreds. "Even Mick has to try and survive it. Marco is incredibly unpredictable. If I were Mick, I would be saying my goodbyes today."

"You think Marco would kill Mick?" I ask with hope and confusion. Why would Marco kill one of his guards?

"He marked you with a whip, and I've learned to expect anything with Marco. I won't ever underestimate him. We need to get down there. Are you ready?" Jake asks.

I nod and we walk downstairs to the meeting. Jake was right. As soon as we make it to the office, Mick is there, and as soon as my eyes land on him untouchable rage surges through me. I attack.

Sprinting toward him, I swing my fists out, connecting with his head. Pain radiates up my arms, but I don't care. I need more. I need to draw blood.

Mick grunts and covers his face with his hands trying to avoid my nails scraping his cheeks and neck. I scream a war cry. To me, this is war, and this is a fight to the death. Only, I'm soon pulled back into a hard chest.

I glare with every ounce of hate in my body. I spear him with my loathing and wish for God to strike him down.

Jake turns his back to Mick and places me on my feet, still holding me from behind with my arms caged to my front by his iron hold. My chest is burning from my heavy breaths.

Jake softly growls into my ear, "Pull it together."

He walks me to the opposite side of the room. Before turning me around, he asks, "You good?" I nod. However, I'm not good. I will never be good around that man.

Jake turns us, lets me go, and stands to my side but still in my space, ready to grab me at any moment.

I try to calm and take in Mick's appearance. Shoulders hunched, his hands are shaking. He's shit scared of this meeting with Marco. I smile, loving the fact that I may see him suffer today.

Marco walks into the room with two guards I saw at the party. Everyone freezes. Marco comes straight for me and places his hands on my face. I tense and Jake flinches. Marco's eyes dart to Jake, and my heart drops at him seeing Jake's reaction.

Marco's eyes come back to me, and he looks into my eyes while rubbing his thumb gently over my chin. I feel repulsed by his touch. I stay silent. There are a storm of emotions swirling violently inside of me at seeing this man, the one man who created all of this evil.

Marco drops his hand from my face and speaks. "Jake tells me you were hit with a whip. Show me," he demands.

I turn slightly to my right and pull the lace strap down just enough for him to see the swollen cut.

Marco hisses through his teeth.

"I see you still have fire in your actions. Any other woman would wear it for show, looking for guilt, for apologies. Instead, you choose to hide it, as if it's not even there." His tone is one of respect. "Something at least," Marco mutters.

He stays standing in front of me, looking into my eyes. "Your sister made a mistake trying to escape from me." I still at his words. "I see you have taken her death badly. You look like death yourself. Your eyes have dark circles, and your appearance seems messy." This guy is un-fucking-believable.

Marco shakes his finger in the air as if just coming up with an idea. "I will fix this for you."

Marco turns to Mick and walks over to him. Marco and Mick are clearly the same size and height, but Marco exudes danger and power. Mick oozes nothing but weakness, a sheep who follows in the footsteps of people he only wishes he could be. Mick is a coward, and it's written all over his face.

Mick starts stuttering. "I- I- didn't mean to kill her. She was on- only supposed to get hurt enough to give up who helped her get in and out of the trunk."

Still looking at Mick, Marco speaks, "Jake, please tell Mick what you told me yesterday."

Jake begins as if already knowing Marco would ask this of him, his voice matter of fact. "After looking over the video, Sasha and one slave girl got into the trunk on their own. And it is easily seen they do not lock it down. The two girls would have held it down with their hands all the way to town and then opened it on their own when they thought it was clear for escape."

Marco begins speaking, "So Mick, if you had watched the fucking tapes, like you should have, you would have seen for yourself no one else fucking helped them. Now I have my doctor, one slave girl, and a guard out of action till God knows when because you are fucking incompetent. I'm surprised my son hasn't killed you yet."

Mick stares at Jake then back to Marco, apparently realising his epic mistake.

Marco's hands clench and unclench, and suddenly Marco grabs Mick by the back of his neck, pushing him to me, his face inches from mine. "Look what you have done to my collection piece." He shakes Mick's head hard, to look at me. "Look at her eyes. They are dead. No fire. I would rather you have broken her arms than break her spirit. A woman with injured arms can still open her legs. A damaged woman with dead eyes holds no want from any man." Fear takes hold of my whole body at hearing for myself just how sadistic Marco is.

He pulls Mick back and throws him to the ground. "What do you think will happen when she is standing on my stage, with no spark in her eyes," he ends on a roar. "They will bid lower for her. That's what will happen," Marco says, breathing heavily.

Oh, God, he makes me sick. His whole world revolves around money and power. My sister dies, and all he can see is how much money he might lose.

"So," Marco says as he appears to calm down and rubs his hands together as if he's about to watch a good show.

"Lily, what will it take to get that fire back in your

eyes?" I'm shocked and look to Jake, not sure what Marco is asking me. Jake looks at me, seemingly confused as well.

"Come now, Lily. No need to look to Jake like a scared little animal. Won't getting revenge for your sister's death make you feel better," Marco asks, but it's more like a statement.

I swing my gaze back to Marco and nod, unsure what I'm agreeing to.

"Wonderful," Marco smiles at me. "As I can't give you a gun, since I'm sure you will aim it at me, I will—" he stops talking and looks back to Jake and back to me. "No, since I can see you and Jake have become quite attached in my absence, Jake can do it for you." I freeze.

My emotions are battling each other; The intense need to see Mick pay for killing my sister and my fear for Jake at Marco seeing through us so easily.

Jake steps forward straight away. He takes the gun out of his holster from behind his back and under his bomber jacket.

Jake doesn't spare a glance my way. He walks straight over to Mick. I move to the left wanting to see the last look on Mick's face. He looks right at me. This time with utter fear and resignation. He knows he is about to die, and all I can do is smile.

Marco stands next to me and whispers in my ear, "There she is."

Mick stands and backs up against the wall. He begins to beg for his life, "Jake, please, don't do this. Marco, I've learned my lesson. This will never happen again."

Jake raises his gun to Mick, but suddenly Joseph storms

into the room shouting, halting Jake's actions.

"Where is he?" Joseph yells.

"Where is the cock sucker who dared touch what is mine?"

All eyes are on Joseph as he wildly looks around the room then levels his piercing gaze at Mick.

"There you are." He points his finger at Mick.

"You are a dead man." Joseph doesn't seem to notice what is going on around him, and that Mick was just about to die.

In a flash, Joseph is standing before Mick. He pulls a gun from behind his suit jacket and pushes it to Mick's chest, right over his heart. Rage so powerful pulses around Joseph, his body shaking from his anger.

"See you in hell, motherfucker," he sneers.

I don't look away. The gun goes off, and in lightning speed, the bullet enters straight into Mick's heart. The life leaves his eyes. He slumps against the wall, blood pouring from the hole in his chest down his body.

I can't help but be captivated by the heinous and brutal death. My chest feels marginally lighter having one small amount of justice for Sasha. I close my eyes and think of my sister, hoping she got to watch him die as well.

I'm pulled from my thoughts by Marco clapping. He pats Joseph on the shoulder. "Well done, son." Joseph looks around confused by all the people standing in the room.

Jake is looking at me. I see the question in his eyes. He wants to know if I'm okay, but I keep my expression blank.

Marco motions to one of his guards. "Have the slave girls come up and clean the wall." The guard leaves the room instantly.

Joseph appears to be waking up from his murderous fog and his eyes swing to Marco. "Father, your business has gone too far. I'm taking Alexa and leaving, and this time, you won't stop me." Joseph's voice is low and angry.

He starts to leave the room when Marco booms a furious voice across the room, "Fine, leave. Your mother will miss your hero antics when she gets my fist. And don't think you can take her with you. I will find you wherever you go, and I will make sure Alexa pays for your desertion."

Joseph's expression is furious. He growls, "I've grown tired of this game father. We are done." Exuding the hate he has for his father, he storms out of the room just as fast as he arrived.

Marco shouts after Joseph, "We will never be done. You are my son and you will follow in my footsteps." Marco waves his hand in the air and mutters, "Ah, he will be back."

Marco looks to Jake. "I'll be back tomorrow, Jake. We need to talk then." He looks from Jake to me, then back to Jake. "You're doing a good job, Jake. She looks well, apart from her grief, but she needs to move on from her sister. Explain to her the importance of being a part of the collection versus being removed from the collection."

All I can do is stare at him. Stunned, appalled, aghast, they don't even begin to explain how I'm feeling.

The guard returns with two slave girls and a guard I

remember as Phil. They go over to Mick, and Phil picks up his limp and lifeless body, throws him over his shoulder, and walks out of the room, not saying a word. The slave girls start cleaning the wall and carpet. Soon it will be as if it never happened and a man never died there.

"I need to keep moving now. These fuckers who want to take what is mine just never fucking give up," Marco announces. He walks past Jake and me, and leaves the room with his two guards.

As soon as the front door slams closed, Jake takes my arm gently and walks me to my room. Before I know it, the door is closing and I'm in Jake's arms. I cling to his shirt, tears falling, but I have no idea what feelings I'm having. Relief at seeing Mick pay for Sasha's death? Scared for Marco realising something is between me and Jake? Or fear I won't be able to feel alive again and I will be removed from the collection? Sasha was my only reason for living after my parents died. Now she's gone, and she took that part of me with her.

Mine

JAKE

I FLINCHED. I FUCKING FLINCHED. I COULDN'T HELP IT. AS soon as he touched her, my mind screamed *MINE*. I wanted to rip his cold, murdering hands off her beautiful face.

As soon as we were hidden away in her room, I had to have her in my arms. Lily hangs onto me tightly.

"Baby, are you okay?"

She shakes her head no, and I feel her tears soak through my shirt. "Oh, baby, it's going to be all right."

I pick Lily up and carry her to the bed. We lay together; Lily still holding onto me firmly. I pull her closer to me, thoughts rushing through my head of what tomorrow and my conversation with Marco will bring. Have I fucked it all up? Have I blown my chance to still be in his top guards? Shit, what if I have? What will I do then?

Lily slowly calms down. Seeing her in pain is excruciating. I fucking miss her smile and her sassy attitude.

Her eyes peer up to me in question. "What is it, Lil?"

With silent tears still falling down her gorgeous face, she asks, "Sasha's body, where is it?" Her question comes out of nowhere and surprises me. I hope Lily doesn't freak out when tell her what I did.

"I was the one who took care of Sasha's body. Everyone including Marco thinks she was sent off to get cremated."

Lily gasps. "She wasn't, Lil," I say quickly. Continuing, I hope she won't be furious with me, "But I had some outside contacts collect her. She will be flown home to Australia. I have someone there who will keep her safe for you as long as you need." I wait to see how Lily takes the news. Her gaze moves to my chest, and she seems lost in her thoughts for a moment. She then jumps at me and hugs me tightly.

"Thank you. Thank you so much. Knowing she is away from here and going home where I can bury her one day, gives me a small amount of peace."

My shoulders relax, feeling relieved. I wonder when Lily will realise I would do anything for her, well, almost anything. I know the moment is coming when I will have to choose between everything I've worked for and the woman who has stolen my point of direction.

I sit up on the bed, my legs straight out, my back to the headboard. Lily takes off her shoes and sits up on her own, her legs crossed. I start rubbing up and down her back, hoping to relax her more.

"I'm scared, Jake," she whispers, barely audible.

I want to take all her sorrow and make her forget she ever hurt in the first place. I move in behind her and hug her to my chest as she relaxes into my body. Fuck, this feels amazing, like she was always meant to be mine.

"I know, Lil. I wish I could tell you everything is going to be okay, but know that you will get out of here, in time."

"Your outside contacts, they can't help you, us?"

"No, Lil, just walking away from Marco isn't, or ever will be, a possibility." I know Lily will assume I'm talking about running from this house, but that's not what I mean. I could never walk away and leave without killing Marco first. But I need that damn fucking location first.

"What will you do when you get to his house?"

Burn it to the ground. I want to tell Lil the truth, but now, after Sasha, there is no way she will understand. I'm afraid of her reaction, telling Marco or another guard to get back at me. There is no forgiveness for what I have had others sacrifice for me to get to the secret location. I just have to take what little time I have left with Lil before she finds out just how much of a monster I really am.

Luckily, there is a knock. I quickly get up off the bed and go to the door. I open it and see a slave girl standing there. She pushes the table cart at me, and I take it from her and nod. I roll the cart to the bed.

"Come on, Lil. Time to eat." I'm thankful it's lunchtime. It gives me reason to leave and get my head together. If Lil keeps asking me these questions, I need to come up with some ways to get out of answering them.

"There is no way I can eat after just seeing someone shot through the chest."

"Well, I'm heading downstairs to have mine. I will see you in a bit." I go over and kiss her forehead.

"Jake," she says softly, and I know she's asking me to answer her question.

I sigh and lean my cheek on her hair. "I'm sorry, Lil. There are some answers I can't give you right now."

"But soon?" she asks.

When she finds out what I've done, she's going to rip my world apart. Fate has had the worst timing for us. "Yes, soon, Lil," I promise her.

I leave the room and shut the door, looking at the deadbolts. I know I'm walking a fine line. I could fail at getting to the secret location, or I could lose everything I thought I didn't deserve anymore. But I need both. I can't live without both.

LILY

AFTER JAKE LEAVES, I CHANGE OUT OF THE LACE DRESS, AND into denim shorts and a dark blue long-sleeved top, forgoing the bra and only putting on some undies. I know the only thing I will be doing for the rest of the day and night was reading and sleeping.

Boredom is the worst here. It's when thoughts of Sasha, and the pain of losing her creep into my heart and mind. Those moments feel like I will never get to the next hour without falling back into the dark, but Jake has given me a sliver of hope, a small light through the keyhole in a dark tunnel.

I want to follow Sasha back home and bury her, put her to rest. That will be my focus now, and then after, I will decide if I can go on. Again, my baby sister is the reason I keep fighting.

Jake is evasive about why he is here. Am I being a fool trusting someone who I've only known for a short time, who clearly doesn't trust me, but at the same time protects me and comforts me? My mind screams yes; however, my heart screams no, but isn't that what all women's hearts say right before they get broken? This isn't love though, is it? *Yes.* I hear the words in my head, but I push them away. No, I may be falling, falling hard, but I won't let myself fall all the way. .

Still awake and restless, I hear my door open and Jake walks in. This time, he's out of his bomber jacket and just in jeans and a white shirt. His hair is messy like he's run his hands through it the whole time he was away from me. My mouth instantly waters at how good he looks. Why does he have to be so damn attractive? How does God expect us females to resist that!

Jake smirks at me as if he knows what I'm thinking. Darn, caught for the second time today. "Baby that look in your eyes when you see me walk into a room drives me insane. I fucking love how much you want me." Jake walks over to the bed still smirking. "Shift over, gorgeous."

I shuffle over instantly for him, and he encircles me with his arms, and instantaneously, I feel warm and at home. Damn him.

"Ah, I need this," he says. "This ache in my chest just won't fuck off, unless you're in my arms." Damn it, every word out of his mouth makes me fall further and further.

"I'm afraid, Jake. I'm falling for you, and I'm scared I'm going to lose myself, or that I have already," I quietly tell him. Not knowing why I'm opening up to him, but it feels good to finally get that out, consequences be damned.. I would rather risk my heart than to never fall at all.

Jake lifts my chin to look at him. "Lily," he breathes my name out like a prayer. He kisses me tenderly and lays his body on top of mine.

I start unbuckling his jeans, while he starts grinding against my clit. He's rock hard. His erection straining against the denim.

"Fuck, Lil, seeing you under me with that sexy look of desire and heat in your eyes, screaming at me to fill you with my cock. It blows me away baby, I can't wait to be back inside you either."

He's right. I can't wait. It was the only time the world felt perfect, the only time my life seemed wonderful. Even if it is only a lie, I will take it.

Breathing harshly against my lips, Jake grows impatient and takes over removing his clothes. He pulls a condom out and quickly stretches it over his length.

He grins down at me. "Every minute I'm not inside you is a wasted minute." I laugh at his cliché and lame comment, catching myself at the end. *I laughed. I smiled.*

A naked Jake lays his body over mine and strokes my cheekbone with his thumb, gliding over my lips. "Your smile breathes life into me, baby, I can't wait to see you smile again, these two seconds have already been too long."

A single tear escapes my eye at his sweet words. Jake wipes the tear away and makes quick work of my top, panties, and shorts, groaning when he realises I'm not wearing a bra.

He kisses down my neck, across my shoulder and down to my nipples, smothering them both with his hands and mouth. "I love your tits, Lil, the greatest fucking ones I've ever seen."

I grind up against his hard cock, ready for him to enter me, his words setting my body on fire. "I need you, Jake, now."

Jake pushes up and takes my mouth. The kiss is hard and passionate, showing just how hungry we are for each other. You can almost see the desire surrounding us like an aura, intermingling and weaving through our bodies, fusing us together, creating a bubble neither one of us ever wants to leave.

Jake breaks the kiss, his eyes staring down at me as he adjusts his cock to my entrance. He slips in. I close my eyes at the incredible feeling.

"Eyes on me, baby," Jake says softly.

I open my eyes and see Jake watching me with reverence.

"Jesus, Lily, I love how wet you get for me," he groans.

Jake's hands caress each curve of my body, his fingers

leaving cherished sensations on my skin. Our tongues tangle together like a slow dance to a love song. His thrusts are slow and tender. Unable to look away, his eyes capture mine. We're stuck staring at each other. *He's making love to me.* Tears fall silently as Jake lovingly takes me and brings me over the edge. I arch my back and Jake catches my scream with a tender kiss. He ends the kiss suddenly and growls a deep long groan into my neck, his hot breath exhaling heavily onto my skin for a moment before he kisses his way up my neck and jaw. Flicking his tongue out at my lips, I oblige by opening for him. Our kiss is long and perfect. We eventually break apart, both of us breathing deeply.

Jake kisses my temple and gets up from the bed. He heads into the bathroom just like our first time. I close my eyes not from tiredness, but to live in this moment for a little bit longer. I feel whole, and I don't want to let that go.

I hear Jake walk back to the bed, and I open my eyes to watch as he climbs up onto the bed, spreads my legs and starts sucking on my clit. I inhale deeply, surprised by the incredible sensation of his mouth on me. He growls with each suck and push of his tongue inside my pussy. Heat rises up my legs. The trembling begins, and I go off, a silent scream forced from my mouth. Jake slows and licks me lazily for a moment before he climbs off the bed once again and comes back to me with a warm washcloth. He cleans me and heads back to the bathroom, turns the light out, and climbs into bed with me. He holds me close to his body, my face to his chest. Cocooned in Jake's protective arms, I drift off to sleep with a smile on my face.

Lies

JAKE

I **WAKE TO MY ALARM GOING OFF ON MY PHONE. I NEED TO** get up and get ready for Marco's visit. I know he will have words about my actions yesterday, and I need to make him believe there are no feelings between Lily and me. I will deal with whatever he throws at me today. What I need to know is when Lily and I will be leaving for his house.

Laying eyes on a sleeping Lily in my arms, she seems so peaceful and happy, a light smile to her lips. Waking up to her every day would be amazing, but right now, impossible. I'm jealous of the daylight that will get to see her eyes when she wakes. I want to see them first. The fiery eyes that captured me are slowly coming back; I saw them last night. They caught me, and now I am the one who is caged. Just as trapped as Lily is—more so, because even if she ever set me free, I could never leave her.

I need to get my head in the game and remember why I'm here. Now I'm not just here for one reason, but for two. The weight on my shoulders is heavy.

I pull myself from Lily. She rolls to her side and stays asleep. I tuck her in, move her hair from her beautiful face and kiss her temple. The scent of vanilla hits my nose and my dick comes alive. Fuck.There is nothing in this world I have smelled or tasted as delicious as Lily.

I pull my jeans and top on then head for my room, straight into the shower. I turn the water on and wash my arms and chest as memories of last night flood my mind. Lily's whimpers and the way her eyes light up right before her orgasm. When she admitted to falling for me, my world tilted. It's exactly what I'd wanted. I just didn't want to admit it to myself until recently, but I want Lil to fall for me, hard, and I want her to keep falling until she is in as deep as I am.

I dress in jeans, a grey shirt, and my black bomber jacket. I grab my boots, and I'm heading downstairs as my phone rings. I don't have to check who it is. "Marco," I state.

"I'm coming up the driveway. Meet me in my office." I turn the corner at the bottom of the stairs and head toward his office.

"On my way." I hang up.

I get to his office and take a seat on a black sofa just to the right to the office doors.

Two minutes later, Marco strides in with purpose, his two personal guards from yesterday with him. I'm wondering how yesterday went. If he got the people following his collection. Should I ask? Or would that draw suspicion. I decide to leave it for now.

Marco stands behind his desk and nods to me. I don't nod or say anything as he goes straight to the vault and starts keying in a code. I've tried to crack it, but he changes it often. I've glanced inside before. There just seems to be money, no documents that might lead to his private location.

"Fuckers are getting too close, Jake. We need to move Lily and soon."

My heart speeds up. This is it.

Marco pulls out bundled-up cash, row after row, shoving it in a duffle bag.

"I can't keep coming back and forth. It's getting harder and harder to shake them. I had to drive three hours out of my way yesterday just to lose the bastards. I didn't even make it to the collection or my family home. The pricks are going to pay if they keep delaying me from my business."

I stand up fast. "Lily and I are ready. We can leave with you today," I state confidently.

Marco hands his duffle bag to one of his guards, and then walks over to me. "Can't be today. I've got men boarding off every entry into this city. We go in two days when I know it's clear for her to leave." Marco watches me carefully as he adds, "Plus I have someone who is paying me a lot of money to see Lily tomorrow night." *What the fuck is he talking about?*

"Who is coming to see her?" I ask, trying to keep my anger and curiosity at bay.

Marco crosses his arms still staring at me, watching for any indication I care. I keep my shit together. I have to.

"A man who had a magnificent time with her at the last party. He sounds desperate to see her again and is willing to pay me a lot of money to have her again so soon."

To have her again. My heart stops.

What the fuck am I going to do, so close to getting to his secret location and this sick bastard is the only thing standing in my way? If I intervene, he will tell Marco, and I'll blow any chance of getting to the collection as a personal guard for Lily. And if I let the sick fuck at Lily, I will lose her forever. FUCK! There's no use even pretending I could ever let that happen. I would kill him from just remembering how rough he was. He made my girl bleed. I'll come up with a plan.

"Jake," Marco sternly calls me. I look up, not realising I looked away from him while I was thinking.

"Are you getting too close to Lily? If you are, I get it. I do. Goddamn, I don't touch my own merchandise, never have, but she is the one who has come closest to tempting me." Marco pauses and pins me with his eyes. "I need to know. Have you touched her?" Marco's tone is calm, but I'm not a fool. I know Lily and I will have his wrath if he finds out we were together.

"No, I haven't touched her at all," I lie, I have no problems lying to a psychopath.

"But you have feelings for her. I saw your reaction

when I touched her yesterday." He narrows his eyes at me.

"After losing her sister, I felt sorry for her. But that's as far as my feelings go for her. She's not my type or worth sacrificing my place at your side for." Another lie.

Marco stares at me for a moment. I see him assessing me. "Good, but just to be safe, I'm leaving Davis here to watch the two of you, and oversee her visitor tomorrow night. He'll report to me, and then I'll decide if you will still accompany Lily to the collections home."

Fuck! My life just fucking nosedived into a pile of shit.

"I understand you feeling for her, Jake. She's exquisite, but I can't have you getting attached. I have found in the past, the guards find it very hard to turn off their feelings at the parties, and if you cost me money, then you lose your life, understood?"

"I do. There are no feelings, no attachments." I state, convincingly.

"Good, then Davis will report what you are telling me is the truth, and you will become a part of the collections' guards."

He walks up to me, puts his hand on my shoulder and whispers in my ear, "Don't disappointment me, Jake, because if Davis reports back that you are lying to me, Lily will be the one to pay, and she will pay dearly while you are dead at the bottom of the sea." He lowers his hand and walks out of the room.

I wait until I hear the front door close and turn to walk out. The man Marco left behind, Davis, is standing in the doorway, blocking my way out.

He's the same height and weight as me, black hair shaved close to his head. He's wearing boots, slacks, a buttoned-up shirt, and a trench coat. Standing there with his feet together, and hands clasped in front of him. Pussy. I could take him and fuck him up in less than a second.

"Can I help you?" I scowl at him, my mood darkening more and more by the minute.

He smirks, "Jake, I'm only following orders. If you have nothing to hide, why so angry, hey?"

"I don't need a babysitter. Piss off out of my face. Go get laid or something, but stay the fuck out of my way," I demand, walking past him, wanting to get to Lily; however, he stops me in my tracks with his words.

"Tsk tsk tsk, you know I can't do that. I want to meet this Lily everyone seems so fond of. Take me to her," Davis requests.

"She's sleeping." Shit, I know as soon as I say it, it was the wrong thing to say.

Davis arches his eyebrow at me. "And how do you know she is sleeping?"

I come up with a reason, fast. "I'm her guard; that's how. I check in regularly, which includes when I get up in the mornings. Any more questions, asshole?"

"Jake, I can be your friend or your enemy. You had better decide which one you want and fast, because with that attitude, it will be an enemy and you don't want that now, do you?"

Fuck, no I don't. I relax my shoulders and shake my head, letting him know I'll calm down.

"Excellent, now that's fine. I'll wait until later today to

see Lily. I'm going to and go fetch myself some breakfast." Davis walks past me and heads for the kitchen.

Oh God, I'm going to lose her. I thought it might happen eventually. It's just happening earlier than I hoped it would.

My chest aches. I have to break her heart. I need her to believe I feel nothing for her. Lily isn't like me. She can't hide her feelings behind a deceptive front. She's too pure. She will glance my way with desire in her eyes. Davis will see it. This is what he's trained to do, to see what everyone else would miss. I can't lose my chance when I'm so close. There's too much riding on me getting to that location. And if Marco finds out anything happened between us, he will kill me and throw Lily to the wolves.

I love Lily. I love her with everything I am, but it's not enough. I have something else I love just as much, something I can't sacrifice for my love. Torn doesn't even come close to how my heart feels. I'm sorry, Lily. I'm sorry my love for you isn't enough to save you.

◆◆◆

LILY

LAST NIGHT WITH JAKE WAS AMAZING, EARTH SHATTERING. I felt the pieces of my heart start to slowly re-assemble. Not entirely, but I have hope that one day my heart will heal. I have a smile this morning, just a tiny one, but that's huge for me and that makes me smile even bigger. When Jake gets me out and I can go home and bury Sasha, I hope to find my peace.

Stepping out of the shower, I hear my bedroom door open. I wrap a towel around me, and as I open the bathroom door, I smile, thinking I'm about to see Jake. Oh, my God, I'm on a roll today.

Jake closes and locks the door. My stomach drops at the expression on his face; he looks like someone just died. He lowers his gaze to the ground, pinching his nose and closing his eyes tightly.

"Jake?" He raises his head to me, resignation in his eyes and that same lost look I saw so many times when I first got here. "What's wrong?"

Jake blows out a big breath. "Things have changed, Lily."

"What things?" I ask, my hands starting to shake. "Marco has offered me something I can't refuse, and I'm taking it, which means I'm not going to help you. You're on your own now." I'm staring at Jake, trying to make sense of what he just said. My brows lower and my forehead creases. Did I hear him right?

He looks back down to the ground. I step up and place my hand to his cheek. He jumps back like I burned him.

"Don't do that!" he commands in a thick voice.

I don't need to look in the mirror to see my skin has gone pale. "But everything we shared, everything you said." I try to keep my voice calm, but it shakes slightly.

"They were mistakes, and you can't ever bring it up again. Do. Not. Tell. Anyone. As far as I'm concerned, Lily, they never happened. I'm warning you. If Marco or anyone finds out we were together, Marco will throw you to the wolves, and by that I mean to his friends, who love to torture and share their toys." Jake's voice is cold, his expression uncaring to my quivering lips.

Crack

My heart's re-assembled pieces start to fall apart.

"But you said you'd protect me, get me out of here," I say, my mind too stunned to know what else to say.

"I lied!" he shouts.

Crack

"I wanted in your pants, so I lied. Guys do it all the time, Lily." Lily. No more Lil.

Crack

A tear escapes and falls to my cheek. I wipe it away quickly. Confusion and disbelief pounds at my chest.

"I don't understand," I say, stronger this time. I search his face for something, anything to tell me he is lying. Something must be wrong. I shake my head back and forth.

"No, no, no, something's happened."

"Something has happened. Marco offered me something I want more than you." Jake's tone is bored, and he keeps looking to the door. He wants to get out of this room, away from me.

My head keeps shaking in refusal to believe what he's saying. Is this a dream? A nightmare inside a nightmare?

"Lily, this was all a game. What did you think would happen? You slept with the bad guy. I'm not a prince here to save you. I'm here to keep you caged. Oh, well, it was good while it lasted." He looks around the room, not once looking me in the face while he slays me with his hurtful words.

SHATTER!

The last part of my heart is gone. My mind clears. My tears dry. I have nothing left.

A knock sounds from the door. I'm frozen on the spot. I can't think, can't breathe.

Jake opens it, and a slave girl brings breakfast in.

He takes the cart from her and growls, "Out."

She quickly exits the room. He puts the cart beside my bed. "Eat something," and with that he leaves and the lock echoes around the room.

I don't know when, but I come to, standing in the same place with dried tears on my face and my mouth parched. I go to the cart like a robot and start my breakfast. I think of nothing, and I just keep telling myself to eat.

I finish my food and put the table cart at the door. I knock twice. The door opens, and without looking who it is, I turn and go into the bathroom.

I strip off my clothes and turn the shower on, hot only. I get in and don’t feel anything as the scorching water hits my skin. Numbness becomes so easy when it takes you after the first time; it's like saying hello to an old friend.

I pick up the soap and washcloth, and scrub myself raw. I stop when I feel stinging from the cloth touching my red raw skin. I don't know how long I’ve spent in the shower, but the water is now warm.

I turn off the water and step out, my skin sensitive from the constant rubbing. The first thing I see is my reflection in a foggy mirror. I wipe it with a towel and just stare at myself. Is that my face? It looks so sad, so lost.

Examining myself all I see is someone weak. "Pathetic,"

I say to my reflection. I'm losing it. I can see it, hear it, but I can't stop it. Hope soaked my soul in heavy want, then lit a match and watched me burn.

Sobs rip from my chest while tears burn a path down my face. I begin screaming and smashing my fists against the vanity again and again. Anger digs into my skin and starts to fester. Why am I so pathetic? Why am I so dumb? I punch at my chest. How can I still feel this hurt? Another punch, harder this time.

I don't want to feel anything!

I scratch at my chest, wanting to tear it open and die right here. I want them all to see what they have done to me, that they've ripped me apart. Despair and anguish is all I have left within me.

The locked door slams open and hits the wall with a smash. Jake is in the doorway breathing heavily. Our eyes meet: his shocked, mine tortured.

"Lily, what the hell are you doing?" Jake begins to walk toward me, but he stops and freezes. "What the fuck," he breathes out in a hoarse voice.

I focus on my reflection in the mirror and find red and purple marks on the top of my left breast. I notice I'm naked, but the ability to care left me with the last crack of my heart.

"Lily, look at me." Jake's pained tone has me turning to him. "What have you done?" he asks.

"I had to wash you off. I felt dirty." My voice is emotionless.

"Lil." A moment of guilt tries to penetrate my soul at his agonised voice. Then I remember: it's all lies.

A woozy feeling washes over me. I grab hold of the vanity as I become unbalanced.

"I feel sick," I say, barely above a whisper.

My sight forced into blackness, I'm falling, and I land on something soft.

Distantly, I hear a tortured sob boom through the room, but the darkness encircles me in its beautiful warm, safe arms. Oh, how I have missed my dark corner.

Plan

I FEEL WARM AND COMFY UNDER THE COVERS. PULLING THE blankets up tighter, a pain shoots through my chest and shoulder. *Ouch!* I look down and find I'm naked with a big blue and purple bruise. Suddenly, the warmth turns to a cold chill as memories invade my mind. Jake. *This was all a game.* The bathroom, me hurting myself. I lost it.

Through the corner of my eye, I see movement. I whip my head up to see what it is and find Jake sitting on his chair in the corner. He stands and heads for the door. Not facing me, he speaks, "You missed lunch. I will go and get you something to eat."

Not caring in the least about food, or if he ever comes back, I get up and dress in denim shorts, bra and a hooded jumper. My hair needs brushing, so I go into the bathroom. Immediately, my reflection catches my attention.

You lost it, Lily, but you deserved to lose it then. You've been through too much to stay sane. But now it's time to fight and be strong. Jake isn't helping you get out anymore. Now it's up to you, only you.

I feel the adrenalin pumping through me. I will get out of this situation. I will be free. I just need to find my opportunity and be ready to act. Brushing my hair, then my teeth, I head out of the bathroom to see Jake standing with a tray. He puts it on the bed and looks at me.

I take the tray off the bed and walk to the table and chairs. "Thanks. You can go now. I don't need you to stand over me while I eat," I say without a glance in his direction. I place the lid from the silver tray on the chair Jake usually uses, giving him nowhere to sit so he will leave the room.

When I don't hear anything or sense him moving, I look up and see him as he's turning away; however, not before catching the miserable look on his face. A pang hits my chest, but I tell it to shut up, no more caring for Jake. A thought in the very back of my mind repeats the tortured sob I heard when I collapsed this morning, but I push it away, ignoring it.

I nibble at my food while reading a book. I don't knock when I'm finished with my food. I don't care if the cart sits in this room forever. I don't want to see Jake anytime soon.

Reading my book for a while in the chair in the corner, I see now why Jake likes it. You can almost feel invisible, while seeing everything in the room.

When my door opens, it's becoming dark outside. Jake walks in followed by a man I've never seen before. I sit up straight.

"Lily, this is Davis. He's here to help guard you," Jake states, his voice matter-of-fact.

I look to Jake to try and figure out what's going on, but he turns his head away from me, and I lose his eyes.

"And to make sure you don't try running like your sister, so it's more like, make sure you stay locked up," this new man says, grinning.

Well, he's shown his true colours quickly. I narrow my eyes, hostility seeping out of every pore in my body.

Davis strides over to me, lifts the tray lid from the other chair, sits and starts speaking to me, "Lily, Marco has a request for you. Well, really it's a demand. There will be no saying no to this."

At this point in my life nothing can shock me, so I simply stare at the man who walked into my life one minute ago and now has the power to control me. Just another one to add to a long list.

"The man who bought you at the party, he has been hassling Marco to see you again."

Okay, I may not be shocked, but now I'm downright scared. Fear and panic rush through my body. I look to Jake and see him staring down at the floor, his hands holding on to the dresser, his knuckles white. I scowl at him. *Coward can't even look at me.*

"Whoa, so there are those fiery eyes everyone talks about." I swing my eyes back to Davis and realise he caught me sending fireballs to Jake. "What did Jake do to catch your fury, hey?" Davis asks me smiling. Jesus, I hate his obnoxious smile.

"He's breathing," I state, then continue, feeling like this is a good time to share my feelings. "I hate this place. I hate Marco. I hate you, and most of all, I hate him." I point to Jake and see him staring at me. His body language tells me he doesn't care about my words. But his eyes, like always, they tell me differently, and this time they show me sadness. I freeze what I'm doing, stunned, but then Davis takes my attention away.

He's shaking his head laughing. "Marco is crazy if he thinks something is going on between the two of you. I know a woman who detests a man when I see one, and you would never be with someone you hate." He claps his hands together and stands. "Well, that was easy."

What the hell is he talking about? "What the hell are you talking about?"

Jake interrupts Davis just as he begins to speak. "Nothing, Lily, let's move on to tomorrow night."

Confusion muddles my head, and I can't help but continue looking between the two men. *I'm missing something.*

"Oh, yes," Davis says, "your visitor will be here tomorrow night at nine pm, he will be here and gone within a few hours. Don't disappoint him. He's paying a lot of money to see you between parties."

Confusion quickly gone, my emotions turn back to fear. How much does God expect me to take? I'm shaking my head with glassy eyes, but I let no tears escape. "Of course he is," I hiss.

"Now, now, Lily, are you not surrounded by luxury? Fed? Clothed? Marco only asks you to repay him."

I growl, "I would rather be homeless, starving, and dirty than living in this Hell."

Davis sighs, "You will learn."

I ignore him and stare down at my lap.

Out of the corner of my eyes I watch Davis walk to Jake and hear him mutter, "Watch her." With that, he leaves the room.

My emotions want me to scream and throw things around the room, but I'm so sick of feeling like that. I have hurt, screamed, and cried—there's nothing left. Instead, I form a plan.

My hands shake, and I have a lump in my throat. "Jake, I need a drink, a strong one. Vodka? Rum? Can you get me something?"

He exhales loudly and nods. When the door closes, I walk over to my tray still left from lunch. I lift the lid and take out a fork. I clean it with a napkin and place it under my pillow.

They think they can control me. They think I will just let men keep taking me. Well, tomorrow night will be a wakeup call for them. That man will bleed and die before I ever let him force himself on me again.

I move back to the chair and pick up my book.

Jake walks back in with a glass and brings it over to me, "There was some vodka. I added a bit of lemonade, but it's still pretty strong."

I snatch it off him and drain the glass.

I reach out to hand Jake the glass back. Looking to the

ground, I say, "You can go. I'm not going to lose it again." Adrenalin pumps through me. Finally, I have some power over what will happen.

"Lily, it's okay to break about this. I'd rather you did it while I was here than if Davis hears you."

"You think anything else can hurt me? They've already taken everything from me." My voice wobbles, and it pisses me off. "Bring it on. I will fuck that man and make him scream my name, so he never forgets it." *When I stick that fork in his neck, he will scream and never forget me.*

"Lily," Jake growls low and rough.

"What, jealous?" My tone borders on want and desperation. *Give me a sign that you care.*

"No." His voice is hoarse. He heads for the door to make a quick exit.

"I hate you," I hiss, kicking myself for pointing out that I care about his answer.

Jake faces me, his expression hopeless. "Next time, don't give away your heart so quickly, and then you won't be so disappointed."

I pale at his words, realising he's right. I did fall in love with him; however, I didn't do it willingly. "I didn't give you my heart. You stole it." *And now, I can't get it back.*

Jake's face turns ashen.

I stare out the window and continue to talk quietly, if only to myself, "You're an arsehole. I wish I never met you."

I sense him just behind me now, so close I feel heat at my back.

"I know," he sighs. "I know what I am. I wish you'd

never met me, too."

I continue talking quietly to the window, "I'm not a fool, Jake. I know this is about that man, Davis, being here and Marco thinking we had feelings for each other. Either you did all this to save me, you, or both of us, but whichever one it is, it doesn't matter, because you hurt me beyond repair." I feel his hot breath on my neck, goose bumps rise on my skin.

"I know, but I need to get there so damn badly. You have no idea. I'm so fucking close." His tone's laced with desperation.

There. The collections' secret location. I haven't even been there yet and already I hate the place.

Still facing the window, I say loud enough I know he will hear every word, "Whatever you're so fucking close to, I hope it was worth selling your soul to the devil."

Jake reaches one arm out and leans on the windowsill. Softly, he speaks into my ear, "I have no choice but to believe it will be."

He backs away, but I don't turnaround, and I hear his footsteps get further away. The door closes and the lock clicks into place.

When I wake up, I'm shocked I got a great night sleep, no nightmares of what's to come tonight, just numbness and a peaceful sleep. I wonder if God was giving me a reprieve to prepare me for what I'm about to do tonight.

I would never regret it or feel guilty. If Mr Smith thinks he can just take women by force, then he will be getting his karma tonight, and I'm happy to be the bitch.

I'm not saying I'm not scared, because I am, but I'm more scared of what's to come: what man will come next, how many parties will I be forced to when I get to Marco house. What's the point of surviving if, in the end, I will be dead on the inside. They already took Sasha from me, but that's all the blood they will draw from me. Tonight, I will make them wish they never kidnapped us in the first place.

I hop out of bed and shower quickly. I'm jittery with anticipation, hoping the day goes by quickly. I dress in jeans and a black lace short-sleeve top. I step out of the bathroom. At the same time, my bedroom door opens, and Jake walks in with my breakfast.

He looks at me, and I feel a shot straight to my heart, like a machine restarting it. He looks horrible, like he hasn't slept in a month. His hair is messy as if he pulled at it all night long, and his shirt is inside out.

I take my breakfast from him and say, "You might want to look in the mirror before you leave your room."

Jake looks down at himself and mutters a curse.

I walk over to the table, sit, and start eating my omelette.

Jake takes his shirt off, and I stop with the fork hanging just in front of my open mouth. Jake's bare chest has captured my eyes and my attention. *God,* I growl in my head, *so damn hot.* Why can't he be hideously hairy or have pimples everywhere? Why does he have to be perfect? *Oh, Jesus, am I drooling?* I shove my food in my mouth quickly. Chewing, I try to look around the room calmly.

Jake puts his hands through his hair, but it does nothing to dispel the look of a sleepless night.

“I didn’t say to fix yourself up in here,” I state, my tone distant and uncaring. I continue to eat, waiting for Jake to move or say something. When he doesn’t, I huff out an annoyed breath and look up at Jake.

At the same moment, he mutters, “Tomorrow cannot come soon enough,” and starts for the door.

Oh, that’s right. From one hell to another. We’re supposed to be leaving for Marco’s secret location tomorrow. I doubt I will be going anywhere after tonight. But out of curiosity and need to be prepared for anything I ask a question.

“What do I take?” Jake turns back around to me at my question. I have nothing I own with me, but if I was being moved, I would want to know I will have clothes.

“Nothing. Just dress in the morning.” Jake extends his hands to the room and says, “Marco has these rooms in every property he owns. All fully stocked to have collection pieces at any time.

“Good to know,” I say, finishing up my breakfast.

“You seem to be in a good mood today, Lily,” Jake states.

I shrug. What does he think I’m going to say.

“I almost had to search your room last night. One of the slave girls said you didn’t send all your cutlery back.”

I freeze for a millisecond before turning my calm expression to Jake, praying the panic doesn’t show on my face.

"But," he drags out the word, "a slave girl said she already put them in the washing up. Who was it again?" Jake narrows his eyes on me and says, "Oh, that's right, Beth."

Beth, oh God, helping me again. "Well, there you go. They found them," I say casually. I take a sip of my iced tea and stand, putting the lid on the tray and pushing the table cart toward Jake.

"You can take this with you on your way out. Ah, and when you check under the tray I promise the knife and fork will still be there." I wink and move over to the chair in the corner and pick up the book I was reading last night. As I sit, I see Jake still standing there, looking at me.

"This doesn't seem like you, Lily, to be acting so…so, fine on a day like today. I expected you to scream, fight bloody murder about tonight, or I don't know, maybe even beg for help," he says as he flings his arms out, exasperated at my casual attitude.

"And if I did all those things, would you help me?" Jake just stares at me, giving me my answer.

"I'd rather save my energy for getting through tonight, than waste my begging on bastards." I look back to my book and end the conversation.

Jake says nothing. I hear the cart move and the door slams closed.

Sometime later, Davis enters my room, smiling. "Good morning, beautiful. Get a good night's sleep?" he asks, while rubbing his hands together and giving me that obnoxious smile.

I choose to ignore him and give him a blank expression.

I'm getting pretty good at it I think.

"Suit yourself. Ignore me. I know if it was me always locked in a room, I would take every opportunity to talk to anyone who offered a conversation." I continue to pretend to read. "Lily, look up at me and give me some respect before I lose my temper," Davis growls at me.

I sigh, lookup at him and then he smiles. "Much better. Now I can see your beautiful face while I talk to you. We need to cover some details about tonight. Mr Smith will be here at nine pm. I will bring him up and then I will be downstairs with the other guards having a meeting about who will be in charge when Jake and I leave tomorrow. Mr Smith has requested dinner with you first, so I want you dressed in one of those expensive dresses," he waves his hand, gesturing to the closet, "by eight thirty. Mr Smith has instructions on how to enter and exit the property. When your night has come to an end, he has been told to leave straight away."

"So no guard at my door in case he tries to hurt me? Kill me?" I say, arching my eyebrow in question.

Davis smirks. "He's a trusted client, who has been with many of our collection pieces and never harmed any of them, so no, all guards will be at the meeting and Jake will be patrolling the fence line."

He slaps his knees as he gets up, startling me. "Tomorrow morning we leave around nine. Make sure you're dressed and are ready on time."

Davis looks down at me with a sickening smile this time. "Have fun tonight, Lily." And with that, he leaves the room.

Oh, I will have fun tonight.

Chapter 24

Playing By My Own Rules Now

THE REST OF THE DAY DIDN'T DRAG LIKE I IMAGINED IT would. Before I know it, it is eight o'clock, and I'm showering and picking out a dress. I choose a short bright red, silk wraparound dress, wanting to tie in with the theme of the night, blood.

I put my hair up in a high bun. I don't want him to grab onto anything while he's struggling against me. After applying only mascara and lip gloss, I select a pair of black pumps from the walk-in closet. For some reason, and this is probably where I should take notice of how sick my mind is becoming, but I want to look good while I take back my power. I have this image in my head of standing over his body, all sexy in my black pumps, red silk dress and the fork in my grip with his blood dripping down my hand. I'm sure it will be gorier than that, but a girl can dream.

I hear my bedroom door open and go out to see who it is. I stay just inside my walk-in closet and watch as three slave girls' drag in two chairs and a round table. They put a white cloth over the table and two candles in the centre. Great, a romantic dinner with a rapist. Awesome.

Jake walks in not long after and looks over the table and chairs. He looks to the bathroom door which is closed, and I assume that's where he thinks I am. He walks over to the window, leaning on his two outstretched arms he bows his head and stays like that. The girls finish setting the table, and Jake looks over his shoulder and growls at them to get out.

The anger behind his growl has me straightening my back and walking out to defend them.

"Don't treat them like that," I state angrily.

Jake stares at me, looking shocked that I appear out of nowhere. He looks me up and down, grits his teeth, and bends at the knees and groans. He grabs his head in his hands and pulls at his hair, shaking his head while leaving the room, slamming the door.

I'm not stupid. I see the war raging inside him, the one where he's the bad guy and the good guy. My heart believes in the good, but my mind reminds me of the bad. But it doesn't matter what my heart wants; Jake is letting this happen tonight. My heart may always want him, but a part of me will always loathe loving him.

Sitting in the chair in the corner, I stare into nothingness, waiting for nine o'clock to arrive.

Eventually, my door opens, and seeing the same man

from the party brings back all of the contempt I hold for him. The memories flood my mind, but I manage to push them back, remembering he won't be doing that to me tonight; he won't be walking out of this room alive.

"Wow," Davis says as he puts his hand on Mr Smith's shoulder and pats him while saying, "Lucky man tonight, enjoy."

And with that, Davis walks over to the lights and dims them. The lit candles on the table add an air of romance.

Davis leaves the room and shuts the door, no lock this time. I wonder if after I do this, I should try for the front door.

"Gorgeous, Lily." Mr. Smith steps toward me, and I take a step back. He stops and smiles the same sleazy smile as last time.

"Okay, we'll take it slower this time, however, it's going to be hard to keep my hands off you when you look so delicious. Nevertheless, I'll try."

He extends his hand toward the table; the hot food arrived while Davis was here. "Let's eat first, shall we?"

He moves to the table first and removes his expensive looking suit jacket and takes a seat. Walking over to the seat across from him, I sit.

"How have you been gorgeous?" I shiver at his name for me.

"Have you thought about me as much as I have thought about you?" Yep, he is the craziest man in crazy-town. I continue to ignore him.

Mr. Smith reaches over, and I flinch as he pulls the cover off my plate.

"Lily, don't be afraid. I won't hurt you." *Yeah, that's what you said last time.*

I look down at my plate and see roast beef with vegetables and gravy. My stomach rolls at the thought of eating anything right now.

"Go on, begin. The sooner we finish, the sooner we can get to the good part of our evening together." Yep, there goes my ability to eat at all now. I cut some beef and nibble on a piece.

We eat in silence, Mr. Smith staring at me the whole time. Sweating, my palms begin to slip on the cutlery. He places his cutlery down and pushes his plate away from him.

Showtime.

He stands, and I stand quickly to match him, knocking my cutlery from my plate to the table.

He shakes his head with a smirk. "So tense, Lily. Come. Let's move to the bed." I decide that's a good idea since it's where I will have a better advantage to surprise him.

I walk over to the bed. My main goal is not to let him hold my wrists down again. If he does, then I am in trouble. I need to relax him, let him think I'm okay. He'll then give me free reign, maybe even allow me to dominate until I can find the perfect time to use my weapon.

Come on, Lily. Smile and touch him. I form a smile. *Argh, God, this sucks.*

"That's better. You have a stunning face. You should smile more often." *Sicko.*

"Come. Let's lie down," he requests.

I decide to be brave and take the lead. I pull the tie

from around my dress and it undoes; the dress opens and falls from my shoulders to the ground. All I have on is a lace bra, G-string and garter. Mr Smith inhales sharply at my lingerie—the exact reaction I am after. I want him distracted.

I climb onto the bed, turn and lay down exactly the same as I did at the party. Except this time, I put my hand under the pillow and feel the fork there. I wrap my fingers around the handle and force myself to look relaxed and sexy.

Mr Smith climbs on top. He spreads my legs and sits on his knees between my thighs. He looks down at my G-string and garter, and grunts his approval.

My body begins to shake. I'm trying to calm myself, but having him so close is sending warning signals all through my body.

"So perfect, worth every cent I spent on you."

My spirit takes a knock at his words, but I quickly recover and start rubbing my legs along his thighs to get him moving.

Unbuttoning, his shirt but doesn't take it off. Instead, he comes down to my bra and starts sucking on my nipples through the material.

I groan in disgust then catch myself and try to make it sound like a moan.

Mr Smith doesn't seem to catch my mistake as he lifts up, quickly unbuckling his belt and pants with haste.

"I can't wait. I need to fuck you right now. I can't even get all my fucking clothes off." He pulls himself out through his unbuttoned pants and pulls a condom out of his back pocket and pushes it on.

He lays down on top of me, kissing my neck as he tries to pull my underwear down my legs.

It's time. I breathe, brace, and get ready to put all my force behind the fork when I stab him in the neck. He lowers my underwear more, and I can feel his dick touching my thigh.

I take a big breath in, then swing my arm out as hard and fast as I can. But just as I'm about to stab it into his neck, I'm left with air; my arm swings right through the space where Mr Smith's neck should be. With the force behind my arm, the fork stabs straight into the mattress.

I look up quickly and see Mr Smith against a wall with Jake's hand around his throat. My eyes go wide and my mouth drops open.

Mr Smith is off the ground and gasping for air, clawing at Jake's hand.

Jake is staring at Mr Smith. If looks could kill, he would be dead. There is only rage in Jake's eyes. The air crackling with Jake's violent temper.

Jake looks over to me, his eyes quickly find my hand with a fork stabbed into the mattress. He narrows his eyes on the fork then back to my eyes, and he mutters something under his breath. I think I hear him say, "Fuck me."

Jake looks back at Mr Smith and says, "I'm going to let you breathe, fucker, and when I do, you're going to shut your fucking mouth and listen. Got it?" Jake growls his demand.

Mr Smith nods through his gasping. Lowering him to

the ground, Jake continues to hold him tightly to the wall by his throat.

"You're going to put your dirty dick away, button your shirt and then I am going to escort you out of this room and house. You are going to tell Marco you had an enjoyable time with Lily. Got it?" Jake pulls Mr Smith toward him then smashes his body back into the wall. I flinch with the hard hit to the wall.

Mr Smith's eyes clench closed from the hit, but he comes around quickly. "What the fuck! I paid a lot of money to fuck her," he whines, obviously realising he's not going to win against Jake's strength.

Jake gets right in his face and sneers, "I don't give a flying fuck if you gave your pathetic life. It's not going to happen, ever. And you even think about talking, Peter Falcone of 265 Murray Drive, Florida." Mr Smith, now known as Peter, inhales harshly. "If Marco hears about this, I will be gunning for your wife and daughter. Do you understand?" Peter inhales sharply.

"You leave my family out of this," he hisses at Jake.

Oh God, this sick asshole has a family.

"Their lives rest on your shoulders. You say anything to Marco or anyone else, and I will have no problems taking them out." Jake pauses, waiting for any response from Peter. Pulling him forward, Jake then pushes him back into the wall once again, but harder this time. Peter's head bobs crazily.

"Yes, yes, I get it. Fuck," Peter whines.

Jake looks back at me, anger still sizzling all around him. He says nothing, grabs Peter by the shoulder, and sneers, "Now, walk out of here as if you just got lucky, asshole." Leaving the room, the door locks behind them.

Her

ALONE IN THE DIMLY LIT ROOM, I LOOK AROUND, STUNNED. What just happened? Jake came to save me; that's what happened. A second later and he would have seen me kill a man. I come out of my thoughts and realise I'm still holding onto the fork. I pull but the fork won't budge. Clenching my teeth, I pull with all my strength. The fork releases from the mattress with a pop. Well, at least I know I had a good chance of getting it into his neck.

I decide just to leave the fork out on the dresser, no use hiding it now. Grabbing a silk robe, I strip the lingerie off and wrap the robe around my body. On my way back to the bed, wondering if Jake will come back to explain what just happened, my door swings open and slams shut. I freeze on the spot.

Jake stumbles into the room, sinks to his knees and

bows his head, his body shuddering. After watching him for a few seconds, I notice his knuckles have cuts. Lifting his hands to cover his face, I'm floored when I realise he's silently crying.

My body jolts forward. I take big steps and kneel on the floor, making sure to keep a little bit of distance between us.

"Jake?" I ask softly.

He sobs loudly this time and it echoes around the room.

My heart aches at the painful tone.

He speaks with his head bowed, "I'm so sorry, Lil. I'm so sorry I hurt you, but I couldn't stop." Jake's voice is thick and strangled.

He raises his face to mine and I gasp at his anguished expression. Jake's usual deep brown eyes are now bloodshot and glassy.

Tears sting my eyes and I lift a shaking hand to my lips, trying to hold in my cry from watching such a strong man fall apart. The pain radiating off him is suffocating.

He penetrates me with his tortured gaze. "I can't do it anymore," he grasps my hand and pushes it to his chest, right over his heart.

"This beats for you and another." *What?* "I have been walking a tightrope for so long, hoping I could save you both, but all it's done is torn me apart, and put you both at risk."

I stay silent, staring at Jake, waiting for him to give me the answers to his cryptic words.

"I thought when it came down to it, the obvious choice

would be her." Jake pauses and shakes his head wildly. "But I fucking couldn't do it. Thinking of that fucker touching you, it nearly drove me insane." He ends on a shout.

I'm frozen, unable to move as I track each glistening tear that silently falls down his handsome face.

"If that guy calls my bluff and goes to Marco, I've lost her forever." Another violent release of anguish releases from Jake. His fingers lose their grip on my hand at his chest, and my hand falls away.

He lowers his face; his body bowing so low his head almost touches the ground.

"Who is *her*?" I whisper, waiting for the crushing blow where he tells me about this other woman he loves so much.

"Emily," his voice tortured as he says her name. *Emily.* I'm stunned. "My little sister, Emily."

I let out a gasp and my hand flies to my mouth. My mind stalls and repeats *sister.* I fall from my knees to my bottom, not caring the fall causes a sharp pain up my back.

I demand, "Tell me everything, now. No more lies." Tears are now freely falling down my astonished face.

Jake raises his head, blows out a couple of big breaths and lifts the bottom of his shirt to wipe his face. "Em got taken five years ago. My best friend Kanye, Em's boyfriend, called us looking for her. She never came home after seeing a movie with a friend. We called around to her friends, and that's when we found out she never made it to the movies at all, which wasn't like Emily at all; she would never stand a friend up without a message or call."

Jake takes a breath and continues, "She was then classed as a missing person. We searched everywhere for her. Her picture was all over the news, but nothing. Not one single person came forward with credible information. My parents were destroyed. Emily is the baby of the family. She's naïve but in a beautiful way. She always saw the positives in people, never the bad. We knew whatever had happened to her was bad." Pain flashes through his eyes, which tells me the next part has caused him a lot of torment. "Six months after searching for her, the police got a good tip that she had been sold into the black market as a sex slave. My dad tried to kill himself; he couldn't handle his daughter going through something like that. We got there just in time to save him. He tried to gas himself in his car. He's a good man, a good father. It was just too much for him."

I nod in understanding, while small sobs fall from my lips for a man who has had to think about his baby girl going through unimaginable horrors for the last five years. It kills me that I lost Sasha, but to lose her and know she is in pain every day and not being able to do anything would be the true meaning of living in Hell. My heart and soul cries for Jake and his family.

"When I was in the Marines, I completed secret missions, so I decided to get a team together and go undercover to find Em. My parents were torn. They couldn't say no to having hope of finding her, but they were sending their only other child off into the same world. But they knew in the end no one would stop me from trying to find my sister. I got my team together, and we've been working this case for four years, me inside, them outside."

He's lived this life, this persona for four long years, seeing and doing unimaginable things to find his sister. I can't help but regard him with awe and want to comfort him for all the lines he's had to cross. Those marks will forever be on his soul, and he's doing it all for Emily.

Jake pierces me with a stare. "Then you came along, Lily. Marco sent Mick and me to New York to find another piece for his collection. All he asks is to find beautiful women from different countries." Jake pauses, and I see guilt flash through his eyes before he continues, "I spotted you and Sasha as soon as you stepped off the plane at JFK." My eyes go wide; he watched us the entire time we were in New York. "Right away I wanted you. I couldn't keep my eyes off you, and you were exactly what Marco wanted. I had every intention of taking you and your sister. But the more I watched you, the more captivated I became, and I couldn't do it. I told Mick I didn't find anyone." Jake blows out a big breath. "He said he had, and I was so fucking relieved. I couldn't wait to get away from you; you were pulling me away from my mission. And then there you were; tied up in the van, and my world fell apart." I want to cry for his pain and our misfortune.

"I have worked with gangs, bikers, and pimps to get Marco's attention to be asked to guard this house. I knew there was a chance at being selected to guard the collection pieces, but it takes basically losing your soul to prove your loyalty to him. I have been working as a guard for the last three years doing everything Marco asked of me. Some things he has asked of me I couldn't finish, but that's where my team comes into it. They had taken men away and hidden them, so Marco thinks they are dead and buried. Or I have paid off slave girls who have been given to me by Marco."

"Jake," I breathe out, sorrow coats my voice.

"The last few months have been the worst. I started to lose hope. And then Marco handed me everything I had ever wanted. A chance to get to his private house, the secret location where he holds the collection... he handed me you."

The fog clears, and now I understand. Jake needed me to get him to the collection to find Emily. "I just had to keep you here with me until I got to the house, and then I would've freed you and your sister." Jake's voice softens and lowers when he speaks about Sasha. It warms my heart that he knows hearing about her hurts me, so he tries to soften the blow even though that's impossible to do, but still he tries.

"When you went to the party and told me you met the whole collection, I lost it. I finally had someone who could tell me if my sister was alive or not." *Oh Jake, she is alive, but she's dead on the inside.* "Those people following Marco, that's my team Lil. We always hoped Marco would trip up and tell me where the house is, or my team would successfully follow him to his secret location, but he trusts no one. And he has eyes everywhere. He has bought out every town in this state, and while he is visiting, no one gets in or out without him knowing who and why."

As Jake speaks about his team, I slowly realise he could

have helped me a long time ago; he could have helped Sasha. My thoughts race through all the lost opportunities.

"You could have saved her." My voice comes out strangled.

Jake rubs his face roughly. "I tried, Lily. I'm scared to tell you this, but if I don't, you may not see the full picture for what it is." I stare at him, not knowing what to say, not knowing what he means. He continues, his voice thick, "This falls on my shoulders. I should have told you. Please know I didn't think you would find a way to get her out, and I honestly thought telling you about her auction on the day, you would have no time to plan or re-plan anything. That's why I wanted to stay close to you that day, so you couldn't organise anything or risk yourself by trying to run." I'm confused, and he must see it, so he quickly continues, "One of my boys was going to be at the auction, Lil. He was going to buy Sasha, at any cost. The money wasn't an issue."

Broken doesn't even come close to how I feel. There are no words for the kind of pain searing through my veins. My body elevates and my mind sets straight to numb to fight off the slicing pain it's bracing for. My world just shattered for the millionth time.

"Lily," Jake chokes out, and I look up automatically. "Don't go back in your head. All of this, it's fucking bad luck, bad timing, whatever you want to call it. But nothing will change by you hiding away again. Stay strong. We are so close to getting out."

Bad luck, bad timing. That's what Sash's death comes down to? No, for the rest of my life, I will live knowing I sent my sister to her grave while Jake was trying to send her home. This is not my fault. I know that; however, I played a hand, an unknowing one. But her death is someone's fault, Mick's, and he's dead. Marco: he needs to die.

I find Jake's hand and grip it tightly. My strangled voice whispers, "Thank you," I cough to clear the lump in my throat, and say stronger, "for trying."

Jake takes my hand and kisses it, his soft lips warming my body, his eyes never wavering from mine, keeping them captive to his stare.

"Before tonight, Lil, I thought there was a limit to what I would do for you, but there isn't, and there never was. Every chance I got, I crossed a line that put my sister is jeopardy. I just didn't want to see it. I love you, Lily. I love you so fucking much it hurts to be away from you."

I dive into Jake's arms and wrap my body around him, hanging on for dear life. "I love you, Jake," I say fiercely. I kiss his neck and promise, "We're in this together now, and tomorrow, we get your sister back."

On Our Way

JAKE

I'M SHOWERED AND DRESSED BEFORE THE SUN COMES UP, NOT that I went to bed. After escorting motherfucking Peter out of the house, beating his face, which felt fucking good, and finally telling Lil the truth, I was too pumped to sleep. All night all I could think about was today's possibilities; all the things that could go wrong and all the things that could go right. After five years, I may get my little sister back today. My family can be healed and made whole again.

Dickhead Peter was also on my mind more than I wanted; he's lucky all he got was punches to his face. I can't promise I won't go after him later on, but for now, I need him alive and reporting back to Marco that everything went fine.

It could all blow up in my face, and he could go to Marco and then I would have ruined everything, but it would still be worth it. Sitting in my room last night knowing he was with Lily was burning me from the inside out. I don't know how I ever made myself believe I could let anyone else touch her, hurt her.

When I saw him arrive and her bedroom door close, I was pacing. My mind and body at war within me. Then all of a sudden, I just stopped and listened to my heart. It screamed, *she is MINE*. I knew the risk I was taking, and it was huge. But I had to take it. Losing Lily isn't an option.

I charged to her room to tear the fucker off her. When I saw him on her pulling her panties down her legs, my heart almost fucking exploded with rage. I wanted to kill him there and then, against that wall. The only thing that stopped me and pulled me back from the edge was seeing Lily lying there shocked, not frightened. Shocked the man had been pulled off her, and I was confused until I saw the damn fork stabbed into the mattress and the fire in her eyes. My girl is fucking amazing, a fighter till the end. If I ever doubted my feelings for her, seeing her on that bed, half-naked in a garter, ready to kill with a fork put me squarely back in the love category. Fuck, that memory makes my cock so fucking hard.

Opening up to Lily last night was hard. Crying in front of a woman was something I never thought I would do. Lily brings that out in me though, things I never thought I would do for someone. But she's part of my world now, and today I'm going to make sure I get both my girls out and safe.

Staring out the window, feeling the warmth from the sun rising, I hear my phone beep. Pulling it out of my back pocket, I view the screen.

Nightfire, Ironviper, Redwolf in position. Awaiting orders.

Perfect. Today I will get my sister back and make Marco pay for everything he has done to my family and to Lily's.

◆◆◆

LILY

AWAKENED BY SMALL KISSES GLIDING UP MY NECK AND over my jaw, I giggle, knowing it's Jake. My eyes open and I encounter a smiling Jake looking down at me.

Wow, no secrets Jake is magnificent.

"I love your laugh, baby. I can't wait to hear it every day for the rest of my life."

My smile grows at his sweet words. He kisses me again, this time on my lips. It's soft and passionate all at the same time. We break free of the kiss, both breathing heavily. Panic hits me, and my eyes widen. Quickly, I look over at the clock, throwing my head back in relief seeing it's only seven am.

"Don't worry, Lil, we have a few minutes. Now if we had hours, I would strip you bare and take you slowly, cherish every inch of your silky skin. Then you would never question how much I love you."

I kiss Jake's nose and say, "Save that amazing sex for

when we are out of this nightmare."

I scoot away and walk to the dresser while Jake plops down on the bed. I throw on a pair of jeans, white tank top and a black jacket I found in the closet last night. Jake observes me with an arched eyebrow. I shrug. "We can match," I say with a smile.

Jake falls back to the bed and laughs out loud. I'm going to have to get used to that laugh. It's so husky and it makes me want to jump him no matter where I am. The real possibility of getting out of here today obviously has us both in a great mood.

When Jake's laugh dies away, he turns to his side on the bed with his elbow bent and hand to his head. Staring my way, he says, "We need to talk about today, Lil." The seriousness in his tone gets my attention right away. A question jumps to the front of my mind and I can't believe I never asked Jake this before.

"Jake, where are we? What country are we in?

He doesn't miss a beat and answers me straight away, "we're in Columbia, South America."

Oh, my God, South America. But I haven't heard any accents. How can that be? "But no one has an accent?"

"Marco started his empire in the United States over a decade ago. He moved it over here because the people are easier bought for their silence. However, he recruits his guards in the United States. When he sends guards out to find new women, he found they trust English speaking Americans much more over the ones with accents."

The depths of evil Marco has is limitless. He's a monster and unfortunately a smart one at that. Jake gains my attention again with his serious tone.

"I know where we are Lil but I have no idea where we are going. And when we arrive, I don't know what to expect, but I know it won't be long before we will get separated. I will need to be shown around and introduced to the other guards. At the first opportunity, I will start disabling guards and have my team move in."

My body chooses this inappropriate moment to start heating at his military speak. Imagining Jake storming the grounds, his gun firing, killing the bad guys. His muscles rippling with the vibration of the gun. *Oh, God, so hot.* I shake my head, trying to snap myself out of my fantasy.

"Lil? Did you hear me?"

My thoughts clear and I notice Jake is standing in front of me. I nod, and I'm sure a guilty look is on my face.

Jake's lips lift into a smirk as he continues to speak, "I need you to watch out for tense moments, guards on their radios, yelling or becoming agitated. It will point out to you that we are not far off. At that time, I need you to get somewhere safe, and if Em is near you, take her with you. Can you do that for me?"

Em, Hearing Jake's nickname for his sister again causes my heart to trip over itself. "I will, Jake. I'll make sure to keep Emily safe."

Jake stares into my eyes. "I know you will, my little spitfire," he replies and winks at me.

He encircles me in his arms. I go willingly, resting my head on his chest right under his chin. We stay like this for a long moment.

Eventually, Jake kisses my temple and whispers, "I

have to go get ready. Collection guards have a uniform for when they travel with Marco."

I nod and begin to step back, but Jake stops me by threading his fingers through my hair and bringing my chin up to look into his eyes. They penetrate mine before he claims my lips in a possessive, loving kiss. It almost feels like a goodbye.

"The next time I see you, Lil, Davis will be with me, and it will be to collect you."

"Okay, got it. I'll be ready." I give Jake my best, 'let's do this smile.'

"I love you, Lil," Jake softly says. He then places a quick, soft kiss on my lips. "Please be extra safe today. For me to exist, I need you alive and in my arms, because living with this ache would kill me."

Damn, he's good. I jump up and throw my body at him, wrapping him up in my legs and arms.

"I promise, Jake, I will try my hardest to stay safe." Jake sucks on my neck, kisses me in the same place, puts me on my feet, and then leaves the room.

Sometime later, and a lot of pacing from me, my door opens and Davis and Jake walk in. Both wearing black suits, white dress shirts, and black sunglasses.

"Did I just fall into a *Men in Black* movie?" I say sarcastically.

Standing behind Davis, Jake gives me a heart stopping smile while Davis whistles and says, "Looking good, Lil—"

Jake cuts Davis off before he can finish. "Davis, are we clear?"

Davis sighs and says, "Fuck, all right, hold your horses."

He places a finger to his ear and speaks, "Darren, we clear?"

Davis smiles and rubs his hands together. "Must be our lucky day. The dicks aren't tailing Marco for once. He's arriving in ten minutes. The first car will be Marco's guards, then Marco and Darren, then me and Lily, then you will be tailing, Jake."

Jake gives him a quick nod.

"Let's go," Davis says, grinning as he leaves the room.

I go to take a step and then stiffen. Suddenly, I feel like I have to leap over a huge hole in the ground. This was the last place I saw Sash alive, hugged her, and talked to her. My body starts to shake. Davis is out the door first, but Jake stops and looks over at me. He sees my face and comes to me.

"Lil, it will be okay."

I shake my head, trying to talk past the lump in my throat. "This is the last place I saw my sister, spoke to her, and held her. If I leave here, I'm leaving her behind," I lips tremble while I try to hold my tears back.

"Baby," Jake breathes out. He hugs me tightly, and I cry into his jacket, never wanting to let him go.

Jake whispers into my ear, "She's in your heart, Lil, not in this Godforsaken place, and she's home in Australia."

I nod, knowing he's right. I wipe my face quickly and walk out of the room, Jake's right behind me all the way. Reaching the bottom of the stairs, Davis grips my upper arm and walks me out the front door.

I spot two shiny, black cars parked right beside each other. They look like the same cars that brought me and

Sasha here.

Davis opens a back door to one of the cars and orders, “Get in, Lily,”

I get in, fighting my body’s instinct to glance once more time at Jake, but I know right now we need to be careful. We’ve already pushed our luck this morning.

I look out the car window and focus on Jake as he heads toward the car beside mine. The window’s tinted so I can’t see him when he gets in.

Davis gets into the driver’s seat in my car.

“All right, Lily, get comfortable. This is going to be a long drive,” he states, looking at me through the rear-view mirror.

I’m curious, so I ask, “How long?”

“About four hours.” Davis surprises me by answering me.

Since he’s answering my questions, I ask, “And where are we now?” Davis turns in his seat and looks at me. By the crease on his forehead above his sunglasses, it appears he’s narrowing his eyes at me. I know I’m asking him something I already know, but I am wondering just how honest Davis will be with me.

“Why so talkative, Lily?” He drags my name out.

I shrug, “I just want to know what country I’m in; that’s all.”

He smirks and says, “Won’t matter anyway. You’ll be locked away so tight, no one will ever find you, and you will never find a way out.” He gives me his obnoxious smile.

“Yes, yes, I’ve heard all this. Now, where are we?”

"You don't disappoint in the attitude department, do you. We're in Colombia at the moment," he finally replies honestly. I decide to push for more answers.

"So where are we going then?"

Davis presses in his earpiece and says, "Ready, open the gates."

He looks at me through the visor and says, "Now, you shut up and enjoy the drive."

Into The Jungle

ALMOST TWO HOURS INTO THE DRIVE, THE CARS BREAK OFF to the side of the road. We're in the middle of nowhere, and all I can see is a long stretch of road in front of us and on each side is miles of jungle.

"Jake, are we clear? Nothing behind us?" Davis nods and then speaks again, "No tails, clear the path." Davis looks ahead, and a man gets out of the first car. He walks into the forest and starts pulling branches back, and I see it: a dirt road. Oh, dear God, we're going into the jungle.

Once the dirt road gets cleared, we all drive through, then stop again. No one from the front cars gets out, so I look behind me and see Jake get out and cover the spot. He jumps back into the car. At hearing Davis voice, I turn back to the front.

"All covered up. Let's go." And with that, the cars start

driving along the jungle's bumpy dirt road.

I wonder how this sedan is going to go, but the further we get into the jungle, the more I can feel the road stays the same—flat, with small bumps; it's mostly smooth and hazard free, as if gets used all the time. Which it probably does considering the amount of times Marco talked about coming and going, plus the parties and each woman coming back at different times. This road is probably busier than that highway we were just on.

I glance out the window and see nothing except thick jungle. *Oh, God.* We are in the middle of nowhere. Escape would surely mean death of cold nights, starvation, not to mention the dangerous animals that would be out there.

After what I consider almost two hours of driving through the wilderness, I notice the jungle starts thinning out, and we arrive at a clearing. There's a tall barbed wire fence that stretches on for miles. We stop just near it, and I search out the windows, trying to see what's going on.

"Why did we stop?" I ask.

"Simply waiting for the gate to open. Won't be long now and you will be home." I shudder at his words. This will never be my home.

Up ahead, a man wearing khaki pants, jacket, and boots opens a large metal gate. It's square with gaps in-between the metal bars. He swings up a big latch, and it opens. It's a long gate so we have to wait until he walks it all the way back so the cars can fit through.

The first car starts making its way through and we follow behind. I examine a building up ahead; it's a big brown house, nowhere near as great as the mansion we left today. This one looks like it's made out of trees and painted a dark brown. It appears to be a two-storey house, simple with lights all around the outside that makes it seem inviting.

The cars brake in front of the building, all four cars side by side. Davis and the guards exit the cars, while a guard opens Marco's door, and he steps out. He's on his phone. Glancing over to my car, he nods to someone.

My door opens and I see Jake. I smile instantly, but his expression stays blank. He steps back waiting for me to exit the car.

I wipe the smile from my face as I emerge from the car. The first thing that hits me is the thick, humid air; it envelopes me, and almost instantly, a trickle of sweat creeps down my neck. I don't know how Jake is coping in his black suit, but if it were me, I would be trying to rip off all those clothes.

Jake leads me to the house, not touching me at all. We walk through the open front door, and as soon as we enter, the air-conditioning cools my skin.

The door closes behind us. I look back and find Davis. He walks around me and Jake, and we start following him. On our way through, I quickly take in my surroundings. On the right, I find a large lounge room filled with a long, white, L-shaped lounge, a large TV, and a round white rug. There are floor to ceiling windows through the whole lounge room, no curtains or blinds, just an open view of green trees and plants—the jungle at its purest. There is one set of stairs leading to the upstairs area and two exits leading from the room, one I am now walking through. To my left is a dining room with a large, thick wooden square table with twelve seats.

Davis leads us down a long hallway. The hall opens up to a large room at the back of the house, and again all the windows are floor to ceiling. From the front of the house, you would think there is no way to see inside, but most of this house is glass windows instead of walls. The room is huge. It's as long as the dining room and lounge combined, and there is a desk in the left corner with two black leather lounges, and a coffee table to my right. This must be Marco's office in this house.

"I don't give a fuck. He killed one of my collection pieces. I want him found and fucking skinned alive. Then I'll replace her with one of his daughters. That bastard cost me a lot of money." At Marco's words, Jake's and my backs go straight at the same time.

One of the girls is dead? No!

I glimpse at Jake, expecting to see terror on his face; however, his expression remains blank, except his eyes; they looked pained.

Marco growls and turns quickly toward us. "Fucking incompetent pricks can't even find one person."

I decide to ask the question whether I'm supposed to speak or not, nothing mattered more than easing Jake's pain or confirming what he is too terrified to hear. Either way, we needed to know.

"Who died?" I choked out.

Marco looks around his desk distracted and spits out, "Adanya."

Jake's shoulders slightly lower, only someone looking

for his relieved stature would notice.

Tears sting my eyes. I may not have known these women well, but they were still human beings and they were just like me, trapped.

Marco glances up at us and freezes, his gaze fixated on my face. “Don’t worry, Lily. She will be replaced quickly. You will have another friend soon.” He waves his hand around like it’s nothing at all.

My mouth hangs wide open, a whole swarm of bees would have fit in there.

“You are so heartless.” My voice is thick with grief. “She was a human being, someone’s daughter, you bastard.”

“Ah, I see you have your fire back, wonderful. You got over your sister.”

My heart squeezes. I hate hearing her referred to from his disgusting, psychotic lips.

Marco's eyes examine my expression and his face twists and contorts into rage. “Remember who’s in charge here, Lily, and don’t think because I can’t mark you on the outside that I can’t ruin you on the inside.” He speaks low, his tone spiked with icy anger.

A slither of fear bleeds into my courage, and I clamp my mouth shut and lower my eyes to the ground. I know what he wants me to do. I have to remember Jake is here for a reason, and that reason is bigger than me telling Marco what a monster he is.

Going against every fibre in my body, which is screaming at me not to do this, I say, “Yes, sir.”

Out the corner of my eye, Jake’s white knuckled fist gets my attention.

"Good girl. I love that you are a quick learner, yet you still hold the fire in your eyes. We're going to have some fun, you and I, over the coming years." *You wish, arsehole.*

"Davis," Marco speaks.

Davis steps forward in full minion mode.

"Show Lily to her room, and then show Jake around."

Marco shoos us away and distractedly starts searching his desk again.

Davis once again leads us back up the hallway, through the lounge room and up the set of stairs. They twirl around once until we hit the next floor. At the top of the stairs, there is nothing but a long hallway with three bedroom doors on either side. At the end of the long hall is another floor-to-ceiling glass window.

Davis opens the door to a room on the left, right next to the glass window.

As I'm about to walk into the room, I check out the view from up here. All I see is miles of jungle, and an occasional glimpse of the barbed wire fence between the trees.

I enter the room and find it's different to the one at the mansion, just as luxurious though, just in a woodsy and natural way. There's a similar massive walk-in closet and bathroom, but the walls are dark brown. The flooring is wood with a large green rug in front of the bed. The bed has an oak frame with green covers. The windows aren't floor to ceiling in this room, just one standard-sized window with green lace see-through curtains.

Davis speaks, "Jake, give me five. I need to go double check that Stevens is watching my post while I'm showing you around."

Jake nods and Davis departs the room, leaving the door wide open. I go to the door and look down the hall, seeing only the back of Davis as he descends the stairs.

An arm winds around my middle, and I'm pulled back into the room. I know it's Jake, so I don't freak out. He holds me while he softly closes the door and turns me to him.

"Jesus, Lily, did you have to piss Marco off already?" Jake blows out a big breath and rubs the back of his neck. "You are going to give me a damn heart attack."

I smirk and shrug. "I can't help it. I've finally found my talent, and it's to piss off evil arseholes."

Jake grins and kisses my nose. "Well, no more today, baby. You're gonna kill me before I even get you out of here."

My smile drops. "I know. That was selfish of me. I promise, I am now on my best behaviour." I throw up three fingers and give Jake my best scout's honour promise.

Jake laughs and places me away from him. He puts distance between us in case anyone enters the room, but his grin is still ever present on his handsome face. "Damn, I can't wait to get you home and spank you for that sass."

Home. The only home I have is the farm, and there's no way I could live on it now, not yet anyway. The memories would be too painful. So many things have been taken from me, and I just realised I have to add my family home to the list.

"I'm sorry, Lil. I shouldn't have said that." I shrug,

trying to throw off how much his words affected me.

Jake steps to me and declares, "You have me, baby. We will find a new home together."

I jump when we hear heavy footsteps walking up the hall.

Jake quickly whispers to me, "If you see Em, don't tell her I'm here. I don't want her change in attitude to alert anyone."

I nod quickly. Making quick strides to the window, he leans back on the wall as if he's been there casually waiting the whole time.

Davis opens and enters the room, "Okay, Jake, let's get this boring-ass tour over with."

Jake nods and follows Davis out of the room. Before he goes, he winks at me. I wish I could smile back, but the fear of what is about to happen holds my face captive.

Left alone in this new room, unsure of what to do, I decide to wash my face and clean the sweat from the back of my neck. Walking back into the room, I hear something through the walls. It's muffled and hard to pick up what it is. I place my ear to the wall and listen. Someone is crying; it must be one of the women.

I decide to go and knock on the door to the room. Slowly, I turn my door handle and look down the hall once again. This time it's empty. I take four big steps and gently knock twice. I hear rustling then the door opens. Long wavy blonde hair and grey, red rimmed eyes greet me, Megan.

Her eyes widen when she sees me. She pushes her door, and it opens all the way for me to enter. "Oh, gosh,

Lily, you're finally here." Guilt crosses her features. "Sorry, I mean, we didn't know when you were arriving. There's been a lot of talk about you coming, but we didn't know when that would be." She gives me a small, sad smile and says, "I'm sorry you're here." Her grief-stricken face clearly shows her struggle to stay composed.

I move and bring her in for a hug. Her sobs start immediately. "I'm so sorry about Adanya."

She nods and I rub circles on her back over her red flowing dress. Megan calms, and we break from the embrace. A shaky smile graces her face, but nonetheless, this time it's a real one.

"Come on. Let's go and see the other girls. In this life, there isn't much to be thankful for, but I know the girls will want to know you are safe and well, as safe as you can be in all this anyway." She clasps my hand, and we walk to the next door across from mine.

"Emily, come to the lounge," Megan shouts. Then without waiting for a response, Megan moves me on to the next door. I want to stay put and wait for Emily, but I keep moving with Megan to the next door, "Xiūxí shì Cho" she does this to one more door, before pulling me down the stairs to the open lounge room.

First thing I notice is how Megan relaxes into the lounge as if anyone would in their own home.

Footsteps coming down the stairs have me whipping my head around. Cho is first off the stairs, dressed in shorts and a white top with her black short hair and her blue eyes sparkling.

Natalia is right behind her in a white floor-length

summer dress, her red hair tied up in a bun on her head.

They both come right to me with smiles on their faces and embrace me in a warm hug. I smile back at them, happy to see they are healthy and alive.

Cho speaks first, "Nin hao."

"Hello, Cho," I reply with smile. I notice Cho has red-rimmed eyes. She moves back to the lounge.

"Lily, hola," Natalie says with a small smile. I can see tracks down her face as if her tears have washed away her makeup. She takes a seat on the lounge next to Megan.

I look up and see Emily descending the stairs. Watching her walk to me, it's like seeing and meeting her for the first time. I see it now: Jake's brown eyes, dark brown hair, and sharp jaw. Standing in front of me, Emily looks confident, composed and not at all teary.

Desensitised

Emily spoke of women disappearing before. It's easy to see she numbs herself to the emotions this life brings, and I completely understand why she would do that. I did it.

"How are you, Lily?" She clutches one of my hands and wraps her other around, encasing my hand in her warm grip. *Your brother's here.* I want to scream it to the rooftops.

"I'm doing okay."

Emily nods, understanding there's not much else I could say. "Your sister, how is she?" My chest collapses at the mention of Sash. I have to force myself to breathe. A few tears escape my eyes and I see Emily's face fall.

I shake my head. Emily squeezes my hand and softly says, "I'm sorry." It's probably the only time I've seen emotion on her face. She understands the bond between siblings. Wait until she finds out how much Jake has done for her.

Emily lets go of my hand, walks to the lounge and sits; she has returned to her composed, expressionless demeanour. I wonder if Jake knows how alike he and his sister are.

"So, what do you girls do for fun around here?" I ask, and everyone laughs, except for Emily.

Megan answers me, "Cho and Emily love to be in the kitchen. They are amazing cooks. Natalia and I like to walk outside. There are paths we can take. If we're lucky, Marco lets a guard take us just outside the fence. It's truly beautiful out there." I imagine it would be; it's untouched land.

"Oh," Megan says and jumps up from the lounge, "we have every board game you could ever think of." She opens a long drawer at the bottom of the TV unit, and she's right; there are hundreds of games in there. "Want to play one?" she asks enthusiastically. There is no way I can say no to her grinning face.

"Yep, let's play one." Megan pulls out Monopoly. "This is my favourite. Plus it takes a while to play so it passes the time quicker," she shrugs, smiling.

We all play Monopoly for a while. About an hour or two later, Cho jumps up and down laughing; she's reached a million dollars first. Emily, who through the majority of the game doesn't say a word or show one moment of emotion, is also staring up at Cho, smiling, openly content her friend is happy.

Just as we decide to play again, Marco walks into the room. He's visibly irritated. Searching the room, he doesn't bother to look at us until he fails to find what he's searching for. Looking down at us, his mood suddenly changes and he smiles at us all.

It's creepy and scary how unhinged this man is. "Ah, my collection pieces, all together and having fun. This gives me great pleasure, all my pieces together."

I bite my tongue, begging my mouth to keep itself shut.

Again, his mood shifts into another gear and he stares straight at me. "Lily, where is Jake?" he demands, all politeness gone.

So Jake is missing. Should Marco know that already? "I have no idea. He left with Davis earlier for a tour of the property, and I haven't seen either of them since." The hairs on my neck stand up. Is this the tense moment Jake was talking about? Damn, I'm not sure.

"Okay," he says distractedly and takes the stairs to the bedrooms.

"Who is Marco searching for? I've never heard of one of the guards by that name before?" Emily asks.

"My guard, he came with me from the other house," I tell her, but I'm distracted, trying to listen out for the sounds which will let me know it will be time to go and hide.

Marco's steps thunder down the stairs and he marches back through the lounge room, yelling on his two-way radio, "I don't fucking care. Get more guards out there. Something isn't right. They should have been back ages ago. Move, now!"

We all look around at each other. Emily is the first to speak. "Something's wrong." Yep, this is definitely the tense moment Jake warned me about.

I whisper to the girls, "We all need to get upstairs and into a room, now," I demand.

They look at me with confused expressions, but at this point, we all hear doors open and close, heavy boots running, then four heavily armed guards dressed in army green gear enter the lounge room with Marco right behind them. *Shit!* I need to move the girls.

Marco is still yelling into his radio, "Well fucking find out. Where the fuck are Jim and Pete?"

Silence, then someone speaks through the radio. "I don't know. Trent went to look for Davis and Jake, then when he didn't come back, they went to see what was going—"

A loud bang is heard followed by a masculine *humph* through the radio. A smacking noise comes through as if the two-way dropped to the ground.

I grab my chest trying to slow my heart from the fright. In the quiet that follows, static air crackling through the radio is the only sound.

Time To Die

"STEVENS?" MARCO CALLS THROUGH HIS RADIO. NO ONE replies. "Fuuuuck," Marco shouts. "Ken, you there? You hear that? What the fuck is going on?" Nothing, just more silence. "Ahhh! Goddammit, is anyone there?" Marco roars down the radio. When there is no response, he throws the two-way to the wall, and it smashes into pieces.

He turns to his guards and says, "Some bastards have found us and they have taken out all the fenced guards. Do not let them in this fucking house. Do not let them anywhere near my collection."

My heart soars. Jake is on his way.

"Kill these motherfuckers. Do you all understand?" he growls at them.

The guards nod and start moving within the house,

taking up residence at different windows, cocking their guns and notifying when they are in place.

Marco storms down the hallway and there is a long silence. He returns, holding a shotgun. My palms sweat instantly seeing this heartless man wield a gun. *Please be careful, Jake.* My heart is beating rapidly. Suddenly, the situation is becoming very real, and the thought of losing someone else I love is unbearable.

I observe my surroundings and realise all of us women are now standing on the Monopoly board, huddled together, holding on to one another. Fear's apparent on each of their faces. Then I remember they don't know these men are coming to save them.

"All of you," Marco growls at us, "stay here. Do not move. I am not losing another fucking pay cheque this week." He then leaves the room.

"Prick," I mutter.

Megan's chuckle at my comment gets all our attention, until Natalia whispers, "What do you think is going on?"

I open my mouth, but Emily beats me to it. "Someone is infiltrating Marco's house. I can't believe it," her voice awed. "All these years here, not one single time did anyone even get close, and now there are people just outside those doors. I think we need to prepare ourselves for what they want. They could want revenge on Marco or they could want us. Either way, we need a plan."

Emily's bravado and leadership surprises me. I'm starting to see why she has lasted so long in this empire. Courage and quick thinking, she's a fighter, just a silent fighter. She fights to last through her time, not to fight every battle that comes at her.

I decide it's time to tell them they are being saved, and I know who the men outside are. "Those men—"

Suddenly, all hell breaks loose. Guns firing, glass shattering everywhere; the sounds are deafening. I cover my ears and drop to the ground on my knees. I curl into my body to try and protect myself.

Cho and Megan's screams cut through the gunshots. I glance up and they're covering their heads and crawling around panicked and scared.

Emily is crawling toward them. Natalia is beside me frozen with her hands to her ears, completely still.

I search around for a safe place. We need to move out of the open space. I pass my gaze over the lounge room and look into the dining room. I then spot what we need: the thick wooden dining table with the big wooden chairs for protection. Under there, that's where we need to go.

I poke Natalia to get her attention. She glances at me with utter fear on her face. I point to the table and shout, "Hide under the table." She nods and heads straight for the table.

I yell to Emily, but she doesn't hear me over the guns going off. I crawl closer and scream again, "Emily!"

She finally catches my voice and looks over to me. Her arms are around Megan and Cho trying to protect them. At that moment, she earns all of my respect. There is no doubt in my mind: she is a fighter. I point to the table and Emily nods in understanding. She starts pulling the girls to get their attention. Finally, they look up, and she points to the table. They all start moving.

We're all under the table with the chairs pulled in, sitting on our knees, jumping scared as more gunshots go off. Cho is rocking back and forth. I'm trying to calm her by rubbing her arms, which seems to be working. Natalia and Megan are calming down with Emily's help. A silent message passes between Emily and me. We are the strongest here right now, and we need to think about what we should do next.

Abruptly, the gun fire and shouting stops. Cho is whimpering and I'm trying to quieten her. "*Shh, shh*, please, Cho, try and calm down," I whisper into her ear, having no idea if she even understands me. Thankfully, she must. She puts her head up and nods to me, tears cascading down her face, but no sound is coming from her lips.

We all freeze when we hear heavy footsteps walk through the dining room. The two steel-capped boots stop right next to the table, and a man's raspy voice says, "Clear." He then moves away from the table.

We all sag at the same time just to freeze again as another set of boots passes the table. All we can hear is glass crunching under their boots. Then he speaks, "Blackbear, this is Redwolf. First floor is clear. We're moving upstairs, over."

The boots move away and out of the dining room. Dammit, why didn't I find out from Jake what his team members' names are? I have no idea if the good guys just passed us.

I glance around the girls for help with what those names might mean, but all of them seem just as confused as I am, except Emily. Her hand over her mouth and her eyes wide, tears spilling down her face, she lets out a loud gut-wrenching sob, one that sounds like she's held it in forever.

"Emily," I whisper, but just then there are more gunshots, this time from upstairs.

Abruptly, a chair is yanked back and thrown across the floor. Marco kneels and stares at us with murder in his eyes. He scans over all of us then narrows his murderous stare at me.

His lip curls up in a sneer. He grabs my wrist and starts pulling me out from under the table. I try to whip my hand back and forth to loosen his grip, but his fingers are tight and punishing.

Emily grabs for me, but as Marco stands, he whips me straight out from under the table in no time, and all I feel is a whisper of Emily's fingertips on my legs.

He screams at the table, "The rest of you fucking stay there. Do not move while I deal with this motherfucking traitor."

So he figured out Jake is behind this.

He lets go of my wrist, and his hand instantly grips my hair hard and rough. A whimper leaves my mouth at the pain.

My hands immediately go to my hair, trying to push down what little hair he's not pulling to ease the stinging.

Marco walks me back toward the lounge room, and we stop. He waves his gun around as he snarls in my ear, "Shouldn't be long now. One of those fuckers will be along soon, I'm sure."

Ideas of how to get Marco off me race through my mind. *For me to exist, I need you alive and in my arms.* Jake's words float through my mind. However, I'm at a loss of how I can protect myself right now.

I decide to take a chance. I bring my knee up. Then with a grunt, I push my heel back and kick Marco hard in his thigh. He roars and throws me against the wall. Hitting it hard, I fall to the ground. I hiss when glass slices into my hands and stomach. Marco has me up before I can even see how much glass is imbedded in me.

He wraps his arms around my shoulders, holding me to his chest, his fingers digging into my skin with a punishing grip. He walks us backwards until I feel him stop right before a half-shattered glass window.

After a moment, the sound of glass crunching under boots gets my attention. A man in khaki camouflage clothes turns sharply into the room, gun aimed and ready to shoot. If it weren't for the yellow band tied to his left bicep, I would think he was one of Marco's guards.

Marco pulls me in tighter to his front and presses his gun to my temple. My eyes close tightly, praying he doesn't shoot me. Fear driving my actions now, I try to move away from it, but he just presses it into my head harder. Whimpers expel from my mouth from the pain.

My eyes open as the man with the yellow band speaks low and calmly, "Downstairs lounge room, assailant and victim." He doesn't move a muscle while speaking.

Marco lets out a sickening crazy laugh behind me. "Yeah, bring that traitor to face me. Fucking asshole better be ready to lose his pussy. He will learn what happens when he chooses cunt over loyalty." *Oh, God.*

Another man comes into view wearing the same green camouflage with a yellow band, his gun also aimed at me and Marco.

He speaks loud and clear into the room, "Nightfire and Redwolf in position. Blackbear move in."

Marco tightens his hold on me as Jake steps into the room. Wearing the same gear as his team, Jake walks in aiming his gun. Shock colours his expression when he sees it's me being held by Marco.

He lowers his gun immediately and demands, "Let her go, Marco, now," his voice low and guttural.

I cry out as Marco pushes the gun impossibly harder into my temple. Tears fall silently down my face, and I watch fear take root in Jake's eyes.

"You're trying to steal my collection from me. It's only fair I get to take what you want!" Marco shouts at Jake.

Jake moves into the middle of the room. He calmly holsters his gun. His eyes bore into Marco; I see hate and anger in his beautiful brown eyes.

Jake's eyes shift back to me. He does a sweep of my body and freezes at what I'm sure is my blood dripping down my fingers. His eyes dart back to mine. The fear is still there but rage is now dominating his features. His eyes shift back to Marco, and this time, there's fire there; he's ready to give this man his justice.

"Give it up, Marco. You're cornered," Jake growls. He's right, two men have their guns aimed at him; even if he kills me, Marco isn't getting out of this room alive.

"Who said I'm going anywhere. I've been playing this

game a long time, Jake. I know when I've been outplayed, but I won't be going out alone."

Marco clicks the safety from his gun. At this point, I'm unable to stop the sobs even if I tried. I'm shaking violently, my voice trying to say no but the words get stuck in my throat. My mouth is filling with saliva, and I know what that means; I'm about to vomit any minute. Terror has set up home in my mind and body.

I close my eyes and think at least I will get to see Sasha. I will get to be with my family now. I open them again to look at Jake and say my goodbyes. He's staring right into my eyes, and I see his lips lift up and he tilts his head to the right. I'm confused and pissed. I tilt my head to match his wondering what the hell is so funny right now. My eyes narrow at him telling him this is not the freaking time to smile!

Jake's lips mouth 'now' but no sound comes out.

The room is completely silent as I feel a hard thump to my back and warm liquid bursts on my face and hair. My eyes go wide, and the gun Marco is holding falls to the ground.

I look over my shoulder as Marco starts to fall on top of me and find half his head is missing. I start shrieking and try to get out from under his falling body.

Two big hands grab my arms, and pull me forward. My heart violently beats against my chest as I watch Marco fall to the ground with a thump.

"Lily," I hear, but all I can do is keep screaming and looking at Marco's half blown-off head.

I'm turned around and forced to look up at Jake.

"Lily," he says louder this time. I stop screaming and try to swallow past my now sore throat.

I swing my head around to the broken window and see a man in the same gear as Jake with a sniper rifle, and he's grinning. *Grinning!*

I wiggle out of Jake's hands and sink to my knees, gagging. "Get me a bucket," Jake shouts to someone. I have blood and brains in my hair! Oh, God, I'm going to go all girly and faint.

"Lil, baby, please listen to what I'm saying." I'm blowing out big breathes, desperately trying to keep the vomit down.

"I need you to calm down so I can see why you're bleeding."

More deep breaths and I manage to quickly say, "Glass. Cuts."

Jake picks me up and lays me down on the couch my back to the seat cushions with my legs straight up in the air laying on the back of the couch.

I start feeling better almost straight away, Jake lifts my shirt, "Fuck," he hisses.

I pop my head up to see what he's cursing at and see my stomach covered in blood with small glass pieces stuck inside me.

"We need to get you to the hospital."

He checks my hands and hisses again, “Shit. Fucker is lucky he’s already dead," Jake growls.

Laying upside down, I see Emily run up behind Jake. She looks shocked and pale.

"Jake," her voice is small and anxious.

Jake spins around rapidly and looks up at Emily. He stays frozen for only a second before he stands, grabs her, and picks her up, hugging her tightly.

She wraps her arms around his neck sobbing.

"Em," I hear Jake softly say, "I didn't think this moment would ever come." His voice is thick and strangled.

He places her down on her feet, and they just stare at each other for a moment.

A man, Redwolf, I think, steps forward, drops his gear to the ground, and stares at her with utter shock on his face.

"Emily," he breathes out.

Emily searches for the voice. Finding the dark blond-haired man, her lips tremble, and she starts falling to the ground. The man catches her and they grip each other tightly. The agony and torment from their sobs echoes around the room. Picking Emily up, the man carries her out of the room.

Jake watches the man walk away with his sister, and then with purposeful strides gets to me, picks me up and carries me through the house.

"I feel like I just watched Romeo and Juliet reunite," I comment.

Jake laughs and says, "Yeah, well that's pretty damn close."

We exit the house and a black SUV speeds up the driveway. It brakes suddenly and clouds of dirt floats into the air.

"Come on, Lil. Time to get you to the hospital. Your cuts have stopped bleeding and most don't look too deep. But there is one I'm worried about, and I don't want to pull the glass out without you having something for the pain," Jake explains.

"What about the other women? We need to help them." I insist. They need to go home too.

Jake swoops down and kisses my lips long and hard. "They are safe now Lil, my men will take care of them." I nod, feeling warm and safe in his arms.

The man, who first entered the lounge area when Marco had me, walks over to us and looks to Jake. "Orders?" he asks.

"I'm taking Lil to the hospital. Kanye and Em will come with us. First take Em to find the girls and explain to them that you and Dom will get them out of here safely. Then bag up Marco and burn the building to the ground. Then meet up with Joseph and his team at the manor and finish the mission. Report to me when completed. We'll meet up at the hospital in civilian gear," Jake instructs. The man nods and walks away.

Joseph and his team?

The car door opens and Jake takes a seat in the back of the SUV with me still in his arms. He holds me carefully, trying not to touch my stomach or hands.

Jake checks my injuries again.

"I'm okay, Jake," I assure him.

"I know, baby. I'm just making sure I didn't miss anything."

I smile, loving the way he's taking care of me.

After about ten minutes, I hear car doors open and close, and then the car starts driving and Jake demands,

"Drive fast."

I tuck my body further into his, and with Jake's lips kissing my temple where the gun was pointed and his powerful body and warm hands around me, I don't even feel the pain at all.

Chapter 27

I Forgive You

I HEAR A WINDOW BEING OPENED AND A CHAIR SQUEAKING. Slowly opening my eyes, a handsome man with short, dark blond-hair looks down at me with a large cheeky grin.

I rasp out, "Redwolf?"

He laughs and says, "You can call me Kanye, sweet cheeks."

I remember arriving at the hospital, Jake carrying me inside and demanding a doctor. I started whimpering as a stinging sensation ran around my tummy. With the adrenalin wearing off, I was beginning to feel all the glass that had pierced my skin. I felt a prick in my arm and I must have drifted off to sleep.

The soft material on my body tells me I'm dressed in a hospital gown. I try to sit up, but struggle, realising there are bandages around my hands. Kanye helps me, and I clench my teeth at the stinging sensation on my stomach.

"Yeah, careful there. You got some stitches."

I look down through my hospital gown to find my body completely naked, and one bandage stuck to the left side of my stomach. I can see other cuts but nothing serious.

"Jake's gone out to call his parents with Em. He'll be back soon." He says her name so adoringly. I remember him with Emily. It's hard to explain what I watched as he embraced her, but I know they both must love each other very much.

Kanye walks to the side table and starts pouring a cup of water. I take a quiet moment to look him over. He's wearing jeans and a grey thermal shirt. He's the same height as Jake, and it's obvious he's just as fit, but Kanye has a more handsome look about him than a powerful one like Jake. He hands me the water, and I drink the whole thing. He refills it for me without me even having to ask.

"So how long have you known Jake and Emily?" His face lights up at their names. It's easy to see they mean a lot to him.

"Since Jake and I were in first grade, we both threw out our strawberry yogurt, been best friends ever since." He winks at me, and I giggle. This guy is adorable.

Still grinning at me, he says, "Jake is going to be pissed when he finds out you woke up to me and not him," he laughs. "I can't wait to tell him." Warmth floods me, and I smile at his playful manner with Jake.

Music starts playing from somewhere, and Kanye's face breaks out into an enormous grin. He pulls his phone from his back pocket. The song playing is 'Bad Boys'.

Kanye shows me the phone and says, "This is Jake. He'll be checking up on you. He only left ten minutes ago."

I can't help but laugh at his ringtone for Jake. I also try to shake my head at the same time, trying to tell him not to tell Jake I'm awake. I want him to have his moment with Emily and his parents.

"Hey Jakey, Em good?" Kanye nods, then a frown appears. It disappears as he looks down at me and he grins massively. "Hmm...let me think. If she was still asleep, would I know she has gorgeous green eyes and a stunning smile?"

A boisterous laugh bursts from Kanye, and he pulls the phone from his ear. "He hung up on me. My guess is he's running through the hospital right now. You probably have about two minutes of peace left for the rest of your life."

A massive smile breaks out on my face thinking about Jake getting here any minute. Then I frown when I remember the blood and brains in my hair. My bandaged hands fly up to my hair. It's wet but it feels clean.

Kanye must see my confusion. "They washed your hair while you were getting your stitches.

"Thank God. That was the most disgusting thing that could ever happen to any living person."

Kanye chuckles but stops immediately when we both see the door to the room swing open.

Jake enters, his strides purposeful and his eyes trained on mine. "Out," he growls. Kanye laughs as he leaves the room.

Jake walks up to me, his breathing heavy, obviously from his run. He cups my cheeks and I lick my lips, dying to have him kiss me. He gently strokes my now wet lips with his thumb, and then his thumb is gone. His lips are on mine. A possessive, punishing kiss filled with so much love my heart almost explodes.

Jake releases me from the kiss and places his forehead to mine, my bandaged hands hanging onto his wrists.

Still breathing heavily, Jake says, "You scared me so fucking much, baby. When I saw that gun to your head, I thought my world was going to end right in front of me."

"It's all okay now, Jake. You saved me and your sister. You did it."

Jake takes my mouth again, this time softly with gentle strokes of his tongue.

A memory flutters to the front of my mind and my blood starts to heat. I pull away from the kiss. "You grinned at me while a man had a gun to my head!" I almost shout.

Jake grins and his eyes soften. "I had to make a decision. I didn't want to shoot Marco from front on. There were too many ways that could fail and you would get hurt. Even if you didn't tilt your head, you would have been fine, but I knew Marco's head would fly forward into yours, and I didn't want you hurt at all. So I took a chance, and you did what I thought you would do. You tilted your head, confused and pissed at me."

"I got blood and brains in my hair, Jake. How was that not hurting me?" I whine. His laughter echoes through the room, and my whiny mood disappears at hearing it. I will never get tired of hearing that.

Jake lifts my whole body effortlessly and moves me over on the big hospital bed. He scoots in beside me and turns me on my side, wrapping his arm around my body, he hugs me close to him.

I lean up on my elbow to find out something from Jake, something I want to know right now. "Jake, what happened to Natalia, Cho, Megan, Beth, and the other slave girls?"

Jake's expression grows thoughtful. "They're free, Lil. Every single one of the girls are being taken home as we speak."

"What about the guards?" I need to know every single one of those bastards is locked up or dead.

"The guards at Marco's private house are dead. They were trained to fight to the death, and none of them were ever going to surrender. And the slave house, not many made it out alive. The ones who did have gone into custody. Although, being known as a guard for Marco, they won't last long. A lot of important people will want to keep their secrets, just that way, secret. They won't know just how secretive Marco was and that all of their secrets also died with Marco."

I nod, comfortable with knowing most of the evil men from the empire are dead or will be soon. “And did I hear you say Joseph and his team earlier?” I want to know if it’s the same Joseph.

"Yes, Marco’s son Joseph also helped take the mansion, and he burned it down, with Marco inside."

I gasp, "Joseph burned his dead father in the house."

He nodded. "It's fitting; he burned where so many others died at his orders."

"I didn't know Joseph was helping you?" I state, shocked Joseph would help Jake, but then I didn't know Joseph at all.

"Joseph has known I was undercover for just over a year now. He despised his father and I took a chance and told him who I was and what I was doing. Unfortunately, Joseph knew even less than me. Marco didn't even tell his own son where his private house was. If Joseph found out anything regarding locations, he would always pass the information to me and my team would look into it, but it always lead to dead ends. Marco was a smart man. He knew not to leave any trace he was there or where he was going.

"Unfortunately, Joseph helping me created a rift between him and Alexa. She wanted to leave a long time ago, but Joseph refused until we successfully found Em. Joseph tried to get Alexa to go without him. He had ways of hiding her from his father, but she refused to hide away and let Marco punish Joseph for her disloyalty." Jake looks down to the end of the bed and continues to talk, "I always felt sorry that she was trapped there because of me. I understood why she needed to go. She saw every new slave when they arrived, when they got beatings, and when they died."

“Seeing all that and not being able to do anything must have been killing her," I add, feeling bad at remembering how I treated her.

Jake continues, "The day Joseph killed Mick, I knew his

argument with Marco was serious, and this time he was going to flee. Joseph came to me later that day and told me he was disappearing with Alexa and his mother. I understood and wished him well. Unfortunately, when he went to collect Alexa to disappear, she was already gone. He has been looking for her ever since, only stopping to help take the mansion."

I stare up at Jake and ask, "Will he keep looking?"

Jake laughs a deep laugh. "Hell yes, the one reason Joseph didn't push her to hide away in a different country is because he couldn't bear to be away from her. Not knowing where she is now is taking its toll on him. The boys said he's in bad shape. He even beat his dead father before leaving him to the fire. The boys had to pull him off Marco before he almost burned alive himself. He's on the edge, and I think the only thing that will pull him back is finding Alexa."

My mind torn, I feel for a man who is clearly in pain, but I still need to come to terms with the fact Joseph was one of the good guys.

Jake brings me out of my thoughts with a serious tone, "Lil, we need to talk."

My eyes find his and my body tenses when I see fear there. He finally finds his courage and begins speaking, "I want to move forward with you, Lil, with us. I want a life with you." He pauses before continuing, "But I understand if you can't do that. I lied and trapped you. I don't know how you can ever forgive me for not saving Sasha in time." His voice comes out strangled, and he coughs to clear his throat. "I know I hurt you, Lil, but I promise you, from now on, there is nothing left but the real me. I want to show you who that is. I want to give you everything you deserve."

He's begging me to give him a chance. My body relaxes, and I sit up and stare into the eyes of the man I love.

"Jake, I want a life with you too, and I forgive you and so would Sasha. Nothing is more important than your family. I did the same. I risked other people's lives to get Sash out. I understand why you did what you did, all of it. And you succeeded: you saved your little sister." I pause to try to get my words out pass the lump in my throat, with tears threatening to spill. "But I didn't. I failed my sister, but I know Sash; she knew everything I did was for her. I can live knowing my baby sister died knowing I loved her more than life itself, and I can forgive myself because I know she would forgive me too."

Jake wraps me in his arms and lays us down together. I cry into his chest for what feels like hours. He strokes my hair and kisses my forehead. My crying slows to just hiccupping. Then my eyes drop and I sleepily ask, "What now, Jake?"

"Now we take you home to your sister," he replies.

JAKE

WATCHING LIL SLEEPING DEEPLY IN MY ARMS, MY MIND finally stops racing with what ifs or what could have been, my world finally feels at peace. My whole reason for living was to save my sister, but along the way, my life changed, and Lily became my purpose, my reason for breathing.

To watch her strong spirit and sassy attitude for the rest of my life would be an honour and a blessing. To have children, strong and beautiful, just like her, fuck, I would be in heaven.

And I'm going to make that happen. I just got out of hell and the only thing I'm focusing on now is making heaven with her.

You Loved Me At My Darkest

THE NEXT DAY, I MANAGE TO GET MYSELF SIGNED OUT OF the hospital early after some manipulating and fluttering of my eyelashes to convince Jake I was ready to leave. The only clothes I could get my hands on were the jeans I wore to Marco's house and a spare white shirt Jake had. My hands are now bandage free. They are healing nicely with only a small sting when I close my fist.

We went right to the airport. Jake's parents commissioned a private jet for us all to fly home in; they are desperate to get Emily home as soon as possible.

Jake's up front, talking to the pilot when Emily walks onto the plane. I'm sitting in a four-seater and Emily takes the seat across from mine. We smile at each other.

Emily speaks first, "I'm glad you're okay, Lily."

"I'm glad you are too. Have you spoken to the girls

since leaving the house?"

Emily shakes her head no. "Dom and Nick let me know when each of them reached their homes; I imagine they will be spending these first few days back in the real world with their families. I think, for now, we all just want to pretend it was a bad dream and forget it ever happened."

I wish I could take away all of Emily's memories of the collection. "Dom and Nick? Were they the other two men with Jake and Kanye?"

Emily releases a soft laugh. "Yes, Dominic, Nick, and Kanye are part of Jake's team. They have all been friends since they were little kids. I knew it was them as soon as I heard the code names. They used to run around my family's backyard with those names, storming castles to save the princess."

A huge smile appears on my face imagining Jake as a young boy saving princesses and killing dragons. "Well, that was good practice then, because this time, they really did save the princess. You're very lucky to have them looking out for you."

Emily looks out the window. "Yes, I am very thankful. I'm just not sure who they think they saved though. I know what they want to see, the Emily from five years ago, but that's not me anymore. The Emily I am today is lost and dirty, inside and out," she ends on a whisper.

My heart dies at hearing her words. "Emily," I say sternly, "you are not dirty. You have been through something most people will never know or even read about, and you survived it. I saw you. When the guns starting going off, you went straight for Cho and Megan. You didn't think about yourself. You covered them with your own body. You're a fighter, Emily. No matter how much you think you aren't that girl from five years ago, I saw flashes of a very different girl to the one you try to pass yourself off to be. You may feel lost now, but it won't always feel like that. Keep fighting and one day you will find yourself again," I say with conviction, hoping with every fibre of my being that this will come true for her.

She quickly wipes away a few stray tears and then recomposes herself. "My brother seems quite taken with you, Lily. I can see why."

I lean forward, grab her hand and squeeze. "I'm here for you, Emily. If you ever need to talk, please, all you have to do is tell me and I will listen."

Her eyes grow glassy. We sit like this in a comfortable silence until Kanye walks on to the plane and sits next to Emily. She stiffens slightly, releases my hand and turns, looking out the window.

Kanye looks to Emily and I see the pain in his eyes. He has no idea how to help her, and it's clear he's hurting. I wonder if Emily can see that, or if she's too caught up in her own nightmares to notice.

"So where is home for you guys?" I ask.

Emily, still staring out the window, doesn't seem to hear me so Kanye jumps in and answers, "Hastings, Minnesota." He glances to Emily quickly then back as Jake walks over.

Jake sits down next to me and pulls me to his side. He notices how quiet we all are. As he looks around, he arches an eyebrow as if asking, 'what's up?'

I decide to redirect the awkwardness away from Emily and say, "Kanye just told me you all live in Minnesota."

Jake slowly nods, looking at me.

"The boys and I have a business there. When Kanye and I got out of the Marines, we got into security. We employed guys who we grew up with and trusted to work for us. They travel all over Minnesota for parties, clubs, and big events. We handle the security. Our business is well-known and sought after. The boys have kept it afloat while I've been away, but it needs a lot of work. It hasn't been our priority for a long time."

I know Jake and I talked about building a life together, but we haven't talked about the details past taking me home to bury Sasha. Suddenly, I'm nervous. Jake lives half a world away from me. How would we build a life together? "You're going back there." I clear my throat and say, "I mean, you're going back there to live after you take me home?"

Obviously sensing the awkward conversation Jake and I may be about to have, Kanye announces, "We'll go sit up the front."

This time Emily is looking at us and understands. She moves with Kanye to a two-seater right at the front. Emily's head turns toward the window while Kanye's is turned in her direction.

Jake's hands find my waist, and he lifts me to sitting on his lap, my front to his front, each of my knees touching his thighs. His cock grows hard, so I squirm to feel more of it.

Jake stills me with his hands at my waist. "Baby, you need to stop that." His voice is gruff.

I smile at being able to make him hard just by sitting on his lap.

"I love your smile, baby, and right now, there are many other things I would love to be doing but we gotta talk first."

I nod, bracing myself for his next words. Whether they are good or bad, I know I will be all right. After everything I have been through, I know I can handle whatever life has left to throw at me. Being with Jake would be life throwing me a life vest, but I've come to expect the unexpected.

"Lil, let's get one thing clear, okay?"

I nod slowly, nervously waiting for his words.

"Where you go, I go. We are not separating, baby, ever." His voice is stern, and his eyes shine with love.

My body relaxes at his words. "We will be together in Australia or Minnesota," he announces.

My eyes go wide. "Live in America?" I say softly. All I've ever known is Australia.

"Yeah, we can live on your farm if that's what you want, or we can move to my home in Hastings. Maybe we can do both? Six months in each? The work I do, I don't need to work the whole year, and it pays pretty fucking well. Plus, when we're on your farm, we'll be working it, so money won't be an issue. It's up to you, baby. I love you, Lily. I go where you go. Forever."

Thoughts race through my mind. "It's my family's farm. I could never sell it, but I also can't live on it, not yet anyway. The memories, being reminded of them all the time, will be too hard at the moment."

My eyes search Jake's for what I should do, but he isn't giving anything away. He wants me to make my own decision. I can't quite believe he's willing to give up his family and friends to be with me. That gesture alone already decides my answer.

"I want to do both, six months at each."

Immediately, he answers, "Done."

Happy tears fall from my eyes, and I giggle at the thought of Jake on my farm.

Jake's eyes soften and he kisses the side of my mouth. "Love that smile, baby. It breathes life into me."

Every time he says things like that, a piece of my heart heals a little more.

"I love you, Jake. My home is with you, wherever you are."

Jake's hands twist up into my hair gently and he kisses me hard. He groans into my mouth when I grind my heat down on his erection.

"Baby, you're killing me. As soon as we are alone, I'm going to show you just how much I love you."

I smile brightly. Finally feeling like my life will one day see the light again.

◆◆◆

Eight hours later, we finally arrive in Hastings. The trip included listening to Jake and Kanye joke around and make me laugh a lot, eating lunch and a taking a nap, on top of all of us watching Emily worried as she simply stares out the window almost the whole time.

We all say our goodbyes as the plane is refuelled. Jake hugs Emily and kisses her hair. For a moment, I don't think he will let her go. I feel guilty. He just saved her and now he is leaving her again. I want to tell him to stay with her, but I am too selfish. I don't want to go home and bury my sister alone.

Kanye gives me a small hug and tells me to take care.

The boys do a big, manly one-second hug followed with hard pats on their backs.

Jake says sternly, "Watch her. Call me with updates."

Kanye nods, and with that, he and Emily exit the plane, and Jake shuts the door.

He goes up front to tell the pilot we're ready to go, and then we buckle up. As the plane takes off, I watch Jake and Emily's parents run out to Emily and embrace her in a very emotional family hug.

"So your sister and Kanye, it seems like there is more than just history between them?"

Jake huffs out a sigh, "Yeah, there is. Before Em got taken, they were together and in love. They had been since she was sixteen. They hid their relationship from everyone for two years.

"Kanye had crappy parents. Actually, they weren't crappy, they were horrible. He was a kid from the wrong side of the tracks. He got into trouble a lot, but usually it was stealing food to eat or taking text books from school so he could study. My dad had no problems with Kanye and I being friends, but he hated his parents. Kanye's parents were into drugs, and when my dad found out he and Em were together, he banned Kanye from our house and from me and Em. It's a long story. One I will tell you one day, baby, but just know, it all worked out, until five years ago. Right before Em was taken, Kanye was preparing to ask her to marry him. She was only twenty-three and he was twenty-six. My parents thought they might be too young, but I knew Em would be over the moon and so did my parents, so they gave Kanye their blessing. Then she disappeared and he was shattered. We all were, but Kanye stopped existing."

Jake's eyes grow pained. "When we got the tip about the sex slave industry, he lost it, smashed up his and Em's house. It wasn't until I told him my plans that he started to focus again. He had a purpose, a way of finding Em. He worked just as hard these four years searching for her as I have. Dealing with scum and beating information out of men involved with Marco."

"But seeing Em with him now, I don't know; she's stiff and flinches when he's near. She seems like a different person. Em used to be smiling all the time. She was carefree and loved to hold hands, cuddle. She was always touching Kanye. Even when my dad was around, and she knew my dad was gonna go ballistic, but she didn't care. She loved Kanye just as much as he loved her."

I should tell Jake about Em's earlier comments. He needs to know she won't be the old Em anytime soon, or ever. "I talked to her earlier, Jake. She's not good. She's lost and thinks all anyone sees is how dirty she is from what she's been through."

Jake's raises his voice, "That's bullshit."

I calmly state, "I know, Jake, but what has happened to

her has changed the way she views herself. You still see that same girl from five years ago, but she isn't the same. To Emily, she doesn't think she's good enough. That won't change. Not until she learns to let go of what happened to her. It's going to be a long and bumpy road. I hope Kanye is up for it."

Jake shakes his head and says, "I hope he is too, because I know he won't cope if he has to lose her all over again."

The planes seatbelt sign dims, and right away, Jake unbuckles my seat belt and pulls me from my seat. "No more talking, baby. I haven't been inside you for days and my cock is begging me to take you."

His words set my body on fire, and my clit starts to tingle.

Jake carries me to the back of the plane and through a door. I'm surprised to see a bed in the middle of the room.

I smack his chest. "Jake you should have told me there was a nice comfy bed to sleep on when I was napping on you."

"No way, Lil, I like it when you sleep on me, and I don't want you out of my sight for a long time yet."

Jake places me on my feet. We're standing next to the bed, Jake's legs and shoulders almost touching the wall and bed with his big size.

"Strip, baby, I want to see what's mine," he whispers into my ear. A shiver runs through me. "Fuck, baby, I love feeling you tremble for me."

I unbutton my jeans and pull them down my legs. I'm not wearing any underwear as the hospital only had plastic ones, and they felt horrible.

I hear Jake groan, "Christ, you're not wearing panties, fuck."

And with that, Jake lifts his shirt off my body and discovers I have no bra either. He groans again and rubs the front of his jeans.

"Fuck, Lil, this is gonna be fast, but after that, I have twenty hours to take it slow with you, and we will do just that. I'm gonna lick, taste, and devour your whole goddamn delicious body."

I moan at his words. Just remembering how Jake touches me and how he feels inside of me creates wetness between my legs.

I reach out and unbuckle Jake's jeans, pulling his zipper down slowly. I push his jeans down then his briefs. He kicks them away with his feet and whips his shirt off.

I feel ready to burst, just looking at his erect cock. God, I feel like devouring it with my mouth, and then at the same time screaming to the world it's mine, and if anyone ever tries to go near it, I will scratch their eyes out. *Wow. So this is what possessiveness feels like. It's intense.*

"Lay on your back, baby." I sit down and crawl backwards on my elbows and bottom. I lie down and spread my legs. Jake moans, deep and guttural.

"Shit, Lil, look at you. I can already see you glistening." Jake pulls a condom out of his wallet in his jeans pocket and covers my favourite part of his body.

He starts kissing up my body, starting at my thighs, up to my bandage covered stitches on my tummy, then to my breasts. He sucks on my nipples and it feels amazing, like the sun hitting my skin for the first time in forever.

Jake groans as the head of his cock slides inside me. Then he looks down at me and smiles. "Ready baby? This is gonna be hard and fast."

I nod and smile brightly at him.

"I love you, Jake," I say on a whimper as Jake fills me completely.

"I love you more, Lily Morgan," Jake growls as he starts moving inside of me.

"You loved me at my darkest, baby, just wait till you see me at my best," he promises.

Until We Meet Again

JAKE
(one year later)

PLEASURE IS THE FIRST THING I FEEL WHEN I WAKE, ONE warm hand stroking my hard cock up and down. Heaven. I open one eye and see a smiling Lily staring up at me naked, her glorious just-woken-up hair tied at the top of her head, and that damn smile, it stops my heart. It's also the reason for restarting it.

Her warm hand cups my balls. I close my eyes and groan, "Fuck, that feels amazing, baby." Lily giggles, and my cock grows impossibly larger from the sound. Hearing my woman laugh is the only thing in this world that truly makes me feel like a man. My chest expands and I want to punch it and yell to the world that my girl is happy.

I gently grip her chin and pull her toward my face. I kiss along her neck and jaw while she continues to stroke me. The strokes are slow. She turns her hand around the head of my cock, glides her fingers down, and then twists all the way around at my base. It makes my cock twitch like crazy. I'm close and I do not want to come in her hand.

"Turnover, baby, I want you from behind this morning,"

She quickly flips to her tummy, moves up the bed, grabs hold of the black metal bed frame and raises her ass up in the air. Shit, I want in that raised pussy so bad right now, but I want to play a little first. I want Lily as ready as I am.

I pull her dark blonde hair free from her head, and it flows freely down her back. I wrap the silky strands around my fingers and gently bring her head backwards and to the side. I take her mouth in a punishing, possessive kiss.

I reach around to touch her clit and we both inhale at the touch. My finger circles her clit slowly, knowing this is Lil's favourite thing. She moans into my mouth, and I need to release her so I can get my cock inside her. I won't last much longer feeling her pushing back against me and swallowing her sexy whimpers into my mouth.

I release her hair and grip her hips tightly. "Ready, baby? I'm so close and I'm not even inside you."

She nods and whimpers as my cock enters her.

"Fuuuuck, so wet, always so wet for me, Lil," I growl.

I push all the way in and then pull out, almost falling

out of her. Lil whimpers at feeling the loss of my cock. My chest expands at knowing how much she loves me inside of her.

I thrust into her and she screams out in ecstasy. I begin thrusting hard, keeping up the punishing pace, her knuckles turning white from holding the bed frame so firmly. Her pussy clenches around me; the first sign she's almost there.

"Oh, my God, Jake, don't stop. Don't you dare fucking stop," she breathes out through her moans. I'm so close. I need her to hurry. I reach around and rub her clit, and she goes off almost instantly, screaming my name.

With her walls tightening around my cock, my legs start shaking, and I roar out her name, "LILY!" while still pounding hard as I come deep inside her.

I fall on top of Lil, both of us breathing heavily. After a long moment, my heart calms and I slide to the side, taking her into my arms. The ache is long gone. Now all I have is a swollen heart that on most days almost explodes with the love I possess for this woman.

I decide it's time for breakfast. I slap Lil's ass, turn her to her back and kiss her stomach. Staring intently into Lil's eyes, I say, "Hopefully, we made a baby this time."

Her eyes grow glassy with tears, but now Lil only cries happy tears. She takes these moments and savours them. We appreciate every second of our lives. We both know how quickly they can get ripped away.

"I'm going to go make my fiancée some breakfast," I say, kissing her tummy one more time, before dressing and heading to the kitchen.

LILY

AT TIMES LIKE THIS, I FIND IT HARD TO BREATHE WHEN I realise what kind of man Jake is. The most loving, caring, protective man alive. Something so amazing and beautiful spurned from evil, and I'm thankful for it every day.

A year ago, when Jake and I arrived back in Australia, he took me right to his contact and I was able to collect my sister. We buried Sash the next day, just Jake and I with the same priest who spoke at my parent's funeral.

It was the hardest thing I have ever had to do. I thought burying my parents was hard; but the world once again showed me that heartache has no limits.

Seeing my baby sister lowered into the ground was almost unbearable. Jake held me up when my legs gave way. I cried for Sasha and everything she went through, and for every day I won't have her with me.

We stayed for a week. That's all I could handle. Everything around me reminded me of the family I had lost. A few times, Jake found me in our willow tree, crying. I wasn't getting better. I was getting worse. I needed space and time to recover.

We left for Minnesota, and soon enough, with Jake, his family and friends around me, I began to heal. It was little things every day, one more smile than the day before, one more happy memory of my sister that didn't send me to tears. I can now think of her and our years together and laugh. My heart still holds a small amount of sadness that will always be there when I think of my beautiful little sister, but it's bearable. I now thank God, every day that he gave her to me, even if it was only for a short time.

After two months in Hastings, I was ready to see my family home and try again. Jake packed us up as soon as I mentioned it.

But again, I only lasted a week. It was still just as hard. Two more months passed and Jake informed me we were going back to Australia. I was excited and apprehensive, afraid I wouldn't be able to spend more than a week at my family's farm.

However that time, the memories didn't cripple me, and it got easier every time after that. And without fail, every two months, Jake would make sure to take vacation time and bring me home.

We're on the farm for a month this time. Jake wants our children to spend our family vacations here, and if a heart could burst from love, mine surely would have. I could never explain to him what that means to me.

So Jake's building onto the house because I want there to be room for his whole family to come with us. Jake has already spent too much time away from his family.

Jake's parents are loving and caring. They took me in and made me a part of their family instantly. Their hugs feel like the hugs my parents used to give me.

"Lil, breakfast is served," Jake yells from the kitchen.

I pull myself out of bed, pull on some panties, a bra, denim shorts and a white tank top.

I make my way to the kitchen spotting a massive

amount of French toast on a plate at the kitchen bar. I sit on a stool and almost get the delicious hotness to my mouth; but Jake beats the toast and kisses me sweetly.

He pulls back and smiles a cheeky grin at me. I laugh and shake my head at him.

"The guys just got here for work. I'm gonna go out and help. You wanna come with?"

I shake my head and say around my mouthful of food, "I'm going to go and visit the willow tree first."

Jake's eyes flash with pain before he whispers to me, "Okay, beautiful, take your time."

He kisses me on the forehead and puts another plate in front of me. This one is full of fruit.

I look over to my fiancé who is looking at me with a huge grin on his face. I laugh, and then start eating my huge breakfast he is obviously hoping is for two.

I look down at Sasha's gravestone, an angel with a sword, the meaning is justice. I bend down and wipe away the leaves and clean away the dirt that has blown on from the wind.

"I miss you, Sash, but I know you're always here." I place my hand over my heart.

Sasha's grave sits underneath our favourite childhood place, our willow tree. We would play here every afternoon, and on the weekends, we'd climb the tree, role playing, inviting our friends to play. The tree was where we told each other all our secrets and all our dreams for when we grew up. Memories float through my mind of

Sasha's laughter, her hair flowing in the wind as she runs to the tree...

Sasha squeals with laughter and starts running over to me as I sit on a branch in our willow tree. "Lily, did you see Matthew O'Conner at lunch today? Did you see him sit with me and ask me to hold hands?" I look over at my excited little sister and grin at her. "I did and I saw you take his hand and hold it too. What was it like? Did it feel gross and sweaty?"

Sasha stares up at me in the tree and looks me right in the eyes and says with a faraway expression on her face, "No," she breathes out, "it was wonderful. His hand was soft and cool." She starts climbing the tree to sit on a branch near me. "I'm going to marry him one day," she announces.

I giggle. "You can't know who you're going to marry in grade four, Sash."

"Yes, I can, Lil. He's the one. I just know it. Holding his hand was like magic. I saw our whole future, a huge white wedding, a big house with purple and pink curtains and a big white fence to keep our dog and cat in." Sasha wrinkles her nose and says, "I'm not sure how many kids yet." I giggle again at thinking about pink and purple curtains.

In the distance, I hear our mum call us in for dinner. We both start climbing down the tree in a hurry. I get to the bottom and say to Sash, "First one to the house gets to pick the TV show we watch during dinner." As soon as I see Sasha's feet touch the ground, I dash off, running as fast as I can. I smile brightly at hearing my little sister running behind me, laughing.

I'm taken out of my thoughts by a cool breeze

caressing my neck. I look down to the angel gravestone and a smile graces my lips. I touch the inscription gently with my fingertips...

BELOVED DAUGHTER AND SISTER
UNTIL WE MEET AGAIN, SWEET SISTER,
I WILL BE WAITING FOR YOU AT THE WILLOW TREE.

Evie Harper is an Aussie author who lives in Queensland, Australia. She is a bookaholic, who is never found without her kindle, if by chance she doesn't have it, she has severe separation anxiety.

When Evie isn't writing or reading, most of the time you can find her playing board games or watching her favourite TV series with her husband and two children.

You Loved Me At My Darkest will be followed by:
You Loved Me At My Weakest, releasing November 2014, and
You Loved Me At My Ugliest releasing February 2015.

STALK EVIE HERE:

FACEBOOK

https://www.facebook.com/profile.php?id=100008340076053

GOODREADS

https://www.goodreads.com/author/show/8276648.Evie_Harper

acknowledgements

To **my husband**. To the man that drives me crazy and loves me like crazy. Thank you for putting up with my late nights, not eating with the family, making school lunches every day, washing clothes. Basically just doing everything for the last few months while I stared at my computer screen. But mostly thank you for getting pissed at me for not being around and missing me. Nothing says you love me more than wanting me with you to watch our favourite shows together. For my next book I will be getting a laptop so I can sit next to you and write while you watch our shows lol! I love you baby!

To **Mel** & **Amber**, you both know I'm so not the mushy type until I've had a few drinks lol! But I'm teary already. Saying thank you here just doesn't feel like enough, but I will try. From the moment I said I wanted to write a book you both encouraged me and read every horrible chapter I sent to you. I'M SORRY! Your words of encouragement and always finding time to read chapters for me made my heart grow to an impossible size. Your comments of loving even my very first horribly written scenes makes me smile. You've put up with my endless talk about books and now my writing. You have always been there for me and I know through any ups and downs past and future you'll be there with me when we are old and grey, trying to escape the old home to go find a bar to party in! I hope to always be there for you both and give you back what you've given me, lifelong friendships worth fighting for.

To my C.O.W's. **Ash, River, Alissa** & **Bel** - This is going to be tough and my eyes are already glassy lol! Okay, I wake up every day and one of the first things on my mind is to log on and chat to you girls. It's built into me now like it's always been there. EVERY DAY I smile, I laugh, I almost wet my pants because of you girls. It's like a girl's weekend every day! You have all supported me and encouraged me on this journey and I THANK YOU all so much for that. I love you all very much and I can't wait for the many years of friendship to come.

And THANK YOU to **River** for answering my many questions and understanding my very confused questions and anwers lol! Thanks for seeing me through the maze that is self publishing and giving me someone to be able to always turn to, to ask questions. I appreciate your help A HELL OF A LOT! Mwah!

To **Bel**. Even though our friendship has only just began, you went out of your way to help me. You hold the record for reading my book the most and finding the most mistakes lol! Your honest opinions, ideas and encouragement pushed me to be a better writer. Thank you so much for always fitting me into your busy life and going the extra mile when I needed someone.

To my Betas, **Gill**, **Ash**, **Alissa**, **Bel**, **Sue** & **Amanda**. Thank you for reading my story and finding my mistakes, plot holes and just for putting your lives on hold to help me. Each of you gave me an enormous amount of help and guidance and I thank you all for that.